Estelle Ryan

D0507459

The

Roubaud Connection

The Roubaud Connection
A Genevieve Lenard Novel
By Estelle Ryan

First published 2018

Chapter ONE

"DOCTOR LENARD! I need to speak to Doctor Genevieve Lenard! Where is she? Canada has five hundred and sixty-one lakes. Doctor Lenard!"

I stepped away from the closing elevator doors onto the plush carpeting of Rousseau & Rousseau's foyer. This had been my place of work for six years as an insurance investigator, using my analytical skills and expertise in nonverbal communication to detect any and all attempts at insurance fraud.

Then my life had changed five and a half years ago. A number of people had blasted into my carefully organised existence to help with an investigation. My autistic mind had rebelled against their neurotypical chaos and unconventional methods. But I hadn't been able to deny the success we'd achieved working together. Three years ago, we'd moved our team room from this building to the one adjacent, all the while investigating crimes most often related to art. Today those interlopers were not only my team. They were my family.

Another panicked shout came from the direction of the conference rooms and I looked at Vinnie.

"Told ya so." The tall man was my best male friend and

self-appointed protector of our investigative team. He was wearing his usual dark combat trousers and a tight long-sleeved t-shirt that accentuated his muscular build. He rolled his eyes in a manner befitting the young adult voice yelling from the conference room. "He's been here for ten minutes and has not stopped his fact-screaming."

"This is not normal." Colin, my romantic partner and international thief consulting for Interpol, took a step closer to the conference room. "He hasn't lost control like this in many, many months."

"True dat." Vinnie's *corrugator supercilii muscles* contracted in a concerned frown. "Usually Phillip manages to calm him down in a minute or two. Nothing is working at the moment."

"Doctor Lenard! The Dead Sea is sinking about one meter a year! Doctor Lenard!"

I'd met Caelan Dupre three and a half years ago when he'd noticed a pattern of kidnapped students. The first time I'd seen him, he'd not received any care or guidance whatsoever to manage his autistic behaviour. After the conclusion of the case, my team had worked hard to get Caelan the care he needed.

Phillip Rousseau, the owner of the high-end insurance company we were currently in, had ensured Caelan had behavioural therapy with the best experts in this field. He and Colin had helped Caelan finish his high-school diploma and enrol in university. They'd even helped him change his surname when he'd insisted on having his own identity—completely removed from his past.

I didn't see him often. Even though he worked extremely hard to manage his autistic behaviours, I found it uncomfortable to be around him. For obvious reasons, it was unthinkable that I would ever disparage anyone for struggling with impulses that were a result of that person's neurological make-up. But his behaviour triggered stimming—repetitive body movement—in me that I'd worked years to control. Therefore I avoided him.

"Where is she? I need her help. Doctor Lenard!" The higher pitch in Caelan's voice alerted me to his distress.

"Ah, there you are." Timothée Renaud walked into the reception area. In the four years he'd been Phillip's personal assistant, I'd not once seen him dressed in a manner that did not measure up to the latest fashion trends. He glanced at me, then studied Colin's designer black trousers, tailored midnight-blue shirt and Italian boots. "Looking good, Colin."

"What about me?" Vinnie put his hands on his hips and moved around like women did when studying a new outfit in the mirror.

Tim tilted his head and raised one eyebrow. "You've got the brutish look down pat, Vinnie." Tim had lost most of his fear of Vinnie. It had taken him years before he could jest like this. He turned and pointed over his shoulder towards the conference room. "Seriously though. Are you going to help Phillip calm that young man down? He needs your help in there."

"Doctor Lenard! Greenland is three times the size of Texas!"

I pulled my shoulders back and inhaled deeply. "Let's hear what is causing him to be so anxious."

"Goodie." Tim's relief was genuine. "You go calm him down. I'll go get him some white food and milk."

We walked past Tim's heavy wooden desk and down the short hallway to the largest of the three conference rooms. I entered the room and was immediately glad Phillip had chosen the larger space for this meeting. Caelan was pacing against the far wall, his shoulders in constant motion as if he was trying to dislodge a weight resting around his neck.

He jerked around when he noticed us and rushed towards me. "Doctor Lenard! I've been calling for you. Why did you take so long to get here? Russia spans eleven time zones!"

I took a step back and raised both my hands. "Stop."

He did. And stared at my left shoulder, his eyes wide. "You must help me!"

"I will listen to what you have to say, but first you need to lower your voice."

His chin dropped and his stare moved to my shoes. "I'm not in control."

"We can see that, superman." Vinnie walked around me and sat down in the first chair. He'd built a strong relationship with Caelan and at one point had given the young man this ridiculous moniker. "Why don't you sit down and take a few deep breaths."

"I can't!"

"Of course you can." Phillip's deep voice brought warmth

to my chest. He'd used that reassuring, yet strong tone with me many times in the decade I'd known him.

Caelan nodded and shuffled to the chair next to Vinnie. He dropped into it and immediately started scratching his thigh. Even though his distress was evident, he appeared well-groomed. His jeans and sweater were clean and fitted him well. His fingernails were short, no longer bitten to the quick, and his curly black hair was cut short.

He took three forced breaths before he exhaled loudly. "Nothing is working. Since Jace disappeared, I haven't been able to get control back. The Atlantic Ocean is saltier than the Pacific Ocean."

"Who's Jace?" Colin pulled out two chairs and waited for me to sit before he took a seat. "Your friend?"

"He's my partner." Caelan glanced up at me, then back at his thigh where he was now tapping a rhythm with his index finger. "He's like us."

"Coffee for everyone and milk for our young guest as requested. And some sugar-free cookies." Tim walked in and put a loaded tray on the table. He winked at Caelan. "I don't think you need anything that will give you more energy, right?"

"Wrong!" Caelan took a deep breath and exhaled slowly. He swallowed and in a more controlled voice said, "I need more energy. I need to find Jace."

"Um. Okay." Tim took a few steps back and glanced at the door. "I'll be at my desk if anyone needs me."

"Thanks, Tim." Phillip reached for the tray and distributed the steaming coffee mugs. "Take a few more deep breaths,

Caelan. Then you can tell us why you need our help."

"Hey, everyone." Daniel Cassel, the leader of one of the best emergency response teams in France, walked in and sat down across from Vinnie and Caelan. He was in full GIPN uniform and shifted until Caelan's eyes were no longer glued to his holstered handgun, but rested on his shoulder. Daniel smiled. "I'm so glad to see you, Caelan. I'm in the middle of my shift and I popped in next door. But then I heard you were here and I had to come and see you. How are you?"

I considered Daniel a friend. Not only was he an incredible leader, he had also impressed me on numerous occasions with his astute understanding and sensitive handling of non-neurotypical people. I wasn't surprised he had come over from our team room in the building next door to meet Caelan.

"I'm not doing well." Caelan stared at his fingers tapping against his thighs. "I can't stop this tic. Last week, I told Jace that I haven't had a shutdown or meltdown in three months and have been able to control my stimming for more than six months."

"What is causing you such anxiety?" Daniel asked.

"Jace is gone."

Daniel looked at us with his eyebrows raised. Colin shrugged. "We were just asking him about Jace."

"Jace is my partner."

"Business partner? Study partner?" Vinnie asked.

"Geocaching partner."

There was a moment of silence in the room. Phillip

carefully put his coffee mug on the table. "Please indulge me by explaining what geocaching is."

Caelan glanced at Phillip's shoulder. "There are caches hidden and we find them."

"Caches of what?"

"Riddles." Caelan shrugged. Then he shrugged again and again until a tear rolled down his cheek. "I can't stop."

"Which mountain is the closest to the moon?" I asked.

"Chimborazo in Ecuador is the closest to the moon. Everest is merely the highest in terms of sea level."

"How many active volcanoes in Japan?"

His shoulders relaxed and he closed his eyes for a second before focusing on my left shoulder. "One hundred and eight."

"How many countries are completely surrounded by another country?"

"Three." He snorted, raised the index finger he'd been tapping on his thigh and counted out on his other hand. "Lesotho, Vatican City and San Marino."

Colin took my hand and squeezed it.

Caelan's dark skin regained some colour, his facial muscles relaxing slightly. He looked at his hands both resting on his thighs, then at me. "I see what you did, Doctor Lenard. It helped."

"I recommend creating hypothetical questions that will distract your mind when you're distressed. You'll be too busy building valid arguments to allow your mind to become severely overwhelmed." I leaned forward to make sure he paid attention. "It might not always work. I'm sure you've already discovered that what works once might not work again. At least not in the exact way it worked before. You just have to continue experimenting until you find what works for you."

"Is that how you manage?" There was hope in his usual monotone.

"Most of the time." I felt tension entering my shoulders. "I hate to admit that it doesn't always work. Sometimes the external stimuli are too much, too fast, too overwhelming for me to put my usual methods in place fast enough."

"That's exactly what my therapist keeps telling me." He slumped into his chair. "I hate it when he repeats himself. It's like he thinks I'm stupid. But maybe I am. I practice all the exercises he's given me, but now that something really bad happened, I've lost all the control I'd gained."

"I assume the bad thing you're talking about is your geocaching partner being gone." Daniel waited until Caelan nodded. "What do you mean by 'gone'?"

"I can't contact him." Caelan's breathing hitched. "We've been partners in geocaching for two years, seven months and five days."

"Has he done this before?" Daniel asked.

Caelan shook his head. "Never. He always answers when I call him. Always."

"Do you have any theories on why he's not answering your calls?"

Caelan's eyes widened. "Theories, no. But I'm convinced his phone is turned off or the battery is completely discharged. When I phone him, the call immediately goes to voice mail."

"Does he ever turn his phone off?"

"Pah!" Caelan snorted. "Never. He's a heavy user. He checks and double-checks everything on his phone."

"Could it be that his battery is depleted, but he's safely at home?" Vinnie asked.

"No." He shook his head. "I knocked on his door until his neighbours told me to leave. He didn't open."

"You said he's like you and Jenny." Colin took a sip of his coffee. "Do you mean he's autistic?"

"Yes. But he's nonverbal."

"Completely?" Despite the many obstacles I faced dealing with being on the spectrum, including my difficulty communicating with neurotypical people, I'd been fortunate enough to be verbal. Even if my words offended people most times I spoke.

"Yes." Caelan's voice hitched and he started tapping on his thigh again. He blinked a few times and inhaled deeply. "The Dead Sea is four hundred and thirty metres below sea level. About ten percent of the earth's surface is permanently covered with ice. There are no rivers in Saudi Arabia."

Vinnie watched Caelan with concern pulling his eyebrows down. When Caelan pressed his palms flat against his thighs and took a shaky breath, Vinnie looked at me. "What is the difference between completely nonverbal and not completely nonverbal?"

"Research has revealed that nearly a third of people on

the autism spectrum use only a few words or even no spoken language. Nonverbal autism is poorly researched and far too little is known about the thought processes of individuals who don't speak. Even though quite a few nonverbal people can't use spoken language effectively, they are able to communicate in different ways. Written or typed language is the most common, but sign language and digital communication devices are being used more often now as well."

"And just because Jace doesn't talk doesn't mean he's stupid or he doesn't understand." Caelan glanced at our phones lying on the conference room table. "That's another reason why he uses his phone so much. He types out messages faster than most people type on a computer. With a hundred percent accuracy."

"No typos and autocorrect disasters." Daniel smiled at Caelan. "Tell us more about Jace. What is his full name and surname? How old is he?"

"Jason Connelly." He paused when Daniel typed the name onto his tablet screen. "Are you looking for him?"

"Just checking if someone else reported him missing."

"No one else would." Caelan lifted one shoulder. "He doesn't have any friends here, his mother is dead and his sister is in Australia. She works there and doesn't like Jace. I'm his only friend."

"You're a good friend." Daniel leaned towards Caelan. "Jace is lucky to have you. Tell me more about him."

"He's three years older than me. He's twenty-five. He's finishing his second doctorate degree. His first was in forensic anthropology, this one is in Persian history. He is fluent in seven languages."

"Goodness." Phillip's eyebrows rose high on his forehead. "Seven?"

"French, English, Gaelic, Irish, Russian, Finnish and Arabic."

"Interesting choices." Most people chose the more romantic languages like Italian and Spanish. "Explain the cache you were looking for. How does such a search take place?"

"We belong to a society of gifted people." He glanced at Daniel, Vinnie and Phillip. "Do you know what it means to be gifted?"

Vinnie frowned. "Someone who has natural talents, like for math or music?"

Caelan sneered. "I was right thinking you wouldn't know. You're talking about talented people. Gifted individuals have certain characteristics that make them different. Their IQs are in the top two to three percent of the population. They are often seen as eccentric or quirky, they are intense and driven, too sensitive and prone to question authority. They are unable to switch off their thinking, are introverted and need periods of contemplation. They are self-disciplined, imaginative, highly curious, perceptive, creative, insightful, flexible, have a wide range of interests and—"

"Stop." I recognised the typical autistic tendency to over-explain and I placed my hand on the table. "You've explained enough. Rather continue about the society and looking for the cache."

"Not everyone is interested in creating the caches and searches. Some—like Jace and I—just want to take part in the search."

"Like a treasure hunt," Vinnie said.

"It's not a treasure hunt." Caelan frowned and turned away from Vinnie. "There's no treasure."

"What is in the cache?" Daniel asked.

Some of the tension left Caelan's face. "A riddle."

Colin smiled when Caelan didn't expand on his answer. "Please explain."

"None of us are interested in finding caches with little superheroes or trinkets in them. And the people who create the caches are far too smart to create something as simplistic as that. So we have cognitive challenges."

"To see who's the smartest." Vinnie leaned back in his chair. "Man, I would be so out of my depth."

"You would." There was no malice in Caelan's reply. "Each cache's riddle leads us to the next cache. There are always three caches in a set. We're given an initial riddle to lead us to the first cache, then we have to find our way to the last cache. With each one, the riddles become more abstract and complicated. Until the final cache which always has the hardest riddle."

"Hold on a bit there, superman." Vinnie's frown pulled his brow down. "You gotta explain it real simple for me."

"Why? You're not stupid."

Vinnie's loud laugh was one of surprise. He shook his head. "Thanks, dude. Okay, my question is this: If you guys get a riddle in each cache, how do you know where to look for the next cache? I mean, how does it lead you to the next cache?"

Caelan took his smartphone from his pocket and put it on the table. "There's a website, but everything about the caches is on an app on our phones. When you solve the riddle from one cache, you enter the answer into the place for it on the app and the GPS co-ordinates for the next cache are revealed."

"Aha." Vinnie leaned back in his chair and folded his arms. "Is there a time limit or some such thing to solve the riddles?"

"No." Caelan glanced at his phone. "The app gives points for each riddle solved and every other action. The faster you solve the riddle, the more points you get. The quicker you get to the next cache, the more points you get."

"And the person with the most points wins what?" Vinnie raised both shoulders. "A riddle?"

Caelan glared at his shoulder. "I'm not sure, but I think you're being sarcastic."

"Sorry, superman." Vinnie lowered his shoulders. "But I would still like to know what you win."

"Nothing. It's knowing that we were the fastest in solving the riddles and getting the caches that counts. There have been a few members who thought it was stupid not to have big prizes, but only a few. The others kicked them out of the group."

"Harsh. Does everyone work in teams?"

"No, but most of us do." Caelan swallowed. "Jace is a perfect match for me. I don't like being outside among other people. I like searching and researching the locations on my computer with the many satellite mapping systems available. Jace loves running through the city or forest or buildings, looking for the caches. He enjoys being outside. As long as no one talks to him."

"Then how do you communicate?" Daniel asked. "Only via instant messages on your phones?"

"Not only. Jace has smart glasses. He wears them very often and streams his footage live to me. That way I can see where he is and what he's doing. When we work like that, I'm on the phone with him, speaking to him."

"GIPN has been using smart glasses." Vinnie nodded towards Daniel. He often joined Daniel's GIPN team when they trained. A few times he'd taken part in their rescues as well. "Pink was going on and on and on and on about it. Just like Franny."

Pink was GIPN's IT expert and shared his passion with Francine, my best friend and a world-renowned hacker.

Almost a year ago, Pink had been grievously injured during one of our investigations. My respect for him had grown exponentially watching his determination to recover physically and emotionally from that event. He'd moved into our extended apartment when he'd been released from the physical rehabilitation centre. I'd observed his optimism and relentless hard work to speed up his recovery. It inspired me.

Two months ago, the department had cleared him for active duty after rigorous tests to ensure that he was indeed able—physically and psychologically—to perform his duties.

"I still prefer the body cams." Daniel looked at me. "If we're going to be recording things, body cams are better."

"But smart glasses do so much more." Vinnie shrugged when we looked at him. "What? I've been listening to Pink and Franny sing these things' praises. And then I tried it. Must say, the fact that these glasses can ID so many things before our brains have time to process them can be very useful."

Daniel sighed. "Vin is right. The smart glasses are pro-grammed for facial recognition. The idea is for law enforcement personnel to be wearing them all the time. The glasses will process everyone crossing the agent's path. If someone is on a watchlist and the system recognises the face, it will alert the agent. If the agent is busy in a verbal exchange with a suspect and focused on his face, he might miss the butt of a weapon peeking out from the suspect's shirt. The glasses will pick that up and alert the agent. There are many life-saving uses for the glasses."

This information was interesting and I appreciated that Daniel kept his explanation short. I knew Francine well enough to be convinced that she would've wasted valuable time going into unnecessary detail. I turned my attention back to Caelan. "When is the last time Jace streamed footage from his glasses?"

"Yesterday morning." Caelan's fists clenched. "It was also the last time I spoke to him."

Something in his tone caught my attention. "But not the last time you communicated?"

"He sent me a photo yesterday afternoon." He took his

phone and swiped the screen. "When I phoned him to ask what this was supposed to be, he didn't answer. He hasn't answered since."

"May we see?" Colin held out his hand towards Caelan's phone.

The young man immediately pulled the phone closer to his chest. "I'll send it to Doctor Lenard. No one touches my phone. Lebanon is the only state in the Middle East in which there is no desert."

I lifted my phone from the conference table. Four seconds later, a notification tone sounded and I swiped the screen. "Is this his flat?"

"I don't know."

"You've never been there," Vinnie said.

"I was there this morning." Caelan's chin dropped. "But I've never been inside my friend's flat."

"Could you forward the photo to us, love?" Colin took his phone from his trouser pocket. "Maybe one of us will see something important."

I tapped the share icon and soon notification tones filled the room. I enlarged the photo to study the view from the floor. At this angle, the only possibility was that Jace had taken the photo while on the floor. It showed a few centimetres of a rug over a dark wooden floor that disappeared under a bed.

I enlarged the photo even more to focus on the space directly under the centre of the bed. "Those are smart glasses."

Colin leaned towards me and I tilted the phone so he

could see what I was looking at. "It sure looks like it."

Vinnie raised one eyebrow. "This means he took the photo with his phone."

Daniel cleared his throat and shifted in his chair. He was frowning at his phone, his muscle tension increased. "I think we need his address, Caelan."

"What's wrong?" It was written all over his face. His attempt to modulate his tone didn't fool me. What had he seen in the photo?

"He's looking at the blood." Caelan's words came out louder than usual. "Show them the blood."

"The very bottom of the photo." Daniel tilted his head, his expression softening with compassion as he looked at Caelan. "We don't know that it is blood. That's why we'll go and check on him."

With my index finger, I moved the image until I could study the bottom of the photo. The image was still enlarged and as I moved the image to the left, I jerked my hand away. What had looked like the grain on the wooden floor now appeared to be blood spatter. It wasn't a fine mist as was often seen in cases of gunshots, but rather long streaks. Seen in cases of blunt-force trauma. I shuddered.

Colin inhaled sharply and leaned forward. "Can't be."

"Can't be what, dude?" Vinnie stretched his neck to see Colin's screen.

"Under the bed against the far wall."

Everyone lifted their phones, fingers stretching the image. Phillip put his phone on the table. "That's a painting."

"A Roubaud." Colin brought the phone closer to his face. "It's too far and too dark to make out whether this is authentic or any other details, but this is undoubtedly Franz Roubaud's *The Battle of Elisavetpol*, also known by the very long name of *The defeat of the Persian troops at Elisavetpol on September 13, 1826*. I would recognise the horses and soldiers anywhere." He looked up. "It's currently in a museum in Baku, Azerbaijan."

Daniel's phone vibrated and he swiped the screen. A micro-expression of disquiet pulled at the corners of his mouth. He looked at Caelan. "Do you have a photo of Jace?"

"Yes!" Caelan swiped the screen of his phone a few times then turned it for Daniel to see. "His hair is very red."

"So it is." Daniel's smile wasn't sincere. It didn't lift his cheeks and crinkle the corners of his eyes. He looked at Phillip. "Could you please take Caelan to your office and get him to write down every small detail he knows about Jace's life?"

Phillip's eyes narrowed for a moment, then he nodded and got up. "Of course. The more data we have on this young man, the easier it will be for us to find him. Caelan?"

He looked at Phillip's shoulder, then at Daniel's, back to Phillip's, then at mine. "Are they lying to me?"

I didn't know what to say. I didn't specialise in working with people on the spectrum. I only knew how *I* processed information. And how desperately I needed as much information as possible. "They are lying to you to protect you. I don't know from what yet, but I will find out."

"Jace is dead, isn't he?" Caelan didn't take his eyes off my shoulder. His breathing was erratic.

I looked at Daniel. "Is he?"

Daniel closed his eyes and nodded. "I'm so sorry, Caelan."

"Russia and China are both bordered by fourteen countries! The Andes form the longest exposed mountain range at seven thousand kilometres!" He got up and looked at Phillip's shoulder through the tears filling his eyes. "I'm ready to go to your office now. Greenland is the largest island in the world."

Phillip's eye and mouth muscles contracted in compassion as he held out his hand towards the door. "I'll get Tim to bring you more milk and white cookies."

They left the room and Daniel opened his mouth to speak, but paused when Caelan rushed back in. He stopped next to my chair and stared hard at my shoulder. "I trust you with my friend, Doctor Lenard. Take care of his body and his memory."

I watched him rush out and exhaled slowly. Typical of people on the spectrum, Caelan didn't exhibit emotion as openly as neurotypical people. Yet the overwhelming pain I'd seen on his face and heard in his voice affected me. I searched for Colin's hand and gripped it tightly before I looked at Daniel. "What do you know?"

"When Caelan first mentioned his friend, I asked Pink to search for anything related to the young man. I'd hoped we'd find him in hospital at worst." He shook his head. "Pink just sent me crime scene photos. The police found

Jace's body in the woods to the south of Strasbourg. Pink is organising for us to go there now. He's also asked the team there to wait for us before they process the scene any further."

"We need to get the old man and Franny to go with us." Vinnie got up, his phone already pressed to his ear.

"I don't want to go." I closed my eyes, my hand tightening around Colin's. "I don't want to see Caelan's dead friend."

"You don't have to go, love." Colin lifted my hand and kissed my knuckles. "We'll work it from here."

I opened my eyes and turned to him. "I didn't say I wasn't going. Just that I don't want to go."

He smiled. "Gotcha."

"The old man will meet us there." Vinnie leaned against the door frame. "Franny is on her way to Phillip's office. She'll get that data from Caelan and start doing her computer magic. Dan, you wanna come with us or go with Pink?"

"I'll meet you guys there." Daniel got up slowly and shook his head. "The younger they are, the harder it is."

Chapter TWO

"THIS IS IT." COLIN drove slowly towards the police vehicles and other cars parked at the entrance of the Neuhof forest. Strasbourg was the only European city with alluvial forests surrounding its outskirts. As one of Strasbourg's three forests, Neuhof was considered a genuine natural monument and was awaiting approval for listing as a nature reserve.

Located south of the city, along the Rhine River, it covered an area of seven hundred and fifty-seven hectares. There were many paths for cycling, jogging, even horse riding. But it also had a reputation for prostitution and late-night illegal activities. I'd been here numerous times, but only during the day.

It was mostly the nature that drew people here during the day, myself included. Especially in the warmer months. This part of the season, some trees were bare while the evergreen trees provided a bit of colour. It had snowed last night, the fresh snow adding to the breathtaking beauty of the nature surrounding us, the ground now hidden beneath five centimetres of snow.

It had taken us sixteen minutes to drive here. Colin had ignored all speed limits, despite my many complaints. The eleven kilometres should've taken us twenty minutes had Colin kept to the road rules. I'd resorted to folding my arms around my torso in a self-hug and mentally writing Mozart's Symphony No.36 in C.

Colin huffed as he parked his SUV next to a familiar sixteen-year-old beige sedan. "How did Millard get here so fast?"

Colonel Manfred Millard was the only member of our team who was formally trained in law enforcement. Currently, he was still employed by Interpol with the understanding that he was running our team who worked directly under the president of France. He was standing next to his car, speaking to Daniel and Pink.

"He must've been close." Vinnie narrowed his eyes as he looked at Manny's sedan. "There's no way the old man drove faster than fifty kilometres an hour."

I relaxed my arms and took a deep breath. The expressions on Daniel's and Manny's faces warned me that this was going to be difficult. I pulled on my thick fleece gloves and got out of the car. The fresh air stung my cheeks and I pulled the zipper of my winter coat as high as it would go.

Winters in Strasbourg were never severe, but the last week had brought an unusual amount of snow as well as lower than usual temperatures. I pulled my scarf higher around my neck and joined Colin at the front of the SUV. Vinnie was already standing with Daniel, Pink and Manny as we walked over to Manny's car.

"All I'm saying is that people are weird. Weird." Vinnie

crossed his arms, his bulky winter coat stretching over his shoulders.

"Why are people weird?" I hated missing parts of a conversation.

"Doc." Manny stared at me for two seconds, then nodded before he looked at Colin. "Frey."

"People are weird because a group of friends come here every single day to walk their dogs." Vinnie threw an arm out and gestured towards the forest. "It's minus twenty, half a metre of snow and my nose is running from the cold."

"It's minus one." I sighed and kicked at the snow under my black boots. "The snow here isn't even five centimetres deep."

"The cover over there is about twelve centimetres." Daniel pointed his thumb over his shoulder.

"Is that where the body is?" Colin asked.

"Yes."

Working with neurotypical people was vexing. They seldom stayed on point in a conversation. I took a step closer to Vinnie. "Why were you complaining about the people walking their dogs?"

"I wasn't complaining about the people." Vinnie grinned. "Only the weather."

"Ignore him, Doc." Manny turned his back on Vinnie. "One of the dogs found our victim. That's why these people are important."

"Did they see anything else?" Colin asked. "Someone dumping the body, driving away?"

Daniel shook his head. "No, they said they got here for a walk after lunch when one of the dogs broke free of his leash and ran off the path. His owner found him barking like crazy at what he thought at first was a pile of clothes. But when he got closer, he saw it was a body."

"Did anyone touch it?"

"I don't know." Daniel turned to his left. "Canet! Come here for a sec."

An officer in his mid-thirties walked to us. He was wearing a police-issued winter jacket, hat and gloves. "Good day, everyone."

Around me, the men nodded and Daniel shook his hand. "Do you know if anyone touched the body?"

"No. The woman whose dog found the body said she immediately saw he was dead." Despite his heavy French accent, he spoke English with ease. He tapped on his temple and rolled his eyes. "Silly woman said she watches lots of cop shows and knew she shouldn't touch the body. She phoned us."

"That's not silly." Why would he say that?

"*That* isn't." He rolled his eyes again. "But then she said there's enough DNA everywhere that she knows we'll find the killer very quickly."

"Hah!" Pink shook his head as he laughed. "She really said that?"

"*C'est vrai.*"

"Of course it's true." Pink nodded in completely fake agreement. "Because the killer always leaves his or her DNA behind for us to find. And the DNA results even reveals his or her motivation and tells us where the murder weapon is."

"Did they give you any useful information?" I didn't have patience for this inane discussion.

"*Non.*" Canet glanced at the group of friends huddled next to a silver Ford Focus. There was nothing in their body language that gave me pause. They all seemed distressed and kept looking back in the direction of the crime scene. "But each one of them has a theory about what happened."

"Let me guess." Pink's smile lifted his cheeks. "They also watch a lot of cop shows."

"*Oui.*" He grinned when Pink chuckled. Then his expression sobered. "I cordoned off the scene, but between the dog, the owner and all her friends who came rushing over when she screamed, any footprint evidence in the snow has been destroyed. But they didn't touch him and neither did we. The body is exactly as they found it." His lips thinned. "It's not good."

"Shall we?" Manny pushed his hands in his oversized coat's pockets.

The officer stayed with his vehicle while we walked into the forest. A clear path had been formed in the snow where the first responders and everyone else had made their way to the body. Deeper into the trees, the snow was pristine, forming a pure white blanket that reflected the weak daylight. At seventeen minutes past four in the afternoon, we only had another two hours before it would be dark.

Daniel slowed down and turned to look at me. "The young man has been brutalised. Please prepare yourself."

My eyes widened and I pushed Mozart's symphony back into my mind. "Brutalised?"

"It would be better if you saw it for yourself. I don't want to influence your observations with my opinion."

I mentally played the first two lines of the symphony.

"Ready?" Daniel waited until I nodded, then walked around a copse of trees and stepped to the side.

I inhaled deeply and held my breath for four seconds. It was the blood that caught and held my attention. The contrast against the white snow somehow made the scene look even starker. I took a step closer, making sure I stayed on the snow that had already seen a lot of foot traffic.

Caelan's friend was lying very close to a large shrub, the low-hanging branches touching his left shoulder and hip. His legs were at an odd angle and his arm closest to us undoubtedly broken. He was dressed in jeans, a t-shirt, sneakers and hooded sweater that wasn't zipped up. No outdoor wear. His red hair was cropped close to the sides and the longer hair on top flopped over his forehead. I gasped when I looked at his face and immediately turned my attention elsewhere.

A large blood pool to the left of his head suggested trauma to the back of his head. Blood had also pooled under his left knee and his right arm. I shuddered at the realisation of what this meant. "He was left here to die."

"That's what the medical examiner said." Daniel's tone

was sombre, his expression fierce. "The killer maimed Jace, then dumped him here to bleed out and freeze to death. The ME will only give us his exact cause of death after an autopsy."

"Poor kid." Manny stepped closer and frowned. "Why would anyone work him over like this?"

"He sure was beaten up badly." Vinnie also walked closer and went down on his haunches to look at Jace's body. I didn't want to go any closer yet. Instead I studied Vinnie's and Manny's body language as they looked at Jace. I knew the moment Vinnie noticed something that concerned him. He pushed up from his haunches and looked at Colin. "Dude. Come look here."

Colin squeezed my hand, then walked the three metres to join the others. They were obscuring my view and I was now curious to know what Vinnie had seen. I took a deep breath and stepped closer.

"Shit." Colin lowered himself and stared at Jace's right hand for a few seconds. Then he leaned a bit to the side to look at the young man's face. My first glimpse of his face had been shocking. I inhaled deeply and forced myself to look at him.

Jace's face was a bloody mess. His left eye was completely swollen shut with a deep cut a centimetre above his eyebrow. His left cheek had a few cuts and was also terribly swollen, bruising still fresh, the discolouration interrupted by death. Whoever had punched him excessively was right-handed.

His left hand was hidden from our view by the shrub.

Looking at his right hand made me take a step back. "He was tortured."

That was the only explanation for why every finger on his hand was broken, some in more than one place.

Colin pushed himself up and nodded. "He suffered greatly."

Soon after I'd first met Colin, he'd been kidnapped by Russians and had been tortured for days before Vinnie had found and rescued him. It had taken Colin more than six months to recover from his injuries. He still had a deep scar on his right leg from that experience. It would explain why his facial muscles indicated distress.

"I don't get it." Daniel shook his head. "He was a sweet young man who liked to go geocaching. What on earth could the killer have wanted from him?"

"We need more data." I always needed more data. "We need to know everything about Jace."

"Francine's already on it." The corners of Manny's mouth turned down. "I have a bad feeling about this one."

I walked closer to the shrub, making sure to stay far away from the blood frozen around his head. I lowered myself onto my haunches and looked at the side of Jace's body that had been hidden from us. The shade from the trees and this shrub combined with the weak daylight made it hard to see detail. I looked at Daniel. "Do you have a flashlight?"

"Not on me."

"I do." Vinnie opened one of the side pockets on his dark combat trousers and took out a small flashlight. He walked over and handed it to me. "Twist the top to turn it on."

I did that and pointed the light at Jace's left hand. His thumb looked completely dislocated and his little finger was at a right angle to his hand. The other three fingers looked unharmed. I moved the light to unnatural indentations in the snow.

"What the hell?" Manny was at Jace's feet looking at the snow illuminated by the light. "Doc, what's that?"

"Numbers." An uncomfortable emotion surfaced and I pushed it down. I'd come to recognise it as grief and didn't like experiencing it. I hadn't known this young man, yet I felt a sense of loss. I stared at the blood-lined grooves in the snow that formed five numbers. "Three, one, seven, one and six. Jace tried to communicate with the last of his strength."

"Good man." Manny narrowed his eyes. "Any idea what these numbers are?"

I looked up at Manny and frowned. "Of course not."

Vinnie grunted and moved away. "I suggest taking loads of pics for Franny to run searches."

"She only needs one photo." I paused. "Not even that. Francine only needs the numbers."

"But I bet you would like the scene to be well documented with photos." Daniel waved at a crime scene technician chatting to Pink while waiting for us to finish. "I'll get them to take a complete 3D scan of the area. Pink also has a 3D scanner in the truck, but I'd rather he come with us. The crime scene techs will send us the scan as soon as it's done."

"Anything else you see, Doc?" Manny looked at the bottom of Jace's sneakers.

I took my time running the light alongside Jace's body and also under the bush. "Nothing."

"Then we'll leave the crime scene guys to do their thing." Manny straightened. "Do we have the boy's address yet?"

"Francine sent it to our phones." Pink walked closer and shook his head when he looked at Jace. "He looks so young."

"Twenty-five, but with more brains than you and I put together." Vinnie put his hands in his jacket pockets. "We need to find out who did these things to this kid."

"Then let's go to his flat." Manny turned towards the parking area. "Maybe we'll find something there that will clue us in."

"And could explain why he sent a photo of a Roubaud to Caelan." Colin took my hand after I gave Vinnie his flashlight. We followed Manny and the others to our vehicles.

No one spoke as Colin followed Daniel's vehicle onto the main road back into Strasbourg. I turned on the sound system in the SUV and chose Mozart's Quintet in A for Clarinet and Strings from the uploaded playlist. Mozart's affinity for the clarinet was evident in this piece, its soothing sound filling the interior of the SUV. I leaned back in my seat and allowed my mind to process what I'd seen.

The injuries Jace had suffered were unlike anything most people would ever experience. I wondered if his non-neurotypical mind had been able to process what was being done to him. Then I thought about his inability to communicate. He hadn't even been able to tell his torturer what had been demanded of him. Or tell him to stop.

It felt like a strong band was constricting around my chest and the urge to start rocking and keening made me stop this line of thinking. Instead I focused on the intimate scale of the Quintet that Mozart executed so masterfully with his chamber music and stared out of the window.

We drove through the port area. I counted thirty-three freight wagons that I assumed were waiting to be either offloaded or filled with goods. The buildings here were huge and mostly shipping companies. We crossed the river a second time, going towards the city centre, and a thought came to me.

I turned to glance at Vinnie in the back. "Why didn't you know about Jace?"

"I didn't know about Jace because Caelan didn't tell me about him."

"But you have been spending so much time with him. How could he not have told you about his best friend?"

Vinnie looked at me for a few seconds. "You spend time with the president's wife, right? Do you tell her about Francine? Or me?"

"Of course not. My friendship with you is not relevant to our conversations." Unless Isabelle asked me directly about Vinnie. Usually, Francine joined us for our lunch meetings which eliminated the necessity to talk about her.

I realised the point Vinnie was trying to make. I nodded. "I see."

Vinnie smiled. "I knew the dude had found some activity that was making him happy. I guessed he had also found someone who shared his interests, so I didn't push when he didn't answer my question about it. I don't know why he didn't tell me."

Colin slowed down the SUV and parked next to Manny's sedan. I settled back in my seat and unlocked the seatbelt, but quickly moved closer to the door when Vinnie leaned forward and punched Colin lightly on the shoulder. "You're cool with all this, dude?"

Colin turned off the engine and looked at Vinnie, his *corrugator supercilii* muscles contracting his brow in a frown. "Why wouldn't I… ah, the torture."

"It was pretty rough on you."

"But it was almost six years ago and I've moved on." Colin cupped Vinnie's cheek in a surprising gesture of intimacy. "You care about me. I'm touched."

Vinnie jerked back. "Oh, fuck off."

Colin laughed and got out of the SUV. Vinnie followed him and punched him again in the shoulder, this time hard enough for Colin to wince. He laughed harder. "I'm fine, Vin."

"Yeah, see if I care." Vinnie stomped toward Daniel's vehicle just as Pink got out, ignoring Manny's questioning look.

"What's up with the big guy?" Manny pulled his coat tighter around his neck. His habit of wearing ill-fitting clothes seemed impractical and even silly at the moment. In these temperatures, surely it made more sense to wear the warm and fitted coat Francine had bought for him.

"Vin's okay." Colin took my hand and we walked to the entrance of the apartment building. It was one of the more modern buildings in an area bordering the older parts of Strasbourg. Manny pushed open the glass door and we walked to the security desk. A man in his late fifties was reading a magazine.

I stayed back and watched Daniel and Manny build rapport with the guard until he was happy to send us up to the third floor. The elevator was large for an apartment building, yet I was relieved when Pink, Vinnie and Daniel said they were taking the stairs.

As the elevator doors opened, Vinnie was waiting for us, his hands on his hips. "Even with an elevator helping you, I'm still faster than you, old man."

"Oh, bugger off." Manny pushed past Vinnie and realised he was going in the wrong direction. "Holy hell!"

Everyone laughed as Manny turned around, marched past us to the left and stopped in front of door number three-one-five. "Well? Are you all just going to bloody stand there or is someone going to open this door?"

Vinnie snorted. "I wish this was an American movie where the building had a super with keys to each apartment." He looked at Daniel. "Don't you think your job would be so much easier if everything was like in the movies?"

"Most definitely." Daniel narrowed his eyes when Colin walked closer and leaned forward to study the lock.

"What are you doing?"

Colin looked over his shoulder and smiled. "What do you think?"

"You can't break into this flat, Frey." Manny pushed his hands in his coat pockets and nodded at Daniel and Pink. "Not when there are law enforcement officers watching you."

"Ah." Pink smiled and turned his back on Colin. "I'm not seeing anything."

Daniel shook his head. "This is a murder victim and we're investigating. Do you need a kit?"

"Yes, thanks." Colin accepted the small wallet Daniel took from his vest. He opened it and studied the set of tools. "I'll only need these two."

He took two thin tools and turned back to the door. He inserted the larger, more curved of the two lock picks and turned it gently. His muscle tension decreased and he inserted the L-shaped tool. Colin's posture was relaxed and confident while twisting the tools. The gears in the lock clicked.

He straightened. "One of the easiest locks to pick and only this one on the door. Jace clearly wasn't concerned about security."

"For the average citizen, the building security would seem more than enough." Vinnie searched the hallway. "If only they had security cameras here as well. It's not going to help if the killer came in through the back door or the basement."

Colin opened the door and turned on the light.

Manny blinked a few times, looked at me, then back into the apartment. "Doc? What are we looking at?"

I was trying to control my breathing and push the panic away from my mind. I looked into the flat and shuddered. A small entrance led to a large open space that appeared to be the living room. Little of the floor space or furniture was visible. The entrance area had piles of magazines, shoes and delivery boxes. At first glance, it appeared chaotic, but I soon saw how neatly each pile was organised. The coat tree was overloaded with coats, jackets and sweaters—all on hangers, arranged by colour. In some places, boxed items reached the ceiling.

"Hoarder." The word came out hoarse and I cleared my throat. "Jace was a hoarder."

Daniel stepped into the flat, his hand resting on his holstered gun. "Let us clear the flat before you guys come in."

Manny unbuttoned his coat, took his handgun from its hip holster and followed Daniel and Pink into the flat.

"I don't want to go in there." I really didn't. My mind functioned better in a much less cluttered environment. It didn't matter that there appeared to be obsessive order to the clutter. I found it most unsettling.

"I hear ya, Jen-girl." Vinnie faked a shudder. "Who lives with all this stuff around?"

"Compulsive hoarders experience great anxiety at the thought of discarding anything, whether it is a useful object, a used object or rubbish. It's clinically recognised as both a mental disability as well as a possible symptom for obsessive compulsive behaviour. People who hoard don't have control over the compulsion." I understood compulsions. "The force of it can rule a person's life."

"Clear!" Daniel's voice interrupted my explanation.

"Jenny?" Colin squeezed my hand. "Want to try?"

"It's not that bad, Doc." Manny stood in the living room and waved his hand towards his right. "This side of the flat is the complete opposite to this crowded bloody mess."

I took three deep breaths and nodded. I walked past the overloaded coat tree, into the living area and frowned. Here, Jace had piled books on top of each other until it looked like it was about to topple over.

"It doesn't smell bad." Usually hoarders found it difficult to throw out food containers and any other garbage. That resulted in a smell similar to a rubbish dump. There wasn't even dust visible here.

There were three piles of books. One was academic textbooks, one books on history and one cookbooks. I thought of my alphabetised bookshelves and wondered what it was in Jace's brain that made these piles more appealing.

I pointed at the rug on the floor, then at the piles of books. "Nothing is unsettled."

"Hmph." Manny glared at the neatly organised piles of bills and notepapers covering the oiled wooden floor. "You're right, Doc. With this little space, a scuffle of any sort would've moved this thin rug and toppled the books."

"In here!" Pink's voice came from the hallway to the right. "Watch your step for the blood on the floor."

My eyes immediately went to the wooden floor, looking for rust-coloured stains. There was nothing in the living area. This flat was spacious for a young man living on his own. The hallway led to three doors, one of which was to the bathroom. It was in front of the bathroom that I saw the first blood drop.

Vinnie pointed at it. "The killer must've carried Jace out to his car to dump him in the forest."

I walked to the bedroom, inspecting the floor before I put my feet anywhere. Pink walked out of the room and headed to the living area. "You guys have a look in there. I'm going to go get my 3D scanner."

The bedroom was large. It looked like it could've been two rooms in the original plans that had been combined to form a space that swallowed up the three-quarter bed pushed in the corner. There were blinds in front of the windows and no décor to give this space any warmth or ambience.

"Looks like this was set up for gaming." Vinnie was standing in front of a corner desk with three large monitors and a game controller next to the keyboard.

"How can this be so neat and the living room such a mess?" Manny scowled at the empty walls. "This is minimalistic."

"It used to be neat." I pointed at the rug. "There was a struggle here."

The rug was bunched up in places and had been pushed out of place. A chair which I assumed was Jace's desk chair was on its side on the rug, one of the legs broken.

There was blood spatter everywhere. On the rug, on the bed covers, even on the empty walls. The dark leather of the desk chair had shiny spots that I was sure were also blood. I shuddered.

"I reckon this is our primary crime scene." Daniel looked at the chair. "This is where Jace was tortured."

The familiar tightness settled around my chest and I turned away from the bed and the chair. I took note of the curled corner of the rug where Jace must've frequently walked to the built-in cupboards.

The minimalism and tidiness of this room was the main reason I didn't feel claustrophobic with the men in the room with me. Manny opened the cupboard doors and grunted. Jace's clothes were neatly folded and all the hangers were white. Manny pushed the clothes aside and started searching through each one individually.

For some reason, Jace had needed this space to have less clutter. I looked at Daniel. "Are the kitchen and bathroom neat like this?"

"Very neat." Pink walked in, a large backpack over his one shoulder and holding out a plastic evidence bag for us to see. "The bathroom is extremely clean. Like white tile advertising clean." He lifted the evidence bag. "I found this phone in the toilet bowl. The water smells like extremely strong disinfectant."

Colin stepped closer to look at the phone and frowned. "It looks like a train went over this thing."

"Yeah." Pink put the plastic bag in one of the many pockets of his uniform. "I doubt we'll get anything from this. Crushed as it is and lying in the chemical water for who knows how long? Well, whoever destroyed the phone knew what they were doing."

"At least Jace had the chance to send Caelan that one photo." Vinnie shook his head. "Poor kid."

Colin walked to the bed. "This is like the photo." Careful to avoid the blood, he got down on his hands and knees and looked under the bed. "The glasses. Oh, my God. And the Roubaud."

Daniel took a step towards the bed, both hands raised. "Don't touch anything yet. Let Pink record the scene first, else it will cause all kinds of problems with the crime scene guys and prosecution."

Colin nodded and looked at Vinnie. "Still have that flashlight on you?"

"Sure do." Vinnie took the small light from his trouser pocket and handed it to Colin.

Colin glanced once more at the blood before leaning forward and pointing the beam of light under the bed. We all watched him. For almost a minute he didn't move, except to slightly change the direction of the light.

"What the bleeding hell are you doing down there, Frey?"

Colin didn't answer. After another thirty seconds, he turned off the light and leaned back on his heels. "This Roubaud is not authentic."

"Are you sure?" Manny looked at the bed. "It's dark down there."

"I'm sure." Colin stood up. "My eyes are not as old as yours."

"Bugger off, Frey." Manny glared at Colin. "Well? Speak."

"Such a charmer." Colin ignored Manny's deepening scowl and looked at the bed. "I'll need to see the painting in proper lighting, but I'm pretty sure I know whose work it is."

"You know who painted that forgery?" Manny leaned towards Colin.

"I *think* I do. Give me the painting to confirm." He held up his hand to prevent Manny from talking. "Then give me some time to track the guy down."

"I want a name, Frey."

"Not until I know for sure it's his work." Colin's lips thinned.

They stared at each other for thirteen seconds before Manny nodded once, then looked at me. "Do you need more time in here, Doc?"

"No." I shook my head and found it difficult to stop. The sadness and depravity of what had happened here was overwhelming. "I want to leave."

"We'll get the crime scene guys here and bring the glasses over as soon as we can." Daniel took his phone from his trouser pocket and swiped the screen.

"And the painting," Colin said.

Pink nodded. "I'll scan the room, log everything and bring the glasses and painting over."

Manny lifted his phone to look at the screen. "No. Pink, you finish up here and go home. It's past six already. The painting and glasses can wait until morning." He turned to Vinnie. "I'm hungry."

Vinnie snorted. "And that's my problem how?"

"We'll see you at our place, Millard." Colin smiled when Vinnie raised both eyebrows. "I saw you prepare the curry this morning. There's enough to feed the entire neighbourhood and one grumpy old man."

"Fine." Vinnie turned towards the door. "But don't let Franny take too long to shut down her computers. I'm not waiting forever to serve dinner."

Colin looked at Daniel. "Join us?"

"I'll help Pink process the scene and get things to the lab." He smiled. "And the painting to the team room. But then I'm going home."

Chapter THREE

"THERE'S ENOUGH FOOD here to feed Daniel's whole team as well." Vinnie nodded towards the two large pots on the stove and smiled at Phillip. "Stay for dinner. Your share won't even make a difference to the leftovers."

I closed my bedroom door behind me and walked to the sitting area of my apartment. The smell of a curry dish filled the open space. Colin was sitting on one of the two large white sofas, Phillip on the other. I glanced around as I walked to join them. There was no one else in our apartment and for the moment, I appreciated the relative quiet.

"Genevieve." Phillip straightened and stared at me. "How are you?"

I sat down next to Colin and wiped my hands on my denim-clad thighs. "Disturbed by what I saw this afternoon."

Phillip's *depressor anguli oris* muscles pulled the corners of his mouth down. "Colin told me what was done to Jace. It's unimaginable."

That was the reason why I'd rushed into my bedroom and had a much longer than usual shower as soon as we'd arrived home. It had taken mentally writing the entire first movement of Mozart's Symphony No.41 in C before the warning signs of a shutdown had dissipated. My concerns hadn't disappeared though. "How is Caelan?"

"Not good." Phillip sighed. "We made it to my office before he had a bad shutdown. Fortunately, Francine was there to help me."

"She's good with him." Colin took my hand and interlaced our fingers. "She's had a soft spot for him from the day he asked... no, begged her to be his girlfriend."

"Hah!" Vinnie set the last place at the table and nodded in approval before looking at us. "I remember that. He asked and asked and asked. He was such an annoying little shit then."

"He's changed a lot," Colin said.

"Most likely because he's had people who took an interest in him for the first time in his life." Vinnie walked back to the kitchen and transferred the curry and rice to large serving dishes. "Franny reckons it's because he's studying and now is more focused."

We'd had this discussion a few times in the past. In my opinion, it wasn't just one thing or person that was helping Caelan function better in society and in life. It was his studies, his professors, Francine helping him with his social skills and Manny's strict and impatient guidance. I didn't know how large my contribution was. I met him only once a month for a game of chess during which we sometimes discussed different ways of coping with a non-neurotypical mind in a neurotypical world. Other times I avoided him.

"Where is Caelan now?" I asked.

"Manny and Francine took him to his flat." Phillip pulled at the sleeves of his bespoke suit. "He wanted to go back to his safe space and have his nightly routine."

"It will settle him." I should know. Whenever my daily routines were disrupted, it left me unsettled and made it even more difficult to deal with usual challenges, not to mention exceptional challenges. Such as the murder of a young man.

The sound of keys in the lock drew my attention to the front door just as it opened. "Honey, I'm home!"

"Hey, little punk." Vinnie walked over to Nikki and took her one-year-old son from her arms. "Hey, tiny punk. Let's get you out of your Eskimo gear."

Nikki shrugged out of her coat and tossed it over her coat tree. I sighed. In the four years Nikki had stayed with us after her father had died, she'd matured a lot. But she'd not become much neater. Last winter I'd reached my limit and had insisted on her having her own coat tree. Fifty centimetres away from mine. That way her layers of coats, colourful scarves and hats didn't touch my coats neatly hanging on hangers or my folded scarves. It hadn't been a week before everyone but Colin had started sharing Nikki's coat tree. They'd said it was 'easier'. I shuddered just looking at the chaos on that tree as Nikki threw her purple scarf on top of the pile.

"Doc G! You won't believe what I bought today." She rushed over to the sofa and flopped down next to me. "A handbag organiser."

I leaned away from her and raised one eyebrow. "And you think that is going to help?"

Vinnie burst out laughing and handed Eric to Nikki before heading back to the kitchen.

Nikki continued to explain how this organiser would help her find her keys and pens the moment she opened her oversized canvas bag. I strongly doubted her bag would stay organised longer than a few minutes after she'd put that silly purchase to use. Nikki was notoriously messy.

Eric wiggled from her lap and balanced himself on two unsteady legs, his hands gripping the back of the sofa. Two weeks ago, he'd taken his first steps with the help of the furniture. The books I'd been reading classified Eric's development as within the norm, but a bit quicker than most. I'd vowed not to mention this again after everyone took credit for Eric's fast development when I'd quoted the statistics last week.

"I'm going to wash up." Nikki jumped up and walked to the side of the apartment she shared with Vinnie and Pink. "Hurry up with the food, big punk. I'm starving."

Vinnie moved as if he was going to chase her and Nikki ran the rest of the way, giggling. He returned to the kitchen and took a salad from the fridge. "Two more minutes and everything will be on the table. And then I'm not waiting for the old man and Franny anymore."

Eric turned around and sat down heavily next to me on the sofa. He looked at me, a smile lifting his little cheeks when he saw me looking at him. He glanced down at the space separating us and shifted closer until he sat flush against me.

I had never expected to be so enchanted with a child. It was still too early to be completely certain, but to all appearances, Eric was neurotypical. Most of the books I'd read described babies as sensitive to their environments and more attuned to nonverbal communication than adults. Some theorised that as soon as their focus changed to words and accurate descriptions, little children started to ignore their innate ability to read nonverbal cues.

The more I observed Eric, the more I considered that theory. For such an undeveloped human being, Eric was incredibly sensitive to my idiosyncrasies. Most days he climbed on my lap and touched me, but days like today when I felt raw from fighting off a shutdown, he would simply sit tightly against me. He would entertain himself with one of his toys or sometimes he would fall asleep against me. I loved him.

"Food's on the table, y'all." Vinnie looked over at us, his expression softening when he saw Eric. He walked over and held out both hands. "Come on, tiny punk. I've made your favourite."

"I swear he's not my son." Nikki sat down at the table and pointed angrily at Eric. "His love for your vegetables is just wrong. He should be eating steaks and burgers."

And so the bantering began. Even though this had been going on in my apartment for years, I still had moments when I was taken aback by it. Ten years ago, my life had been lonely. It had also been safe and predictable. The latter made it much easier for me to cope with my mind so easily overwhelmed by stimuli. Yet I preferred the loud arguments and laughter around the table.

"Tell me about your job, Nikki." Phillip put another spoonful of lamb curry on his plate and smiled at Nikki. "Excited?"

"Yes and no." She looked at Eric, sitting in his high chair next to her, his *corrugator supercilii* muscles contracting his forehead in concentration as he lifted his plastic spoon to his mouth. "It's going to break my heart putting him into day care."

"It will help with his social development." All the books encouraged having infants socialise as soon as possible.

"I know, Doc G. But it's still going to be hard." She helped Eric scoop up the mixed vegetable stew Vinnie frequently made for the baby and held Eric's hand as he brought the spoon to his mouth. Her smile was soft when she turned back to look at Phillip. "I'm really excited about being part of the restoration team at the museum. When I went to uni, I never thought that was where I would end up."

"Where did you think you would go?" Phillip asked.

"I don't know." She glanced at me, her smile embarrassed. "I was young and full of myself. I knew my trust fund would pay out when I turned twenty-five and thought I would just study something until I had enough money to do what I wanted."

"You're still young." Yet I considered her wise beyond her years. With Phillip's help, she'd managed to get the courts to release the trust fund money five months ago. I'd been asked to appear as a character witness. The judge had been convinced by the many respected professionals who spoke in Nikki's favour. She'd received the money and since proven herself to be very responsible with it.

"And you're still full of yourself." Vinnie laughed when Nikki pointed her knife at him, her angry expression fake.

"Now I have all that money and I'm glad I do. It's an amazing security blanket that will help me take care of Eric. But I *want* to work. I'm excited about working at the museum." Her dilated pupils and the lifting of her cheeks confirmed her words. "I've been interning there on and off for the last two years, so it's not like I don't know anyone there. Or like I don't know what I'll be doing."

"You'll be great." Colin winked at her, then turned to the front door as it opened.

"Food!" Francine rushed in and threw her coat over Nikki's. Then she hopped from one foot to the other as she removed her knee-high red leather boots. "I'm hungry. I need food. Feed me!"

"She's been driving me bonkers." Manny took off his coat and put it on a hanger next to mine. He glowered at the overflowing tree of colourful coats and sighed. "Completely bloody bonkers."

Francine rushed over to the table and pulled the curry dish closer before she even sat down. "Ooh, yay. Food that will feed me and make me warm. I love you, Vinster."

"Yeah, yeah. They all say that." Vinnie's chest expanded slightly as he watched Francine and Manny fill their plates with enthusiasm. I didn't need my degrees in psychology to see that he enjoyed cooking, but his real reward came from people enjoying his food.

"Where's Pink?" Manny looked at the empty seat.

"Still at the crime scene with Dan." Vinnie handed Manny the salad bowl. "He said he'll be in late. I've fixed him a plate and it's waiting in the oven for him."

"I miss Roxy." Francine sighed dramatically. "I miss bitching about her horrid shoes."

I shook my head. Their melodrama could be most vexing. Doctor Roxanne Ferreira was an internationally respected infectious disease specialist and Vinnie's girlfriend, her love for him genuine and unconditional. She was disorganised, messy and notoriously tardy. Yet I enjoyed her company. "She's been gone only two days."

"I know!" Francine leaned over and patted Vinnie's hand. "You poor thing. You must be suffering something terrible. And what? She'll be gone another week?"

"Five days." Vinnie caught Eric's spoon a moment before it was going to fall from his little hand and put it back in the plastic plate. "She's enjoying her conference, and no, I'm not suffering."

Manny grunted and slumped in his chair. He too had a low tolerance for the melodrama far too often enjoyed during dinner. He turned to Colin. "Tell me more about this Robot person."

"What robot person?" Nikki looked from Manny to Colin. "Do you have a case with artificial intelligence? How cool!"

"Not robot." Colin turned away from Manny in disgust and looked at Nikki. "Roubaud. As in Franz Roubaud."

"What?" She jumped in her chair and turned to Colin, her eyes wide. "You have a case with Roubaud paintings? Ooh! Ooh! He's like only my most favourite panoramic painter. Ever!"

Manny sighed. "Tell me about him."

Nikki put her knife and fork down, her eyes wide with enthusiasm. "Franz Roubaud was born in Odessa— Ukraine, for those who don't know where Odessa is—to a French family. That was in 1856. He spent a lot of time in Germany organising exhibitions for Russian artists. Then he lived in St Petersburg and taught for many years at the St Petersburg Academy of Arts. But he loved Germany, so it wasn't a huge surprise that he went back to Germany in his later years and died there."

"His art?" Francine looked at Colin. "What are the panoramics Nix talked about?"

"Robert Barker was the one to introduce the world to these amazing works of art." Colin straightened, his face animated. "These are massive paintings displayed in specially built round buildings called rotundas. The painting goes all around the internal walls, depicting different kinds of scenes, often military battles, historical events or landscapes."

"It was the earliest virtual-reality, 3D art exhibition." Nikki smiled. "They were hugely popular in Europe and the US in the nineteenth century. Unfortunately, not all of these survived, but there are still quite a few on display."

"Roubaud became famous because of his giant panorama paintings," Colin said. "They had to build pavilions just to exhibit them. His love for Russia and Russian history came through in his art. A lot of his works are associated with the Caucuses. One of his famous paintings, *The Battle of Elisavetpol*, shows a scene from the Russia-Persian war near the Askerna River. He seemed to have a thing for the Russia-Persia conflicts."

"Now that was an interesting time in history." Nikki wiggled in her chair. "Of course it was also a horrible time, like any time of war. It was the fourth of five conflicts between the then Persian Empire and Imperial Russia. Of all five, this one was the longest and lasted nine years."

"And inspired many artworks." Colin leaned his elbows on the table and steepled his fingers. "One of Roubaud's earlier mentors influenced him to never take sides, not even in commissioned works. In his paintings, he would reveal the bravery of Russian soldiers as well as the heroism of the mountain men equally."

"Ooh." Nikki clapped her hands, her eyes wide, warning me to be sceptical of whatever she said next. "And then there are the theories about Roubaud's art."

"That's nonsense, Nix." Colin shook his head.

"We don't know that." Nikki looked at Francine, her conspiratorial expression completely fake. "There are theories that hidden treasure maps were worked into Roubaud's paintings and in some of his lost panoramas."

"What?" Francine froze, her wine glass a centimetre from her lips. She lowered her glass and leaned forward.

"Tell me everything about these treasure maps."

"Nonsense, Francine." Colin held his hand up, palm towards Nikki, when she inhaled to speak. "Roubaud loved the Caucasus. A lot of his work is associated with the place, the people and the history. His Caucasian cycle lasted for a decade and he was prolific. He painted landscapes, lone horsemen and many battle scenes. He also loved painting river crossings. That was where the first of these ridiculous theories came from.

"The Oxus River was never even close to the areas depicted in Roubaud's art. Yet treasure hunters inspected every millimetre of every painting he ever produced, thinking they'll find hints of where the Oxus treasure entered the river before it started washing downstream. This ridiculousness has been disproved by numerous scholars. There is no substance to any of those theories."

"Dammit!" Francine's shoulders dropped and she leaned back in her chair. "And here I was just getting excited. You're sure there's no fire in this smoke?"

"There isn't even smoke." Colin looked at me. "Need an explanation?"

He knew my tendency to understand everything literally. I thought about it. "I don't care."

Everyone laughed.

"How was Caelan when you left him?" Phillip asked Manny.

"Pouring himself a glass of milk and cutting a few slices of white cheese to go with his white bread." Manny shrugged. "He's struggling, but he seems okay."

"He'll be fine once he goes through his nightly ritual and has a good night's rest." Francine's micro-expressions didn't agree with her statement. She was worried about Caelan. "He'll feel even better when he goes through his morning routine before he joins us tomorrow morning."

"He's joining us?" Manny turned to glare at Francine. "That's news to me. I thought I told you to convince him to stay out of this."

Francine raised one eyebrow. "And since when did I ever follow your orders?"

"Does he have any more useful information?" I couldn't imagine any other reason for Caelan to join us tomorrow.

"Nothing he's consciously aware of." Francine's expression turned serious. "But I do think that he can help us. He was Jace's best friend—Jace's only friend. I also think that helping us will help Caelan deal with this. He's not doing too well."

I agreed with Francine's assessment. I hadn't seen Caelan after his earlier shutdown, but my non-neurotypical mind recovered quicker when I felt like I had control over a situation. Being left out of this investigation into the death of his best friend would leave Caelan feeling helpless and powerless. It would put unimaginable strain on his already overwhelmed psyche.

I only hoped that this case wasn't going to take us too deep into the depravity of some criminal mind.

Chapter FOUR

"LOOK WHO WE found in the lift." The concern underlying the playfulness in Daniel's tone caught my attention and I turned away from the fifteen monitors in front of me.

Caelan was standing between Pink and Daniel. Juxtaposed to the two tall, muscular and older men, he looked young and lanky. He was wearing fresh clothes, had shaved and looked less overwhelmed than he had yesterday.

He walked into my viewing room and sat down in the chair Manny usually used. Daniel walked towards the kitchen where Colin was putting our mugs in the dishwasher. Colin turned and his eyes widened when he saw the painting in Daniel's hands. He rushed over to an easel and waited impatiently for Daniel to place it there.

Pink was at Francine's desk in the team room, handing her a set of eye glasses. I assumed those were Jace's smart glasses—Francine's enthusiasm when she grabbed them confirmed my suspicion.

I looked back at Caelan sitting next to me and narrowed my eyes when I noticed the dark shadows under his eyes. "Did you sleep?"

"A bit. I spent most of the night listing all the mountains

on the planet, from tallest to shortest. Then the rivers from longest to shortest. Then islands from largest to smallest."

"That's gotta be worse than counting sheep." Vinnie was leaning against the doorframe and winked at Caelan.

"Usually it helps me sleep, but it didn't work last night." Caelan scratched his thigh, then curled his fingers into a tight fist and slammed it on the same spot. "I don't know how to cope with this. It feels like my brain is overloaded and is going to explode."

"Overthinking seldom helps." It usually made things worse for me and sent me into a long shutdown. "It might help to focus on something you can control. Like giving us information."

Caelan's fists relaxed and he straightened. "Information. What information? I can give you a lot of information about…"

"Geocaching." I didn't want him to give us useless facts about planets, stars and mountains. I turned back to the monitors in front of me. "Where can we find the geocaching site you and Jace used?"

"It's on TOR." Caelan took his backpack from his back and put it on the floor next to him. He reached into the backpack and came out with two stress balls. This was one of the many fidget toys people on the spectrum used to calm themselves when stimuli began to overwhelm them. He took one in each hand and squeezed. "Do you know how to get onto TOR?"

"Of course she does." Francine walked into my viewing room, her tablet in her hand. "Most of the crimes we investigate have something to do with the dark web. But since I'm here, I'll do it. What's the address?"

"The site won't be helpful." Caelan shifted in his chair in a restless move typical of people on the spectrum. "The site is only for membership screening. Once you're accepted as a member, you're given access to the app. That's where all the information is."

"Okay, superman," Vinnie said. "Can you give us access to your app?"

Caelan hesitated. "It's private."

"Will you use the app without Jace?" I asked.

"No." Caelan hunched his shoulders. "We were a team. I don't want to do this without him. I *can't* do this without him."

"You can do anything you want." Daniel walked to the back of my room and leaned against one of the two antique-looking filing cabinets.

"Okay." Caelan swallowed and gave Francine his log-in details in a hoarse voice. The increased tension in his body made me shift away from him.

"Give me a moment to download the app, sign in and put it all on the screen." Francine sat down next to me in Colin's usual chair, tapping and swiping her tablet screen.

"I checked the painting." Colin walked in, glanced at Francine in his chair and went to stand by my antique-looking filing cabinets. Daniel joined him.

"And?" Manny walked into the room and stopped abruptly when he saw Caelan on my other side. He scowled. "You're in my chair, young man."

The room was feeling crowded now. I was used to the whole team in my room, but Manny's hovering and Caelan's fear took up a lot of space. Francine must've noticed my expression. She snapped her fingers at Manny. "Caelan's our guest of honour. You'll just have to stand next to Dan and Colin."

"I'm not going to the back of the bloody classroo…" Manny's eyes narrowed as he focused on Francine's raised eyebrows. He looked at me and sighed. "Fine. I'll go to the back."

"This is not a classroom." I raised my hand. "Don't explain."

I hoped Manny would see Caelan's distress when confronted with neurotypical conversation. I'd become used to it over the years, but Caelan's fragile mind at the moment wouldn't be able to process this in addition to the stress of his friend's death.

"I think now is a good time to tell you more about the painting." Colin gave Manny a pointed look until the latter pushed his hands into his trouser pockets and joined Daniel and Colin at the filing cabinets. I exhaled in relief.

"Well?" Manny tapped his foot, his lips tightening even more as he glared at Colin.

Colin smiled. "Johan Klein is well-known in the Belgian art community for his excellent reproductions."

"Reproductions? Not forgeries?" I asked.

"Yes, reproductions." Colin nodded towards the painting on the easel. "Johan signed Roubaud's name on the painting. Above his own. Comparing it to the original really shows Johan's skill. The brushwork, the colours, the finest details." He shook his head. "It's as if someone took a photo of the original."

"Have you contacted this Klim?" Manny asked. "I have questions for him."

"Klein." Colin lifted his smartphone. "My call went straight to voice mail so I left a message. I'll follow up. Soon. I also have questions for him. For example, who bought or commissioned the painting that is now in our team room."

Caelan was scratching his thigh again. "I need to give you information. I *need* to."

"Okay, I'm in." Francine pointed at the monitor in the centre. Then she leaned forward, looked past me at Caelan and winked at him.

I pushed back into my chair and looked at the display in front of me. I liked the design of the app. It was uncluttered. The background was a muted olive-green colour, the writing in an unadorned font and all the buttons in a clear layout and large enough for even Vinnie's larger fingers to easily tap. "Show us the last cache you and Jace located. How do you find it on this app?"

"Click on the menu." He stared at the monitor as Francine opened the menu on the app. "Some people never leave their homes, so some caches are online only. That's the second tab. The last tab is the past caches. The first tab is new caches and their categories."

"There are categories?" Colin asked.

"Four categories." Caelan counted on his fingers. "Urban,

suburban, nature and other. Other is for any place that doesn't fit in those categories specifically. They're also the most difficult to find. Jace and I only looked for caches in 'other'."

"How many people are part of this community?" I looked at the many language icons at the top of the page. "Is this international?"

"Yes." He nodded. "This is why the internet caches are the most popular. Gifted people from all over the world look for them."

"Gifted people?" Francine asked.

"People who are in the two percentile scale of intelligence and have certain characteristics."

"What characteristics?" Francine glanced at me.

Caelan repeated word for word what he'd said earlier. Except this time he stopped after listing the characteristics. Then he looked at my shoulder.

"How can the site ensure that their members are gifted?" I asked. It was difficult for psychologists and psychiatrists to diagnose children and adults as gifted since there wasn't any specific test that could determine that. Often gifted people were misdiagnosed as having ADHD, being on the spectrum or having even more severe mental health issues.

"We work on trust and honour." Caelan shrugged. "I've already noticed three people I'm sure are not gifted, but as long as they don't break the rules, no one will complain or withdraw their membership. They have to have higher intellect to take part in the hunts in any case."

"You didn't answer my first question." I still wanted to know. "How many people?"

"This app has one thousand, seven hundred and twenty-three members." Caelan shifted in his chair. "The other sites have the mundane hunts. This site only has caches with complicated riddles that we need to solve before we get the correct co-ordinates. Sometimes the solved riddle gives a secret clue that needs to be decoded and only then do we get the co-ordinates."

"That seems like a lot of work just to get to a final cache," Vinnie said from the door, a frown pulling his brow down.

Caelan looked at Vinnie's shoulder. "It's not about finding the final cache as much as it is about solving the riddles before anyone else. Or faster than anyone else."

"Which then gives you a higher score."

"When there's a countdown, it's even more challenging." He took a shaky breath and lowered his gaze to look at both his hands squeezing the stress balls. "Jace loved the countdown caches."

"Explain these countdown caches, superman." Vinnie's tone was soft with fondness.

"Sometimes when a solved riddle answer is entered into the app, a countdown starts. It could be an hour or maximum twenty-four hours. It's a waiting period before the next GPS co-ordinates are revealed. This way, the cache owners keep the competition high. Even if we were the fastest with the first cache, we'd have to be the fastest with the second cache as well to get to the last cache first."

"Cool." Pink joined Vinnie by the door and looked at the monitors. "A fun way to keep the tension levels up and avoid anyone having a head start."

"I don't like it." Vinnie crossed his arms. "If I worked hard to get a head start, I want the benefits."

Colin waved Vinnie's complaint away. "Caelan, I've been meaning to ask you about your communication with Jace."

"We used his smart glasses and our phones."

"Only?" Colin narrowed his eyes and tilted his head. "Or did you maybe use another form of communication? Not just spoken and written words?"

"Of course. Jace used sign language all the time."

"Bloody hell! Why didn't you tell us this earlier?"

Caelan glanced at Manny's shoulder. "Because signing his words isn't any different than speaking or writing."

I understood how this reasoning made sense to Caelan, but knowing that Jace used sign language was indeed useful information.

Francine had not stopped looking through the app and all the different options. She paused her tapping and leaned forward again to look past me at Caelan. "Are all the caches on the app?"

"Yes. They have to be. Else they don't count." He looked down at the stress balls. "Most caches are in the field, but a lot are only on the site or the app. Not all the members like to leave their homes."

"Like you," Colin said softly. "That's why you teamed up with Jace. With him enjoying the caches outside, you could get to even more riddles."

Caelan nodded. "Some of the clues are not in the app, but come from the surrounding location. That was also why Jace wore the smart glasses and streamed video from them. That way I could also see where he was and find clues that he might miss."

"Huh." Francine blinked a few times at her tablet screen. "Are there comments hidden in some of the caches' html source codes?"

"What are you talking about?" Manny glared at Francine's tablet.

She lifted it. "I'm fooling around on the app and clicked on the link to one of the caches. The html code looked funny and lo and behold!" She paused dramatically. "A hint."

The corner of Caelan's mouth lifted. "She's right. Some cache owners hide hints or clues in the source code. To find a cache you really have to know where to look."

I thought about this while Manny and Vinnie agreed on the outrageous amount of work to waste time with these silly hunts. With so many different places to look for clues, I let my mind wander over all the bits of information we'd gathered from the crime scenes.

"I have a question about the GPS numbers." Pink smiled when Caelan turned to look at his shoulder. "We know that a geographic location has latitude and longitude. The numerical values for these come in different formats, some with fewer numbers. Which one does this app use?"

"All three." Caelan directed Francine to a new cache and pointed at the monitor. "This cache owner used decimal degrees. See? There are only five numbers for north and five for west. But some of the others use degrees decimal minutes and others degrees minutes seconds."

"What the bloody hell does this all mean?" Manny and Vinnie had similar frowns pulling their brows down.

"It means that it could be misleading." The left corner of Caelan's mouth lifted slightly. "If given only five numbers for north and west, a geocacher might think he's using the decimal degrees format, but the cache owner could've given incomplete co-ordinates. Part of the riddle helps complete the co-ordinates, leading to the next cache. We have to figure it out. Add a countdown and it's a really great challenge."

Caelan droned on about co-ordinates, but I stopped listening. I looked at Pink, who was staring at me with an expression I'd seen every time he'd reached a pivotal conclusion. I gasped and turned to Caelan. "Would Jace have given you GPS co-ordinates as a clue?"

"Yes. Jace talked a lot about creating his own cache hunt. He wanted his riddles to be epic."

Manny grunted. "What are you talking about, Doc?"

I searched through the photos of Jace's crime scene and found the right one. The moment I put it on one of the monitors, Caelan uttered a keening sound, dropped the stress balls and started slapping his thighs.

"Bloody hell, Doc. Give a person some warning."

I looked at the photo that I'd taken of the numbers Jace had written in the snow and sighed. I had looked at it enough times to have desensitised myself to the blood smears on the snow. "I apologise."

"No need." Caelan inhaled deeply, picked up his stress balls and squeezed them five times while staring at his hands. Then he lifted his eyes and studied the photos on the screen. I saw the moment his mind registered something important. "I know where this is! The Sahara desert expands at about one kilometre per month! The average iceberg weighs twenty million tonnes!"

"Take a breath, superman." Vinnie walked closer and kneeled in front of Caelan. "Tell us what you know."

Again Caelan looked at the stress balls as he squeezed them slowly and purposefully. He inhaled deeply. "This was Jace's all-time favourite cache hunt. He loved the clues and the location made him very happy."

"Where is it?" Manny turned to the door.

"Very close." Caelan looked at my shoulder. "I don't want to go there."

"You don't have to go anywhere, dude." Vinnie got up. "You just tell us where it is and we'll find whatever it is that Jace left for you."

Caelan took a few deep breaths while staring at Vinnie's torso. "It's in a luggage locker at the train station."

Daniel lifted his smartphone. "Is it one of the lockers where you have to enter a code into a keypad to unlock it?"

"Yes." Caelan gave the number of the locker as well as the code. "I don't think it's possible someone would've changed the code. Jace wouldn't have given me this clue then."

Daniel nodded and left the room, already talking on his phone. Less than a minute later he walked back into the room, his phone still pressed against his ear, but looking at Pink. "Two officers are opening the locker. They'll send you photos of whatever they find in there."

No sooner had he said this than his eyes widened and his mouth opened slightly. "What? Are you serious?"

"What did they find?" Caelan was rocking in his chair.

Daniel looked at Colin. "A statue of a demon. They're sending a photo."

"Got it." Pink tapped on his smartphone screen and a photo filled one of the monitors in front of me. Inside a locker large enough for a big suitcase was a statue filling most of the space. It appeared to be made of stone, but I doubted something that heavy would be stored in the locker. It could be a good facsimile. Its stooped shoulders revealed large wings folded along its back and it was crouching as if ready to jump. Pointed ears, a flat nose, claws and a sneer that revealed sharp teeth were typical of the images frequently portraying evil spirits.

"Holy hell!" Manny took a step back. "What in the blue blazes is that, Frey?"

"It's a gargoyle." Colin looked at Caelan. "Does it have any meaning to you?"

Caelan's rocking increased. "No. The water of Antarctica is so cold that nothing can rot there. I don't know what this means. I don't know. Every year, Alaska has about five thousand earthquakes. I don't know!"

"It's okay, superman." Vinnie looked at me and widened his eyes.

"What?" I wasn't clear on his communication.

"Help the dude." Vinnie nodded towards Caelan muttering to himself and rocking in the chair.

"I don't know how to help him." I leaned away from them, tightness pressing on my chest.

"It's okay, girlfriend." Francine got up and slapped Vinnie hard on the shoulder. "I got this. Vin, go bake some cookies."

"No. No." Caelan's rocking slowed and he squeezed the stress balls a few times slowly, his focus completely on his hands. "I want to help."

"Why don't we take a walk to clear your head?" Pink pointed with his thumb over his shoulder to the elevator. "A bit of movement and you'll be able to understand why Jace left you that gargoyle as a clue."

"I'm okay. I will be okay. I will help." He looked down at his hands, then glanced at me. "It's a riddle. Jace might've created a cache before he died. If I figure out the answer to this riddle and enter it into the app, it should give me the next co-ordinates."

"For the next riddle." Francine tapped a manicured nail against her chin. "Is there a way to check if Jace really created a cache hunt?"

"No." Caelan squeezed the stress balls. "I know all the caches on the app and this one isn't there. That means that Jace hadn't finished creating it." He looked at my shoulder. "I won't stop thinking until I know the answer to this riddle. I will help you, Doctor Lenard."

"I know you'll help." I understood the need.

Francine sat down next to me and picked up her tablet and Manny glared at the image on the monitor. "That is just bloody ugly."

"It's art." Colin smiled when Manny's frown deepened. "There are examples found in ancient civilizations of gargoyles. That's how far back their history stretches. Their mouths were used as water spouts on the roofs of Egyptian temples. The same on Greek temples, but those figures were often lions or other vicious beasts. The whole purpose of gargoyles on the roofs of buildings has always been decorative, but also practical as water spouts."

"I don't care." Manny pushed his hands into his trouser pockets. "It's ugly."

Vinnie crossed his arms and looked at me. "Any ideas what the answer might be?"

I had none. I had no frame of reference for geocaching or these riddles. I didn't even know if the gargoyle was a riddle. I had to trust that Caelan knew his friend well enough to be accurate in this supposition. And I hoped Caelan could calm down enough to allow his mind to find the answer.

Francine shifted next to me and tapped her tablet screen. Her *procerus* and *corrugator supercilii* muscles pulled her brow in and down. It felt as if my stomach turned. The only times I'd seen that expression on her face had been when she'd been about to share something disturbing. I cleared my throat. "What?"

"Hmm?" She looked up from her tablet and blanched at my expression. "Oh, you saw that."

"Saw what?" Manny stepped closer, but Francine raised her hand to stop him. He grunted. "Talk."

Francine leaned forward to look past me at Caelan. "I downloaded all the footage from Jace's glasses."

Chapter FIVE

CAELAN'S *FRONTALIS* MUSCLES pulled his eyebrows high on his forehead. "I don't want to see him die."

"We won't show that." Francine looked at me. "We'll stop before that and warn you."

I also didn't want to see anyone dying, but I knew there might be valuable information that could lead us to the killer. I pushed Mozart's Violin Concerto No. 3 in G major into my mind. "How much footage is there?"

"It seems like your last three geocache hunts are there." She hesitated, then looked at Caelan. "Explain the process you two used to find a cache."

Caelan squeezed the stress balls. "Jace turns his glasses on when he's at a point we arranged beforehand. The glasses connect to his phone's internet, which then transmits the footage to me. I watch live where he's going. As he goes along, we see the clues that are at the site. I process those hints and direct Jace to the next point."

"Hmm." Manny rubbed his stubbled jaw. "Tell me more about these glasses. Can they be hacked?"

"Essentially, anything that connects to the internet can be hacked." Pink took a step away from Manny when the latter frowned at him. "Most smart glasses aren't useful enough to be hacked. Not on their own."

"I sense a 'but'." Manny looked from Pink to Francine.

"A defined butt." Francine glanced at Manny's backside, then winked at him when his scowl intensified. "If I hack Pink's glasses and he's transmitting or connected via Bluetooth or wifi, I can access his system. And wham! I'm all over GIPN's business."

"And because smart glasses are still newish tech, the security is not fantastic." Daniel looked at Pink. "That's why I still prefer button cams."

Pink raised one eyebrow. "The firewalls and antivirus programmes I have on our stuff make it really hard for anyone to hack."

"But not impossible," Daniel said.

Francine asked Pink about the firewalls and soon they were discussing the specifications of the latest smart glasses and their software. Caelan was following the conversation. Vinnie and Manny quickly grew bored with Pink and Francine's explanations of the technical aspects of the glasses, but the more they spoke the more Caelan relaxed. The facts were easier for his non-neurotypical mind to process.

"But the new button cams you guys got are great though." Francine smiled at Daniel. "I even got us a few. These models are amazing. I tweaked ours a bit and now they connect via satellite, which means their transmission is much less limited than those relying on wifi."

"They're also much less obvious than the glasses,"

Daniel said. "Easier to blend with the person's outfit, they're smaller and it would take a lot to slap them off."

"For the love of all that is holy." Manny's fists tightened in his trouser pockets. "Can we stop talking tech and watch the footage?"

"Of course." Francine looked at Caelan and relaxed when she saw him loosely holding the stress balls. "Are you ready, Caelan?"

"No."

"Should I wait a bit longer?"

"No." Caelan squeezed the stress balls once. Hard. "Go ahead."

Francine gave him an encouraging smile and tapped on her tablet screen. "There's quite a lot of footage here. Should I play all of it?"

I thought about this. "No. For now, only play the footage on the day Jace disappeared and died."

"Okey-dokey." Francine tapped the screen and four of the monitors in front of me came to life.

Since the monitors didn't have frames and were positioned close to each other, it was convenient to view something on a larger scale by distributing it over four or even more monitors. At the moment, the image filling the four monitors showed the inside of a huge space.

"It looks like a warehouse," Daniel said. "Where is this, Caelan?"

"It's a self-storage space in the warehouse district." Caelan pointed at a door to the left of the open space. "Jace will go out this door now."

"You're in the wrong place." Caelan's voice came over the sound system.

"It recorded your communication as well?" Colin asked.

"Yes." Caelan stared at the monitor as two hands came into view and gestured in a familiar manner. "Jace used sign language to speak to me like this. But sometimes I had to remind him to lift his hands higher or look at them. He would sometimes sign out of view of the camera. He just said that he knows he's in the wrong place and will go to the correct building."

The image on the monitors changed as Jace opened the door and stepped outside. Three days ago, it had been sunny, but cold. Snow from the night before had been removed from the road between the buildings, but the roofs and footpaths all had a thick white layer.

Jace walked towards the building next to the one he'd exited, raised his hands and signed.

"You're the one who insisted on going out today," Caelan said on the recording.

"What did he say?" Vinnie asked.

"He said it's very cold."

"It might be best if you interpret every time Jace signs," I said.

"Okay."

Onscreen, Jace opened a red metal door and walked into the building. He was at one end of the building, looking down several aisles. Each aisle had numerous red doors, most of which looked like rolling garage doors. His hands came into view and he signed.

"Number six-one-eight," Caelan said on the recording.

He shifted next to me. "We got that number from a clue in the previous cache."

The image on the monitors moved down the aisle to the left as Jace walked past the doors, looking at the locker numbers. He walked past six-one-seven and raised his fist in victory when he stopped in front of six-one-eight. He signed.

"I don't know." Caelan's recorded voice sounded agitated. "There wasn't any clue about a code for the lock."

"He asked what the code was," Caelan said.

"We figured," Manny said.

"Try four-eight-three-two-one-nine," Caelan said online. "We don't have any other numbers to go by."

Jace raised his thumb and entered the six-digit number into the keypad. There was a slight click and again Jace raised his fist. He signed.

"He's saying that using the locker's GPS digits as the code is stupid." Caelan paused as his voice on the recording said, "Yeah, but it made it easier for us. See what's inside."

Jace rolled up the door and jerked back. He signed something at the same moment as Caelan's laughter sounded over the recording.

"I know. Of all the caches, this is the silliest. 'E'. Hah." Caelan continued laughing as Jace stepped into the locker to inspect a large lower-case letter 'e' hanging from the roof. There was nothing else in the room. Just this plastic letter with a small piece of white paper attached to it. Jace stepped closer and signed.

"I see the note," Caelan said on the recording. "'I start with the letter 'e', I end with the letter 'e'. I contain only one letter, yet I am not the letter 'e'. What am I?' You're right, Jace. This is stupid. Put the answer into the app and you can get out of here."

"What did he say?" Manny asked.

Francine paused the recording and Caelan turned to look at Manny's shoulder. "He said this was a stupid riddle. A stupid cache. The riddle wasn't really a challenge, especially the last one. He also said he could create a much better cache."

"Well, I don't know what the answer is." Vinnie didn't appear embarrassed. Just puzzled.

"Let me guess," Daniel said. "It's 'envelope'."

"Hah!" Vinnie slapped his thigh. "I get it. Only one letter in an envelope."

The corner of Caelan's mouth twitched.

"Ready to watch the rest?" Francine waited for me to nod before she continued the recording. It moved as if Jace was shaking his head. He entered the word 'envelope' into the app, put his phone away and signed.

"He said he's going home to upload everything and have lunch," Caelan said before his recorded voice replied, "We're registered as first to get to this cache. We're on top, man."

Jace signed.

"Me too. I'm going to have milk and white cookies. I'm too hungry to cook anything now. Maybe tonight for dinner."

The image on the monitors went black and then paused. I glanced at Francine and saw her finger hovering over the pause icon.

"That was the last time I spoke to Jace." Caelan's fingers tightened around the stress ball until his knuckles turned white. "Is this his last recording?"

"No." Francine's tone was gentle. "There's more."

Caelan released his tight grip on the stress ball and squeezed it a few times. "What? What else did he record?"

Francine tapped her tablet screen. The monitors stayed black for another two seconds before a shaky image filled the screens. The bare walls, floor and lack of windows in the room led me to the conclusion that Jace was in a basement. A lightbulb hung from the ceiling, no lampshade or any decorative finishing visible anywhere. A thin layer of white paint hadn't been enough to cover the concrete walls or effectively lighten the space.

Plastic containers lined the walls all the way to the ceiling, each container neatly marked. A quick glance showed some containers holding magazines, marked by year. Other containers held books. These were marked by year and letters of the alphabet.

Wooden crates in the centre of the room drew my attention away from the combination of hoarding and obsessive organising. Jace's hands appeared in view of the camera. He signed.

"He's saying that he found these in a storage locker in the same aisle as the envelope cache we found. The door was open and this was all that was in the room. The manager of the warehouse was inside, swearing like crazy. He didn't know what to do with the crates." Caelan leaned forward and stared at Jace's hands on the monitors. "He says the manager said that one of their regular clients booked the locker on the same day they expected a delivery.

"The client couldn't be there, so the manager agreed to open the locker for the delivery. Twelve crates were delivered. The client came to pick four up and was going to return the afternoon for the rest and pay for the locker.

"When this person didn't come back, the manager opened the locker to remove the crates. Jace is saying the manager was very unprofessional and full of whiny information. That size locker was the most popular to rent out and he wanted to make it available to customers.

"Jace immediately offered to rent it and the manager was very happy to receive a cash payment for a year in advance. The manager said since that client knew the company policies, he didn't have a problem renting out the locker and giving the contents to Jace. Jace then moved the remaining eight crates to his basement. He planned to store other things in this locker."

Caelan paused. "He says that legally he now owns everything that was in that locker."

The crates were identical sizes and all eight had large stickers warning of the fragility of the contents. The shipping stickers were too far away to read the detail and I wondered if the quality of the footage was good enough to zoom in and read the information on the stickers.

One crate was open, the wooden lid leaning against the

plastic containers lining the wall. On top of one of the closed crates was a dark green glass bottle.

"He took crates of wine bottles?" Daniel's tone matched the confusion seen on the faces of everyone in the room. "Why would he do that?"

"Jace collected stuff." Caelan squeezed the stress ball. "In the beginning, it was hard for him to leave the caches for others to find. He wanted to take each cache we found and start a cache collection. So I told him to take photos of each cache. He printed out all these photos and put them in a book."

"What was he going to do with the wine bottles? Did he enjoy drinking wine?" Colin took a step closer to the monitors and stared at the bottle on top of the unopened crate. "This is not from any reputable vineyard I'm familiar with."

Caelan looked at Francine's shoulder. "Can you take the recording back? I stopped reading Jace's signing when everyone started talking."

"Sure thing." Francine tapped her tablet screen and the video returned to the moment Jace's hands came into view.

For a few seconds it was quiet while everyone watched the gestures. "Now he's saying that he's going to plan a cache hunt for people to find the crates. Each person who gets to the final cache will be allowed to take one bottle of wine. He's very excited about creating his own cache hunt. He's saying the riddles will be epic. No stupid envelope riddles."

Jace's hands disappeared from the monitors and he

walked closer to the crate. He lifted the bottle and tilted it as if to read the glossy label. We needed that information.

As I reached for my mouse, Francine paused the image, zoomed in and took a screenshot. She smiled at me, then pointed with a manicured purple nail between her head and mine. "We share a brain, you and I."

I leaned away from her.

"Do you know where this place is?" Manny was looking at the monitor.

No one answered.

Caelan stared at the monitors. Francine zoomed out and searched the footage for the best view of the room. She took another screenshot and put that on the monitor closer to Caelan. He looked at it for a few more seconds and shook his head. "I know Jace rented a few basements in buildings close to his apartment for all his stuff, but I don't know where any of them are."

"He has more stuff than this?" Vinnie's eyebrows were high on his forehead. "Did the dude never throw anything away?"

"No. But he was obsessively organised and kept his collections in very good condition." Caelan started rocking. "He'll never see his collections again."

Colin glanced at Caelan. "Are you all right?"

"Australia is wider than the moon." Caelan rocked back and forth. "Africa is the only continent that covers four hemispheres."

"Come on, bud." Pink walked over to Caelan's chair. "Why don't we get some fresh air?"

"The Sargasso Sea is the only sea without a coast." Caelan nodded and got up. He looked down at his hands and raised his eyebrows when he noticed the stress balls. He made an obvious effort to relax, squeezed the balls and looked at my shoulder. "I want to help."

"I know." It was unsettling to observe how hard Caelan was trying to cope with the effects of the loss of his friend. I'd learned that the average neurotypical individual often needed reassurance, even if it meant lying to them. My studies and own experience had taught me that non-neurotypical people needed logic. I leaned forward. "I will have more questions that you might have the answers to. When I do, I will need your help."

Caelan stared at my shoulder for another seven seconds, then nodded and followed Pink from my viewing room. Immediately, I felt the relief of having fewer people in my space. Manny's grumbling as he sat down in the chair Caelan had vacated felt oddly calming.

"Ready?" Francine's soft question brought tension to my throat until it felt like I was being strangled.

"Have you watched this?" Colin asked.

"No." Francine turned to look at Colin. "And I can't say I want to."

"None of us want to, Franny." Vinnie crossed his arms, the corners of his mouth turned down.

"Play it." If she didn't start the rest of the video now, I might not be able to hold off the looming shutdown long enough.

"Here we go." She tapped her tablet screen and the

video continued for another minute in the basement. Jace signed something before the screen went dark for a few seconds.

When the screen turned on again, the image moved erratically, pained screaming coming through the speakers. Immediately, darkness entered my peripheral vision. I grabbed the armrests of my chair and pushed as far back against the seat as I could.

The image flipped from the ceiling to the floor, the rug, leather shoes, then it slid across the floor until it stopped under the bed. Where we'd found it.

"Where are they?" a male voice whispered in French. My speciality was in nonverbal communication, but sometimes I could determine intent by the tone of someone's voice. There was no tone to interpret. The man sounded calm, emotionless even.

Another loud scream filled my viewing room. My breathing shallowed, the tightness around my throat increasing. No sooner had the pained sounds slowed than Jace screamed again. I couldn't bear this anymore. I wrapped my arms around my drawn-up knees and hid my face in my arms.

The quiet voice questioned Jace three more times, his questions the same. His French had no discernible accent and his whispering made it impossible to determine the timbre of his voice.

When Jace didn't answer, a tormented scream followed. Once. Then again. Three was my limit.

Mozart was out of my reach, my usual techniques never

intended to help me cope with something like this. When Jace again didn't answer a question because he couldn't, I allowed the blackness to take me before I had to listen to his tormented cries again.

"Jenny? Love?" A familiar warm hand rubbed my forearm. "It's done."

"We shouldn't have watched that." Francine's voice was thick with tears.

"You know we had to." Manny was uncharacteristically gentle.

This was what made me lift my head. "How long?"

"You left us only for about twenty minutes." Colin smiled when I looked at him.

I shook my head. "I wasn't asking about my shutdown." I swallowed. "How long did Jace's torture last?"

"Too long." Colin closed his eyes and pushed his fist against his mouth. He took a deep breath and looked at me. "Fifteen minutes."

"It felt like hours." Francine gripped Manny's hand resting on her shoulder. He was standing behind her chair. Colin had taken Manny's usual seat.

"I really want to find that motherfucker and put a world of hurt on him." Vinnie's fists were pushed on his hips, his nostrils flaring. "He doesn't know it yet, but he won't live much longer."

It was foreign for me to feel reassured by the others' distress. I usually didn't want them to experience any emotional discomfort, yet seeing the effect the video had on them calmed me. I lowered my legs to the floor and rolled my shoulders. "Did you learn anything about the killer?"

"No." Francine wiped her cheeks with the back of her hands. "The bastard was out of view the whole time. And he whispered the whole time. It made everything worse."

"His shoes are quality leather boots, but the type you can find in any high-end store." Colin looked at his own designer boots. "We can't even follow up on that. There are too many of those boots in circulation."

"The thing is…" Daniel sighed when we turned to look at him. "We have nothing. We have a video of an unrecognisable man torturing Jace, but we don't even have any evidence that the same man dropped Jace in the forest. It could've been someone else who took Jace to the forest."

"And left him there to die." Francine grabbed her tablet. "I'm not done with my searches. I will find something that will give us a lead on this guy."

I had no idea where she would look. Despite all the data we had, it felt to me like we had nothing.

"Hey, guys." Pink walked towards us, the elevator door closing behind him. "Caelan decided to have milk and cookies with Phillip. He'll join us when he feels ready. Learn anything new?"

Daniel gave Pink a quick review of what we'd seen on the video. They started discussing the evidence and I returned my attention to the screenshot Francine had taken of Jace's basement room. I zoomed in on the screenshot of the wine bottle and frowned. The bright light was reflecting off the glossy label, making it impossible to read. Ignoring Manny's questions, I shifted closer to my desk and opened the software I used when I needed to enhance footage.

Seven minutes later, I leaned back in my chair. The first view of the bottle was from its side, the label not visible. The reflection of the light and the gloss of the label was an unfortunate combination. "I can't see what's on that label."

"Can you see what's on the shipping sticker?" Colin pointed at the screenshot of the room. "That might give us a place to start."

I zoomed in on that sticker, my muscles relaxing. This sticker didn't have any gloss and the light didn't catch it at a compromising angle. I enhanced the image and nodded. "This wasn't shipped to the storage unit. This is a different address."

"Easy Post. Hmm." Pink took out his phone. "It's an international courier. I have a confidential informant who works there. Last month, we intercepted a shipment of cigarettes from Belarus. All black-market stuff. Give me a sec."

We all stayed quiet while Pink contacted his informant and asked a few questions. Each new question made me more curious about the information Pink was learning. I wasn't alone in this. As soon as Pink disconnected the call, Manny leaned forward. "Well?"

Pink's eyebrows were high on his forehead. "This is interesting shit. Wow. Okay, so my CI works in their admin department. It's a small company, but they do well. He said that the shipment arrived, he scanned it and took a photo like he always does."

"Wait." Francine tilted her head. "He always takes photos?"

Pink nodded. "Yeah. He told me it's to protect himself in case his boss ever accuses him of losing a shipment. Apparently, that's why the admin guy before him got fired."

Manny snapped his fingers. "The photo."

"Yes. He sent me the photo and this is where it gets interesting." Pink swiped his phone screen, stretched the image and turned it for us to see. "One address. Two names."

Vinnie leaned closer to the phone. "Gilles Mahout and Adèle Maxim."

"Hold on." Francine tapped on her tablet screen. "Well, paint me yellow and call me SpongeBob SquarePants. Gilles Mahout is the manager at Self-Storage Solutions, the place where Jace found the 'e' cache. And holy yoga pants! The address on the label is for that self-storage warehouse."

"What is going on here?" Manny glared at Pink's phone. "If this Giggles was supposed to receive the crates, why then did he pretend it was a delivery for someone else? And why did he practically give it away to Jace?"

Pink put his phone in his pocket, took out his tablet and tapped on the screen. A second later, he inhaled sharply. "I didn't see that coming."

"Speak. Now." Manny pushed himself to the edge of his chair.

"Adèle Maxim is dead."

"Bloody hell." Manny rubbed his hand over his face. "What happened to her?"

Daniel was also looking at his tablet, his frown deep. "She was killed. This is an open homicide investigation."

It wasn't his tone as much as his micro-expressions that sent a rush of adrenaline through my body. "How did she die?"

Daniel looked up. "The same way Jace did. Tortured."

"Shit." Colin crossed his arms and swallowed. "Tortured? Why?"

We didn't have enough data to answer Colin's question, so I twisted in my seat to look at Daniel. "Tell us everything."

Daniel nodded. "Adèle wasn't tortured half as much as Jace. The autopsy revealed that she had suffered a few punches to her face and only three of her fingers were broken. The medical examiner concluded that she died from heart failure. She had a pre-existing heart condition."

"And when the stress of being tortured became too much, her heart gave out." Colin closed his eyes. "Poor girl."

"Who is she?" Manny pointed at Francine's tablet. "Find out everything you can about her."

"Sir, yes, sir!" Francine winked at Manny and swiped her tablet screen.

"There's some background in her file here." Daniel kneaded the back of his neck. "She was only twenty-eight. So young. She was born in Paulhan, a tiny town of around two thousand residents in Southern France, went to school in the area and came to Strasbourg around twelve years ago. She had an online business—Freedom Fragrances—selling cosmetics. All her taxes were paid. No red flags."

"Ooh, I disagree." Francine raised both eyebrows while looking at her tablet. "This girl was good. She was never investigated for any crimes, but I will bet all my strappy sandals we'll find loads of naughtiness when we start looking into her life. There is no way her little registered online cosmetics business did well enough to buy her a house in the Robertsau neighbourhood. Not according to the tax records I'm looking at."

"Robertsau?" Colin tilted his head. "That area has some very expensive houses. A house? You sure it's not an apartment?"

"Nope. A house. And we all know how expensive houses are in this ridiculous city." Francine narrowed her eyes as she tapped and swiped her tablet screen. "Hmm. I'm looking at it on Google Maps. It's an average-looking house. Blending in nicely with the neighbours."

"She bought it cash." Daniel's eyebrows were raised. "We'll have to look at her family's financial history, but her father is a handyman and her mother a cleaning lady, so I doubt they could've bought it for her. There's a note here that the parents showed no interest when they were notified of Adèle's death."

"That's just awful." The corners of Francine's mouth pulled down. "So sad."

"Or maybe they didn't care to have a criminal daughter." Manny looked at Vinnie. "Have you ever heard of her while visiting your lowlife friends?"

"You mean my criminal informants?" Vinnie straightened and crossed his arms. "The people who have helped us many times to solve crimes?"

"Bugger off." Manny slumped. "So? Have you ever heard them talk about her?"

"No." He shrugged. "I can't even guess what she was into. Drugs, art, guns, petty stuff, hacking. No idea."

"If she was into hacking, I might've come across her." Francine tapped her tablet screen, then shook her head. "But the IP address from her house has never registered anywhere as a hacker's. Not that it means anything. A good hacker would know how to hide."

"Then I suggest you find out who she was and what she was into." Manny looked at Daniel. "When and where did she die?"

"Six days ago. Her house." He winced. "Her gardener found her in the kitchen, still bound to a chair."

"The house still a crime scene?"

"Yup." Daniel lifted his phone. "I'll arrange a visit."

"You guys go ahead." Francine got up. "I'll stay here and look for her online. See what I can dig up."

"Look for connections between Adèle Maxim and Jace." I thought about this some more. "The age difference is slight, so they might have crossed paths in different ways. She might have a sibling or cousin who has a connection to Jace."

"Will do." She winked at Manny as she walked to her desk and said over her shoulder, "Bring me some chocolate when you come back."

"Why do you need more?" Vinnie pointed at her desk. "You have enough chocolate in your bottom desk drawer to feed a rugby team, Franny."

"A girl can never have enough chocolate. Or diamonds." She perked up and looked back into the viewing room. "Forget the chocolates. Bring back some diamonds."

Vinnie laughed when Manny grumbled a rude response before looking at me. "You coming with us, Doc?"

"You pose it as a question, but your nonverbal cues communicate it as an order." I closed my eyes in annoyance at my observation, then started closing all the windows on my computer. "Of course I'm coming."

I wanted to see how this young woman lived. Jace's flat had given me insight into his character. Seeing Adèle's house would hopefully give me similar insight. More importantly, I hoped to find something that would connect her to Jace so we could find the murderer and stop him before anyone else died.

Chapter SIX

WE DROVE TO the Robertsau area in two SUVs. Mid-morning traffic was light and I could relax. There was more than enough space for Colin to keep a following distance that was comfortable for me. Daniel was driving the SUV in front of us and clearly didn't mind being mere centimetres from the vehicle in front of him.

I looked out of the passenger window at the few people walking the beautiful pathways in Parc de l'Orangerie and thought about Caelan. In the three years I'd known him, he'd shown incredible determination to become as high-functioning in this neurotypical world as possible. The last two days had seen a lot of his behaviour revert, yet he was still much more in control of himself than before.

Autism was such a complex neurological disorder that it made it impossible to have a single treatment that would apply to everyone on the spectrum. Mentally writing Mozart compositions, as I was doing now, helped pull my mind away from whatever chaotic stimuli was overwhelming my senses. It calmed me. For Caelan it was reciting geological facts and more recently using the stress balls. I wondered what, if any, methods Jace had used to help him deal with being nonverbal on top of the usual autistic challenges.

Colin followed Daniel's black SUV into a small street lined with snow-covered hedges. Daniel turned into a paved road that led to two houses hidden from the street. He parked behind a police patrol car on the driveway to the smaller of the two houses and got out. Pink joined him on the driveway, shrugging a large backpack onto his shoulders.

Colin parked behind Daniel's SUV and leaned forward to look at the house. The trimmed hedge surrounding the house was not uncommon in this upmarket area. But the electrified fence was most uncommon. The position of the house so far off the street would make it hard for accidental passers-by to peek into the property.

I zipped up my winter coat, put on my fleece gloves and joined Daniel and Pink on the driveway. The temperature had not increased much from earlier this morning, the air cold against my exposed cheeks. Colin stopped next to me just as one of the two officers standing next to their patrol vehicle by the front gate raised his hand in greeting.

"Dan!" The officer smiled and walked to us, his hand outstretched. The two men exchanged the usual polite pleasantries. I bit the inside of my cheek to stop my impatient demand to enter the house.

Fortunately, Pink pretended to be cold and the officer pressed a remote control button to open the gate. It slid to the side to reveal a landscaped garden covered in snow.

The driveway leading to the house was oddly free of snow, most likely heated. Whatever legal or most probably illegal business Adèle had conducted, it had paid her well enough to allow for luxuries most of France's population could never afford. The short walk to the front door was much more comfortable not having to walk through snow.

Daniel opened the unlocked front door and waved us in. "They said the crime scene technicians finished yesterday and were planning on releasing it today. We can hold this as a crime scene for as long as we need."

The central heating in the house was set a bit higher than in my flat. I took off my outerwear and handed it to Colin when he finished hanging his coat and reached for mine. I walked deeper into the house and entered the living area. Like a lot of modern houses, the kitchen, dining and living areas were combined into a well-designed large space.

Adèle had a minimalistic sense of style. The living area looked Scandinavian in design, the wooden floor had a bleached finish, the furniture was in shades of beige and the coffee table was also bleached wood with a frosted glass top. The black grand piano stood out though. I walked to it and wondered how well Adèle had played. And how often.

The lid was open, revealing the beautiful inside. Two music books rested on the stand, the one in front open to a Chopin Étude. I looked at the copper name stamped on the piano. Adèle might have had a minimalistic sense of style, but she'd had expensive taste. This piano was priced at eighty thousand euros.

I looked back at the living area. The only splash of colour came from a large painting against the wall. Colin was already in front of it, inspecting the vibrant work of art.

A nest-like appearance was created by thick amounts of brown and yellow paint drizzled on top of a rectangular board. I wasn't an art expert, but I felt quite confident that I knew who had painted this.

"This is a Pollock." Colin leaned closer, his muscles tense. "Shit. This is his *Number 5*."

"Authentic?" I asked.

"No." He straightened. "There has been ongoing speculation that this painting was sold in 2006 for a hundred and forty million dollars, but that deal has never been confirmed." He looked back at the painting. "This is a brilliant forgery. Since it's nigh-on impossible to forge Pollock's dribbles, I reckon this is a 3D print."

Previously, we'd investigated a case that had introduced me to quality forgeries created by 3D printers. The technology had since developed and I was certain so had the excellence of the forgeries.

"Check all the other paintings in the house, Frey." Manny walked into the room and frowned at the artwork. "If there is any connection between this victim and Caelan's friend, there might also be a connection between the reproduced Roubaud in Caelan's flat and the forged art here."

I didn't know how Manny could've reached that conclusion, but decided to ignore it. I walked to the kitchen where Adèle had been killed. Every surface in the kitchen had a layer of fingerprint dust on it, making the area look unkempt. But apart from that, it was as minimalistic as the living area. There was no clutter on the counters, no containers holding tea or coffee and no ornaments. Only a coffee machine and a kettle.

To my right was a sliding door that led to a patio now covered in snow. In summer, it would make a beautiful place to enjoy breakfast while overlooking the garden. A round table next to me most likely served as the breakfast nook in the colder months. Usually there would be four chairs around a table like this, but one was missing, the empty space obvious.

"She was found over there." Daniel pointed to the centre of the kitchen area.

I closed my eyes for a second and took a calming breath when I noticed the rust-coloured stains on the cream tiles. Adèle's blood. There wasn't as much blood here as in Jace's flat. I supposed the killer hadn't had enough time to cause injuries that bled before Adèle's heart could no longer take the stress of being tortured.

"Down here!" Vinnie's muffled voice came from the staircase leading to the top floor and presumably the bedrooms.

I followed Colin and Daniel to the stairs. To the left of the staircase was a door that looked like it would open to a cupboard utilising the space under the stairs. The door opened and Vinnie leaned out. "You gotta see what I found down here, Jen-girl. I hit the jackpot here."

"This leads to a basement?" Manny asked.

"Yup. I thought it was a cupboard, but look…" Vinnie came out and closed the door. He held up his index finger and pointed to the door when a quiet click sounded behind the door. He opened it to reveal shelves filled with linen and a few pillows. "Now look what happens when I press this button." He reached inside and pushed a round button hidden underneath a neat stack of towels. The shelves slid sideways into the wall and revealed the stairs going down. "I found this totally by accident. I was searching under the towels when I pressed this and voilà!"

"It's clear?" Daniel rested his hand on his holstered handgun.

"Yup." Vinnie looked down the stairs. "Nobody down there. Just lots to learn."

"She sure as hell didn't want just any visitor to find their way down there." Manny waved Vinnie impatiently out of the way. "Move your big arse."

Vinnie lifted his middle finger at Manny, turned around and walked down the stairs. Manny followed him, grumbling.

Daniel looked at me. "Why don't you and Colin go check it out? Pink and I will take photos of everything up here, then we'll join you. If there's enough space."

"There's more than enough space down here, dude!" Vinnie called from below. "It's the size of a double garage and then some."

"You guys go." Daniel smiled. "We'll be there soon."

Vinnie's reassurance about the space made it an easy decision. I went down the brightly lit staircase and entered the windowless basement. A gray industrial carpet covered the floor and two of the walls were lined with built-in cupboards. An L-shaped desk faced the stairs, a laptop and notebook the only things on the surface.

"Hellfire." Manny was standing in front of one of the cupboards. Three of the four sliding doors were pushed to the side, a large organisational chart surrounded by photos. "Doc, get over here and tell me what I'm looking at."

There were no shelves in this cupboard. The doors appeared to have been put in place to cover this wall. I walked closer and looked at the chart. Colin didn't crowd me, but stood close enough to see most of the chart.

This was an impressive and seemingly comprehensive chart. In the centre of a large pinboard was a green cardboard square with the letters 'FF'. Pink twine was pinned to photos and different-coloured squares surrounding the green one. All the squares had a few words written on them, but none of it made sense. It had to be a code of some sort.

"It looks like this was her business model." Colin was looking at the green square. "That 'FF' must stand for Freedom Fragrances. Adèle's business."

I looked at the many photos on the board. Some were connected with twine to only one square, others to more than one square. One of the photos linked to the blue square caught my attention. I pointed at it, careful not to touch anything. "This photo is of the self-storage warehouse."

"So it is." Colin tilted his head. "The 'SSS' on the blue square must stand for Self-Storage Solutions."

"The place where Jace found the crates." Vinnie was opening every drawer he could find, rifling through it.

"Frey." Manny was shaking his index finger at one of the photos. "Look at this. What is that?"

"Artefacts." Colin pushed in front of Manny and gasped when he inspected the photo. "No way."

"What?" Manny leaned in and I took a step to the side. I would ask Pink to take photos so I could study all of this in depth in the spacious safety and isolation of my viewing room.

"This photo has—seven, eight, nine—nine artefacts that were stolen from a private collection in Iran." Colin's eyes were wide as he turned to Manny. "These are all Persian artefacts."

"Authentic?" Manny asked.

"I can't tell just from the photo, but seeing as these pieces were stolen from Iran and taking into consideration where we are, I wouldn't be surprised if they are." Colin pointed at the next two photos. "These works are Near Eastern antiquities. The market demand is insanely high for ancient artefacts that have been discovered in the area between the Nile Valley, now Egypt, and Mesopotamia, which is now Iraq."

"An area that includes Iran," I said.

"Indeed." Colin looked at the ceiling for a few seconds. "Iran has a history drenched in amazing cultures and obviously their art spans several millennia. There are almost twenty cultural heritage sites in Iran protected by UNESCO and another forty-nine sites on a tentative list."

"So what?" Manny shrugged. "Other countries also have amazing history."

"Yes, but not many countries have been looted by terrorist organisations who then sell these artefacts on the black market to the value of tens of millions of euros to fund their ideologies."

"Tens of millions?" Vinnie looked up from the small chest of drawers he was searching through. "That's a shitload of money."

"Actually, it's reported that the largest terrorist group has made upwards of eight hundred and fifty million euros for their kitty." Daniel walked into the room and his eyes widened as he looked around. Pink followed Daniel in and immediately reached for his phone and started taking photos.

"That amount has not been verified." Colin looked at the photos again. "The players in the black market for these antiquities have learned how to cover their tracks well enough that all we have is a lot of speculation."

But I could see that Colin believed there was a level of truth in it.

"Well, shit!" Colin put on his driving gloves and moved one of the photos. "The Roubaud."

"What are you talking about now, Frey?" Manny elbowed Colin out of the way to look at the photo.

Colin lifted the photo away from the pinboard. "This is Roubaud's *The Battle of Elisavetpol.*"

"The painting we found under Jace's bed? Why would she have a photo of it?"

"Good question, Millard."

"Well, ask it to your Johan Klein." Manny lowered his chin to glare at Colin. "Soon."

"I've left him another message. Now I have to wait." Colin took a step back, his eyes not leaving the photo. "What was so important about this painting?"

"And what the hell have we walked into?" Manny looked around, his brow furrowed. "What do you think about all this, Doc?"

Now that there was more space in front of the chart, I moved closer and studied it. Colin was silent next to me as he looked at photos of the artefacts that were to the right of the chart. Above the chart, lines from the squares connected to photos of documents. I squinted as I looked at the documents, but couldn't make out exactly what kind of documents these were.

Next to two photos of a set of documents was one of a few handwritten notes and a photo of a man walking past a café. A twine linked that photo to two more photos of the same man, one where he was sitting in a restaurant, the other of him talking on his smartphone while waiting at a pedestrian crossing. His face was either turned away or somehow obscured in all the photos. Clearly, he was important in Adèle's business model. We needed to know who this was. It was going to be a challenge since we wouldn't be able to use facial recognition software on these photos.

There was an overwhelming wealth of information here and my mind was rushing to process as much as possible. But everything stilled in me when I looked at the photos to the left of the chart. I pointed. "These wine bottles are from the same winery as those Jace took."

"What on God's green earth?" Manny stepped closer and I moved away. He looked at the three photos, each a full image of a wine bottle. He turned to Colin. "Since when did Iran become a wine-making country?"

"Iran?" Colin's eyes widened and stepped closer to look at the photos. "My God, this wine was imported from Iran. And these artefacts were stolen from a private collection in Iran. And look at the photos of the people next to the artefacts. See this man?" He pointed at what looked like a security video screenshot of an overweight, middle-aged man. "He's Pascal Mayer and well known in black-market art circles for his collection of stolen masterpieces." He pointed at three other photos. "The same with Fabien Riner, Benjamin Picon and Damian Leveaux. These people have fences, dealers and criminal defence lawyers on speed-dial."

"Look what I found." Vinnie smiled when we all turned around. He raised the wine bottle he held in his gloved hand. "Shall we make a toast?"

Colin frowned. "Are there more bottles?"

"Not wine bottles." He tilted the bottle and looked at the label. "Only this one. It comes from that cupboard."

As one, we looked at the other cupboard, three of the four sliding doors pushed aside. Unlike the cupboard with the organisational chart, that one had many shelves and drawers. Manny grunted. "We're going to have to log all of this and go through everything."

"Better get your pencil sharpened, old man." Vinnie pointed his thumb at the shelves behind him. "There are millions of perfume bottles."

"That's impossible. There is not enough space for—" I frowned and gave Vinnie an irritated look. "You were exaggerating."

"Only by a bit." Vinnie showed no sign of contrition. "There are seriously loads of perfume bottles."

"Not all of them have perfume." Pink frowned as he opened another box and took out an empty bottle. "Weird."

I stared from the empty bottle in Pink's hand to the wine bottle in Vinnie's and made a decision. The empty perfume bottles were an oddity that had to wait.

I reached into my handbag and took one of the three sets of latex gloves I always had with me. Once both my hands were covered, I took the wine bottle from Vinnie. The screenshots I'd been able to get from Jace's glasses hadn't been good enough to give any details of the labels. On that footage the label had appeared to have a solid background, but looking at it now, I was intrigued by the many lines crossing the olive-green background.

It was only a shade or two darker, which gave it a water-mark quality. Persia Winery was written in flowing letters above a solid dark green silhouette of a basket of grapes. Colin stood next to me, also staring at the bottle. "I think the wine should be tested."

"Now we're talking." Vinnie smiled. "Let me go get the glasses."

"Not like that, Vin." Colin looked at Daniel. "Did you guys find any wine bottles like this one upstairs?"

Daniel shook his head. "We were talking about the lack

of alcohol in the house. We looked through all the cupboards and there's not one single bottle of any kind of liquor up there. Not even a beer in the fridge."

The expression on Colin's face caught my attention. "What are you thinking?"

"A few years ago, there was a case in Italy where a Brazilian man was caught at Fiumicino airport trying to smuggle liquid cocaine in his running shoes."

"His shoes?" Manny's frown deepened. "How?"

"He'd injected it into the soles of the shoes to look like shock-absorbing gel."

"How did they catch him?" Pink asked.

"Stupidity." Colin huffed. "He packed six pairs of running shoes in his suitcase and nothing else."

"Idiot." Vinnie rolled his eyes. "He deserved to be caught."

Colin lifted his index finger. "Those six pairs of shoes contained a street value of more than two million euros."

"Wow." Pink looked suspiciously at the bottle in my hands. "That's a lot of money."

Colin was also looking at the bottle. "These bottles come from Iran. It's right next to Afghanistan, which produces opium that goes into ninety percent of the world's heroin at the moment. This bottle could contain liquid heroin or cocaine."

"Bloody hell."

I tilted the bottle, but the green glass didn't reveal anything about the colour of the content. "How much heroin could be in this bottle?"

"I would reckon around two hundred grams." Vinnie smiled when I jerked. "With a street value of around sixty to seventy thousand euros. Per bottle. And if this is quality heroin, it can be diluted and sold for much, much more."

I handed the bottle to Vinnie and glared at it. "It could kill so many people."

"Two that we know about already." Pink shook out an evidence bag and held it out to Vinnie. "I'll get this to the lab as soon as we're done here. It won't take long to test for illegal substances."

"So where the bloody hell are the other bottles? Jace said Adèle had taken four crates. And he took the other eight."

"Which are now in a basement somewhere," Vinnie added.

Manny nodded, walked to the desk and rested his hip against it. "Doc, how many bottles in one of those crates?"

"Twelve bottles." It had been clear from Jace's video. "That means Adèle took forty-eight bottles."

"And Jace took ninety-six bottles."

"A total of a hundred and forty-four bottles." I did a quick mental calculation using Vinnie's estimates. "If the bottles contain heroin, it would be a total of twenty-eight point eight kilograms."

"That's a fuckload of heroin."

"With a street value of seven point two million euros." I swallowed.

"Holy hellfire, Doc."

"That's a huge motive for torture and murder." Daniel looked at the photos. "And then there's all this."

Colin pointed at the top photo. "These are people, documents, wine bottles and artefacts." He flicked at the bottom photo, then frowned. "There's another photo under this one."

I walked closer and took care to lift the top photo by only touching the sides. As soon as I saw the photo under it, I removed the pin that held the top photo in place and took both photos to the desk. Manny stood to the side to make space for the photos and for Colin to lean over them.

"Shit!" Colin leaned closer, then stepped back and pushed both his hands through his hair. "Those are artefacts that are part of the Oxus treasure."

"The one Nikki was blabbering about last night?" Manny leaned forward and stared at the photos. There were three small golden statues. Two were bearded men who looked like they were holding something. The other was a small gold figure of an antelope, possibly a deer. "Doesn't look like much to me."

"The value of those pieces is incredible. Most of these will never be for sale."

"You think Nikki was right about the treasure hunt?" Vinnie's smile was mischievous. "Franny will be so happy."

"No." Colin shook his head. "There is simply no truth in there being any treasure maps in Roubaud's paintings leading to the Oxus treasure."

"Are these pieces stolen?" I asked.

"Not as far as I know." Colin shrugged. "I'll have to check with my contacts at the museum, but the last I heard, all the surviving metalwork they'd found from the treasure was on display at the British Museum."

"Then why did Adèle have photos of these pieces?" Manny asked.

The men started speculating and I turned away. I looked at Adèle's chart and let my mind wander over all the questions I had. Not only did I wonder why Adèle hid a photo of pieces of the Oxus treasure, I wondered how it was connected to the wine. I didn't know of any vineyards in Iran, but it wasn't out of the realm of possibility.

I continued staring at the chart, knowing that it would take a while to answer these and the many other questions I had.

Daniel took his phone from one of the top pockets in his uniform. "Huh. The manager of the self-storage warehouse is in the wind." He looked at me. "Gilles Mahout is missing. I sent a few officers to locate and question him, but he's nowhere to be found. The people who rent lockers have full access to the warehouse at all times, but the manager's office is only manned during office hours. It's office hours and he's not there. The place is standing wide open."

"His house?" Manny asked.

Daniel's phone pinged. He smiled at Manny. "They must've heard you. Two officers went to his apartment. The front door was open, clothes missing from the wardrobe and all electronic devices gone."

"At least we have the ID of one bad guy." Vinnie shrugged when all of us frowned. "What?" He pointed at the photos on the pinboard. "We have no idea who any of those guys are."

"Not true." I was becoming vexed with his exaggerations. "Colin identified four of the men who frequently buy black-market art."

"I did." Colin's smug expression didn't hide his amusement.

"Whatever." Vinnie turned to Manny. "What I'm saying is the manager dude wouldn't have run if he wasn't guilty. And I don't think he's very smart. We'll catch him quick sticks."

"Famous last words." Pink glanced at his phone. "The crime scene techs are here."

Daniel lifted his index finger when I took a step forward. "I asked them to record everything carefully and send all of it to you immediately."

"They'll have to take everything here in for processing." Pink narrowed his eyes at the perfume bottles. "Prints, trace evidence of the contents and so on. I'll quickly clone her laptop and send it to Francine before the techs take over here."

"Want to come with us, Vin?" Daniel asked. "We're going to the self-storage warehouse."

"Why?" Colin asked. "Should we come?"

"Nah." Pink put his phone in his pocket. "It's just a routine check. We'll check Gilles' office as well as the locker where Jace found the cache. And the dogs are there. We'll see if there are more drugs." He blinked. "Or more wine bottles with drugs."

Vinnie's smile was immediate. "I love watching those puppies work."

"They're trained officers of the law." Manny turned towards the stairs. "Unlike you."

"I sent you all the photos I took here, Genevieve." Pink looked at the chart. "I didn't get shots of the hidden photos. I don't want to disturb stuff before the techs process it."

"Your photos will suffice." There was so much just on the surface to analyse.

"Thanks, Pink." Colin winked at me. "We'll see you guys at the team room."

I sighed. "Yes. Thanks, Pink."

"Anytime, Genevieve." Pink's smile was genuine and not for the first time did I see affection. Since he'd moved into our apartment, he'd referred to me a few times as his friend.

I didn't ponder upon it for very long. My mind kept drifting back to the chart.

Chapter SEVEN

"WELL, THAT WAS interesting." Daniel walked past Francine's desk and stopped at the door to my viewing room. "Where do you want to chat?"

I glanced back at the images of Adèle's chart filling all fifteen monitors and frowned. "I don't want to chat."

He laughed softly. "Of course not. What I should've asked was where you would like for me to debrief you on our visit to the self-storage warehouse."

"We'll do it in here." Manny got up from his desk and pointed at the round table close to the large windows. "Doc's room is too small for all of us."

I was loath to leave studying Adèle's chart and figuring out the different aspects of her business, but Daniel had already interrupted my train of thought. I got up. "The table is a better option."

"Then I'll make coffee." Vinnie walked to the small kitchen on the far side of the large open space. We were on the top floor of the building adjacent to the one Phillip owned and ran his insurance business from. The elevator to our floor was only for our use and led to the foyer of Phillip's building. Vinnie, Colin and Daniel had taken extensive measures when designing our team room to make it as secure as possible. And difficult to access.

My viewing room was the only closed-off space. The soundproof glass walls and doors not only kept us in sight of each other, but also maintained the spaciousness of the area. Colin had a desk in my room, Manny a desk in the team room and Francine had a large computer station set up across from the door to my room.

Vinnie spent most of his time on the dark green sofa by the windows or in the small kitchen. He reached up to pull down a bin from the top of one of the cupboards and filled a plate with his homemade cookies. By the time he walked to the round table with the large tray of coffee mugs and cookies, we were all seated. "The cookies are just for the worst hunger. Don't eat too much. I'm making lasagne for dinner and you'd better eat it all."

"Count me in." Daniel grabbed a cookie from the plate and leaned back. "Pink got lucky when he moved in with you guys. Good food every day."

I wasn't in the mood for social repartee. I held up my hand when Pink inhaled to answer and looked at Daniel. "What did you find at the self-storage warehouse?"

"Nothing that is of immediate use to our case." Daniel sobered and took a sip of the coffee Vinnie handed him. "The documents in the manager's office show that Adèle paid for five lockers in that self-storage warehouse. Not all of them were next to each other."

"The security in that place is terrible." Pink took another cookie and placed it on a napkin next to his coffee mug. "There are three cameras outside, but nothing inside the warehouse. I would never use a place like that to store something I valued."

"Yet Adèle did." The expression on Daniel's face alerted me that he knew why. He nodded. "Because she took care of her own security. By the time we got there, the regional manager had arrived. He opened all her lockers for us and all five of them had cameras installed inside and just above the doors outside. All top-of-the-range cameras—small and strong." He looked at Francine. "Did she stream the footage to her system?"

"Yup." Francine's fingers hovered over her tablet screen, ready to type in whatever search we needed. "The girl was one strange cookie. She had state-of-the-art security, but her computer is way too easy to access. One password and anyone could be in her whole system. She stored all the video footage from the lockers on an external drive. The crime scene techs found it behind the perfume bottles, but I had already remotely accessed it. Shocking security. I checked the recordings of the last few days and so far haven't found anything suspicious."

Francine was one of the most sceptical people I'd ever come across and I completely trusted her when she said there wasn't something noteworthy. I'd been so absorbed in studying the photos of Adèle's chart that I hadn't given much thought to the self-storage lockers. "What was in the five lockers?"

"The dogs went on full alert in one of the lockers." Vinnie straightened in excitement. "The techs tested the air and said there was residue of cocaine and heroin. But that locker was completely empty. Two of the others were also empty. One had some of her personal stuff, like an old sofa, a bicycle and a few boxes. The techs are going through that now, but the stuff we saw was nothing important."

"He's leaving the best for last." Pink looked at Colin.

Daniel also turned his attention to Colin sitting next to me and smiled. "As soon as the techs are done in that locker, they're bringing the artworks here."

Colin's eyebrows rose. "What artworks?"

"I took photos." Pink took his smartphone from a pocket in his uniform shirt and tapped the screen. "I'll send them to you now. Hey." Pink looked up from his phone, his brow pulled down low over his eyes. "Did any of you know Adèle had a sister?"

"No way." Francine swiped her tablet screen and started tapping. "I didn't find anything about any sister anywhere."

"The case file said nothing about siblings," Daniel said.

"Why do you think she has a sister?" Manny asked.

"Because of this." Pink turned his phone to show us a photo of two young women laughing at the camera. This was the first photo I'd seen of Adèle. I didn't know which one of the two women she was.

They were on an empty beach, the sunset creating beautiful hues of purple and orange behind them. The woman with the short blonde hair and freckles on her nose had a red heart drawn around her face. Above their heads in distinct feminine writing were the words, 'The best twin anyone could ever want. Love you, sis.'

"Bloody hell." Manny tapped his index finger on the table and looked at Francine. "Find her."

"On it, boss." She winked at him.

"What else don't we know?" Manny slumped into this chair. "We don't even have a proper connection between Caelan's dead friend and Adèle."

"I consider the wine to be a very strong connection between Jace and Adèle." I studied Manny's expression. "I'm surprised that you would dismiss that."

"I'm not dismissing anything, missy." Manny grunted when Francine slapped him lightly on his shoulder, immediately returning to tapping and swiping her tablet screen. He inhaled deeply and schooled his expression to his usual scowl. "I'm just saying…"

"These are all artefacts that have been looted from Iran." Colin interrupted Manny and lifted his smartphone. "My God. These works are priceless cultural treasures. They should never be in an unguarded storage locker."

"What are you talking about, Frey?"

Colin pointed at his phone. "The photos Pink just sent us. Two of the artworks they found in Adèle's storage locker are part of the Oxus treasure. These pieces should be in the British Museum exhibition."

"Are these the same pieces in the photos in her house?" I asked.

"Yes." He swiped his phone screen and held it for me to see. "This one and"—he swiped again—"this one."

One of the bearded men and the deer.

"What about the other pieces?" Daniel asked.

"These are all from the Persian era," Colin said.

"And let's not forget that Jace had a degree in Persian history." Pink looked at his phone. "He would've known about this treasure."

"You think that's relevant, Doc?"

I considered my answer for a few seconds before looking at Manny. "I don't want to speculate."

"Doc." His expression was very familiar.

"No need to become irate. In this situation, I think speculation is called for." I ignored Manny's faux relief. "If Jace had seen these artworks, he would undoubtedly have recognised them to be from the period he knew well. But I have to reiterate that we have no way of knowing he'd seen these."

"And it's impossible that he studied this era and didn't know about the Oxus treasure," Colin said. "I also think that Jace would've mentioned it if he'd found this. He would've been much more excited about these artworks than the crates of wine."

"Hmm." Manny narrowed his eyes. "You're sure there's nothing to this Oxus treasure thing, Frey?"

Colin's lips thinned and he exhaled loudly. "It's a theory some treasure hunter started in the 1980s. It's utter nonsense."

Manny pushed his hands into his trouser pockets. "Tell me about this Oxus treasure. Without writing poetry about it."

"It's a collection of about a hundred and eight pieces of metalwork in gold and silver as well as around two hundred coins." Colin's muscles relaxed as he talked about a topic he was so passionate about. "These pieces were found around 1880 in the Oxus River. The greatest value of this treasure is the possibility that some of it dates as far back as 200 BC.

"The exact date and location it was found have never been established, but it is said to have been discovered by local people somewhere on the north bank of the river. That part is now in Tajikistan, but then it was all part of the Persian Empire. The area was a major ancient crossing point for the river."

"I'm sure Caelan can tell us more about the river and how it has changed in the last few centuries." Daniel looked at me. "Where is Caelan?"

"I don't know." Why would he even assume I did?

"He's with Phillip." Francine smiled at me. "He refused to leave."

"Get him up here," Manny said. "His useless facts might be useful for once."

Francine rolled her eyes at Manny and lifted her phone. We didn't need information about the Oxus River at the moment, but I did have questions about geocaching. An unrelated thought flashed through my mind. I looked at Pink. "Have you recovered anything from Jace's phone?"

"Nah." Pink winced. "Between the damage, the toilet water and the cleaning agent, that phone is completely destroyed. We couldn't get anything from it."

"Dammit." Manny sighed. "Please tell me you got something from testing the wine bottles."

"Oh, yes." Pink's smile told me the answer before he spoke. "It's liquid heroin all right. The techs reckon that there's two hundred and fifty grams in that one bottle. It sent quite a shockwave through the labs."

"And the department." Daniel looked at Manny. "Did the chief call you?"

"No." Manny's lips thinned. "The president did. Art and murder is one thing, but this kind of heroin connected to Iran is creating all kinds of political problems. They're all panicking about it."

"It's not just the drugs coming from Iran." Colin put his phone on the table. "It's the anger because the West is stealing cultural treasures from countries they so publicly denounce as terrorists. The sanctions, the travel bans, the"—he shook his head—"the disdain for their culture, yet it is rich Europeans who buy these artefacts."

His expression caught my attention and I leaned towards him. "What did you find out?"

Colin exhaled angrily. "I've been phoning around. Three of the four men I'd identified on the photos on the chart have been asking for unusual artworks. They want things that are extremely valuable, but not mainstream like a Rembrandt or a Van Gogh."

"What do you know about them?" Manny asked.

"Mayer is a property magnate. He's made his fortune restoring old houses, villas and even castles and then selling them at exorbitant prices. He's sharp and known to step on anyone and everyone who gets in his way of a good deal.

"Riner inherited his wealth. He's made himself wealthier by investing in art. I know of three paintings he bought for less than ten thousand euros from some unsuspecting person. Then he sold them a few years later at an auction for millions.

"Lastly, Leveaux got lucky with investments. He started small and built his portfolio by taking incredible risks on volatile markets. But it paid off and he's a multi-millionaire. None of them are notorious criminals, but everyone knows they're willing to push the line of legality when they want something."

"Forgive my ignorance, but how much would a piece like this go for on the black market?" Pink tilted his smartphone to show a photo of the deer statue.

"Millions." Colin's *depressor anguli oris* muscles turned the corners of his mouth down. "It should never be for sale. It should be protected as a national treasure. It infuriates me that the Western appetite for antiquities feeds the looting of ancient sites. These people who pride themselves on their sophistication of taste and appreciation of cultural heritage are the ones who create the demand that leads to the pillage of ancient sites and the trade in black-market artefacts."

"That's...Wow. That's just wrong." Pink looked down at his phone and shook his head. "Wrong."

It was quiet around the table. My mind was rushing through all the pieces of information we'd gathered so far.

"I'm here!" The elevator door opened and Caelan rushed out. "Greenland is the largest island in the world! Doctor Lenard! I solved the riddle! I solved the riddle!"

Phillip followed Caelan out of the lift and smiled when Caelan sat down next to Francine. Phillip walked over to the sofa and sat down. When Vinnie motioned towards his coffee mug, Phillip shook his head and settled deeper into the sofa.

I turned my attention back to Caelan. He was no longer tapping or scratching his thigh or compulsively squeezing his stress ball. The muscle tension in his body was much less than before and his eyes focused. He looked at my shoulder. "I'm here. I solved the riddle." He paused and frowned deeply, still staring at my shoulder. "How much detail should I give you?"

I appreciated his question. Like many people on the spectrum, myself included, Caelan was prone to sharing information in the finest detail. "For now I think just the end result, not how you got to it."

He nodded. "When I solved the riddle, I entered 'Gaudi' into the app and look!" He took his smartphone from his trouser pocket and showed me the screen. A digital clock filled the screen. "This is a countdown cache. As soon as I entered the answer, the countdown started. We have to wait twenty-four hours before we'll get the GPS co-ordinates for the next cache."

"We have to wait?" Manny looked as impatient as I felt.

"That's how it works." Caelan frowned at his shoulder. "Don't you understand how a countdown works?"

"Bloody hell." Manny turned away from Caelan, then turned back. "And what the hell is a Gawding?"

"You're such a Philistine." Colin shook his head. "Antoni Gaudi is only one of the most famous architects ever. His Catalan Modernism influence can be seen all over Barcelona. I can see you don't care, Millard, so I'm going to stop wasting my precious breath on you."

I thought about this cache and looked at Caelan. "Explain how one would create a cache on the app."

"Huh. Yes." Francine turned to face Caelan next to her. "I suppose this means that Jace indeed did create a cache."

Caelan nodded. "His cache isn't complete. If he'd entered all the answers to the riddl—"

"Whoa there for a sec, superman." Vinnie scratched his forehead. "Explain very simply how a cache is created."

Caelan stared at his shoulder. "First Jace would've registered a name for the cache, then he had to enter the steps. Each step needs an answer to a riddle to unlock the next co-ordinates. I don't have access to Jace's account, so I don't know how many steps he completed or even the name of the cache."

"But how is it that we can see it now? He didn't register it."

"It's a glitch. The incompetent app designers haven't been able to fix it. If anyone enters the correct answer to the app, it will automatically publish the cache hunt."

"Yeah, I don't really get that, but whatever." Vinnie frowned at Daniel when the latter jerked at the sound of his phone's notification.

Daniel looked at the screen, his eyes widening. "We have more intel on those crates. Pink's CI at Easy Post did a bit more snooping around to see if there was anything else to be found on that shipment."

"What do you have?" Manny narrowed his eyes at Daniel's phone, then glanced at Francine as she lifted her tablet and swiped the screen.

"This won't come as a surprise," Daniel said. "The crates were shipped from Iran. They were supposed to be delivered to… hold on a sec. The recipients were changed online. The original recipient was completely deleted from the system. Gilles and Adèle are the only names the CI could find connected to this shipment."

"Tell me more about this shipping company."

"I'm checking them now." Francine tapped her tablet screen. "Easy Post. It's a third-party company that simply receives international orders and delivers them to customers. They make it easier for individuals to receive large orders through them. No customs fee, etc."

"This is how the cigarettes from Belarus entered the country," Daniel said. "Easy Post is a small international mailing service, but deals in large shipments and has agreements with a few government agencies to streamline incoming shipments from outside the EU." He looked at his tablet screen again. "These crates cleared customs without any problems, went to Easy Post and were then taken to Self-Storage Solutions."

"Where Jace found them." Caelan's words came out as a whisper.

Daniel gave Caelan a compassionate smile. "Indeed."

"Here's one theory." Colin looked down from where he'd been staring at the ceiling. "The drug suppliers send the wine bottles to their distributor here in France. Somehow Adèle knows about this and intercepts the shipment by changing the recipients. The distributor finds out about her when he goes to Easy Post to collect his crates and goes looking for her. He finds her at the house and tortures her to get the location of his missing crates. I'm assuming she dies after she tells him about her lockers at Self-Storage Solutions."

"He rushes over there." Vinnie leaned forward, nodded at Colin. "When he gets there, he finds the locker empty. Maybe he goes through the limited outside security footage and sees Jace taking away the crates. He finds Jace and tortures him to force him to reveal where he hid the crates."

"But Jace can't tell him because Jace doesn't talk." Caelan swallowed and scratched his leg.

"We need to find the crates that Jace took." I didn't know how correct their hypothesis was, but it fitted the information we had so far. "That will bring us closer to finding the killer."

"Who most likely is the distributor." Daniel looked at Manny. "We find him and we might stop the influx of drugs from the East."

Manny nodded. "We need to be careful. Politically, this is a minefield."

"Could this minefield wait until tomorrow?" Phillip

moved to the edge of the sofa and studied us. "You are all tired. It's quarter to seven and I'm sure you haven't had dinner yet."

I didn't want to wait until tomorrow. I wanted to continue studying the chart we got from Adèle's house. I was sure there was information that could help us find the killer. But from experience, I knew that Phillip was right. My desire to find an answer usually turned into a state of hyperfocus that didn't allow me to eat or sleep.

It took Francine's outrageous flirting to convince Caelan that it would be prudent to continue investigating this with a rested and fresh mind. Twenty minutes later, I was sitting next to Colin in his SUV, looking out of the window as we made our way to our flat. I wondered if Nikki had already bathed Eric and whether she had remembered to use the sponge alphabet letters to teach him while playing.

I felt conflicted. On the one hand, I was looking forward to sitting on the sofa and having that little body snuggle up to me after dinner. On the other hand, my mind kept returning to the chart, the mystery of Adèle's business and the person who had tortured and killed her and Jace.

Chapter EIGHT

"FABIEN SAYS THEY'RE ready." Daniel walked into my viewing room and stopped behind my chair. Colin was sitting at his desk behind me and looked up when Manny, Vinnie and Francine followed Daniel into my room. Daniel continued reading the message on his phone. "He says Claire is not coping well, but she wants to help."

I felt rested after an evening and morning that allowed me to go through my routines. I had come to accept that as much solace as I found in every day being exactly the same, life simply didn't afford me that luxury. Yet it was still extremely hard for me to overcome the discombobulation when my routine was interrupted. When I had mornings like this one though, my mind was at ease and I felt better equipped to deal with investigating Jace and Adèle's deaths. I also felt less disturbed by the people interrupting me.

I closed the images of Adèle's business chart on the monitor in the centre of the fifteen monitors in front of me and clicked on the video conferencing link. Francine had discovered that Adèle's twin sister lived in Paris. It was noteworthy how well hidden that connection was.

Daniel had wasted no time contacting Fabien Leveaux, his counterpart in Paris.

It had taken the Paris GIPN team less than an hour to find Claire Pichet, but Fabien had then needed another two hours to calm her down after they'd given her the news that her sister had died. I entered the contact information and was about to put the call through when Daniel cleared his throat. "Hold on a sec. I think it's best if only you and I are visible on the camera. I don't know how Claire will react to facing a room full of people interrogating her."

"I agree." I would never presume to know how a neurotypical person processed such intense grief, but an interrogation such as this would certainly not be easy.

"Okey-dokey." Francine stopped next to me, turned around and joined Vinnie at the door. Colin got up and stood next to Manny by the wall opposite the door. Manny hadn't said much when he'd entered my room. He was leaning against the wall, his hands in his trouser pockets and his expression a clear warning not to engage.

Daniel sat down next to me. "Please make sure the camera is only focused on us, then put the call through."

I adjusted the camera and clicked on the call button. We connected immediately. On the monitor in front of us were three people. I assumed the man in the uniform was Fabien and the woman sitting next to him Claire. A man was standing behind her, both his hands resting on her shoulders.

Claire and Adèle had obviously not been identical twins.

Claire's nose was slightly broader and her cheekbones not as high and pronounced as her sister's. Her brown hair was much longer than Adèle's and was currently in a ponytail. Either she never wore makeup or all the makeup she'd put on this morning had been cried off. Her eyes were red-rimmed and the tissue she clutched in her hand confirmed her deep sadness.

"Daniel, this is Claire Pichet." Fabien's French had the hints of some areas in the south of France where the endings of words were often dropped. He turned to the man standing behind Claire. "This is her husband, Arnaud."

"I'm so sorry that we're meeting under these circumstances." When Daniel spoke French, his voice dropped a tone, his pronunciation softer. He sounded even more empathetic than when he spoke English. "Please accept my most sincere condolences."

"Thank you." Claire's chin quivered and she swallowed.

"This is Doctor Genevieve Lenard." Daniel turned to me. "She's helping us find out what happened to your sister."

She nodded. "I don't know how I can help, but I'll do anything I can. I'll tell you everything I know."

"Tell us about your relationship with your sister." Daniel's tone was gentle as he asked a question that would not have been my first. I'd observed her micro-expressions and wanted to know what it was she knew and seemed eager to tell us. But experience had taught me that Daniel's way of starting with less invasive questioning would be more effective in getting the most information.

"We were close." Her voice broke on the last word and she took a few seconds to regain control over her emotions. "You know we are twins, right?"

"Fraternal twins." Daniel smiled. "Who was the oldest?"

"Adèle. She was born six minutes before me." She grabbed her husband's hand on her shoulder and held onto it as if it was a lifeline. "We talked every day, sometimes three times a day. Even though I live in Paris and she lives… lived in Strasbourg, we didn't feel the distance."

"We didn't find a lot to connect you guys online."

She nodded. "It was on purpose. Adèle insisted on it. She knew her life could put me in danger, so we never posted anything online to connect us. Only my closest friends know about Adèle. She told me that she made sure no one knew about me, not from her side anyway."

"What about school friends?"

"We went to school in Paulhan. Most of those people are still in town, working in the local shops."

"Ah, the beautiful south of France. Picturesque villages and countryside." Daniel's smile was reassuring. "But you and Adèle escaped to the big city."

She paused and narrowed her eyes. "You're trying to be polite." She took a shaky breath. "I know Adèle was dealing drugs. I will tell you exactly how it happened. But I don't know the details you will want."

"Okay." Daniel sat back in his chair. "I'm listening."

Her expression grew hard, the corners of her mouth turned down. "You know the kind of people who have bad luck following them everywhere? Well, those are my parents. Everything that could possibly go wrong in their lives has gone wrong. At the moment, they're living on my uncle's farm in a small cottage. My dad is helping my uncle on the farm and my mom is cleaning a few people's houses to get by. Adèle and I stopped helping them a long time ago."

"Why?"

"Because even with help, they managed to screw everything up. When we were kids, we learned to look after ourselves at a young age. My dad would be off working on a new opportunity and my mom would be in a new job that she was bound to lose within a month or two. By the time we were going to middle school, Adèle and I were the only ones in the house cooking meals. My mom was and still is a cleaner. The house was always spotless, even when things were falling apart. And when I say falling apart, I mean it literally.

"When we were fifteen and in high school, we realised that if we wanted a better life, we'd had to make it happen ourselves. We were talking about getting scholarships to study, but we soon realised that we wouldn't get that. That's when Adèle devised a new plan. It was one of the few times she didn't share her ideas with me. Not until she had the plan already working. It took her a year and by that time, she'd made up her mind."

"About what?" Daniel asked.

"That I was the one to go to university and she would make sure that we both had money to escape our parents' lives. Once I graduated and was settled, she would start her studies. We argued about this for days." She swallowed. "I was so angry. Adèle was the genius of the two of us. Sure, I did well at school, a bit higher than average, but she was way above that. She was the one who should've gone to university first. But she refused. When she told me about her plan, she'd already saved over five thousand euros."

"Drug money?" Fabien asked.

She nodded. "She was smart. She registered a small business, selling perfumes online. At first, she was selling cheap knock-offs until she could afford the more expensive brands. She also started with small amounts of drugs, but she didn't start with softer drugs. She started with heroin and that was her main trade."

"Do you know how she operated her business?" Daniel asked.

"I figured it out and she reluctantly told me I was right. Her perfumes were a front for the drugs. She sold the high-end perfumes at prices five to ten times more than anywhere else on the internet. The buyers would buy a bottle online and she would ship the heroin to them, neatly packaged in the original perfume boxes. She'd found a way to empty the perfume bottles and fill them with heroin without damaging the bottles."

This certainly explained the numerous empty perfume bottles Vinnie had found in the cupboard in Adèle's basement.

"She used a courier?" Daniel waited until Claire nodded. "That's how there was never any suspicion about the packages. Especially if she sold only in France."

"She sold in other EU states as well, but most of her business was here." Claire sighed. "She told me once that she felt conflicted. On the one hand she was proud that her business had built up such a good reputation for a superior-quality product. And on the other hand she was ashamed that she was proud about selling drugs."

"You feel guilty." I could see that emotion clearly on her face.

"Of course I do." She waved her hand in the air. "Adèle did all of this so I could study and make a better life for myself. She was so stupidly selfless. You know, she never used any of that money to go on vacation or buy herself nice things. Everything she bought was for the business." She paused, her eyes filling with fresh tears. "Now that I think about it, she never went on holiday."

"Did Adèle deal only in drugs?" Daniel asked.

"Yes. Why?" She inhaled sharply. "Oh, God. Did you find something else? You must have. I wonder... You know, about six months ago, Adèle told me that she'd procured some valuable things for someone who was her ticket out. And of course, she refused to tell me what these valuable things were.

"I also don't know if it were these valuables, but she said this was going to change everything. She was working on one huge deal and then she was getting out." Her expression softened. "She was going to study music. She started taking piano lessons six years ago and was really good.

"Last month she told me she'd saved one and half

million euros, so she never needed to work again. She just wanted to play the piano and this last big deal was going to double her savings. She was excited about it. I had graduated and was settling down and it was her turn. Now… now it's all for nothing."

Daniel waited while she wiped fresh tears with her tissue. He cleared his throat. "Did she say anything else about the huge deal? Names, places, anything?"

Claire thought about this for a moment, all the while slowly shaking her head. "Nothing concrete. I'm… I *was* always so worried and curious about her life and work that I grabbed every small detail she ever shared. All I remember is that she mentioned two men. Not their names, just that she co-operated with them. My impression was that these men didn't know each other. I got the impression that she controlled only one relationship. I can't remember what gave me that impression, but I was convinced she was scared of the other man."

I leaned forward, closely watching every single micro-expression. Claire Pichet was telling the truth.

"Any idea when she'd met this man?" Daniel asked.

"The one she was scared of? No. The other one I think she'd known for a few years. She'd only recently started talking about the scary man. The other one… years?" She paused, her eyes going up and left—she was recalling memories. Then she nodded. "Yes, it's been at least four years. He helped her getting the drugs into the country. She'd… wait! One day she said something about a warehouse." She paused. "Does this help?"

"A lot." Daniel had barely managed to hide his excitement. He'd most likely also come to the conclusion that the one man was probably Gilles. "This warehouse. Do you remember anything else?"

She took her time to think about this. Her shoulders dropped. "No. I'm sorry."

"Please don't be. This is truly helpful." Daniel paused when Claire's expression changed.

She frowned and blinked a few times, her fist pushed against her mouth—deep in thought. Her eyes widened and she turned her attention back to the camera. "Six months. I remember now. Six months ago, Adèle said she'd had a run-in with a scary man. By then, I'd learned not to react and tell her to be careful. When I did that, she just stopped sharing."

"What happened six months ago?" Daniel asked.

"I lost a patient and was very sad. This is why I remember that day. I didn't want to talk about my job or myself and focused on Adèle. She told me she'd made a mistake and thought this guy was on to her, but she'd managed to avoid being discovered. You know? Now that I think about this, I don't think she'd ever met this man.

"The few times she talked about him was usually about making sure that he never found out where to find her. The very little she said about him led me to believe that he was her supplier. I never managed to figure out where she got the drugs from, but I was sure he was either the point of origin or the next step. I also never figured out exactly how the drug-dealing business worked."

Her chin contracted and her voice grew shaky. "Adèle kept all that from me. She said she didn't want that life and those people ever getting close to me. Especially the scary man. She was adamant that he would never find me."

"She loved you." Daniel waited until Claire regained control over her emotions. "Why is it that your parents didn't tell you what happened to Adèle?"

Her sadness turned into anger and her husband rubbed her shoulders as he leaned a bit closer to the camera. "We broke contact with them three years ago. Those people are toxic."

Claire gripped his hand. "Arnaud helped me break those ties. It was liberating. Adèle was stronger than me. She stopped speaking to our parents the moment we left Paulhan. I still spoke to my mom a few times a year after that."

"And every time it devastated her." Arnaud's nostrils flared. "That woman had nothing positive to say to Claire. Ever. And she never made the effort to phone or make any contact. If it wasn't for Claire phoning her, they would've never talked."

"She's an angry and sad woman." Anger forced colour into Claire's cheeks. "She blamed me for Adèle having a heart condition. As if I caused it. Adèle was born with it."

"Did you know about all of this?" Daniel asked.

"Who? Me?" Arnaud touched his chest. "Yes and no."

"I told Arnaud everything about my childhood, my parents and Adèle." Claire bit her lip, guilt pulling at the muscles around her eyes and mouth. "I told him that

Adèle paid for everything in my life and that he should never ask where the money came from."

Arnaud's lips tightened. "I asked only that once. It was the first time I looked at Adèle's business website and realised things were off."

"I begged him to let it be."

His expression made me lean forward. "You didn't."

Arnaud blinked and moved away from the camera. Claire frowned, then turned to look at Arnaud. "What is she talking about?"

"I love you, Claire." Guilt was now the dominant expression on his face. "But I worried and wanted to make sure you are safe."

"What did you do?" Her question was breathless.

"I created a dummy account and ordered perfume from Adèle." He relaxed, his smile small, but genuine. "She figured out it was me and came to my office."

"She came to Paris?"

"She did. And she told me about the drugs." His smile widened. "Then she told me in graphic detail what she would do to me if I ever told you she came to me or that I knew."

Claire was sobbing. "Oh, Adèle."

"It was easy to see she had a heart of gold." He reached out and wiped tears from her cheeks. "So I let it be."

"You're right." Claire took a shuddering breath. "Her heart wasn't weak. It was strong. And big. I'm the one with the weak heart."

"We weren't able to find any records of Adèle receiving any medical treatment." Daniel surprised me with that information. He'd been very proactive. "Did she use an alias?"

Claire nodded. "She had two aliases. One she used for her work. Her drug-dealing persona was Élodie Baille and the one for her medical stuff was Janine Durand."

From the corner of my eye, I saw Francine lift her tablet. We had two more names to teach us more about Adèle.

"Was Adèle interested in art?" Daniel asked. "Or maybe she considered investing in art?"

Claire tilted her head and narrowed her eyes. "If you're asking whether she sold stolen art or forgeries, I truly don't know. But I honestly don't think she would've. She made a lot of money with her drugs. She always said that one shouldn't change horses mid-race. And she was close to the end of her race. So no. I don't think she dealt in art. That being said, it's very possible the valuable things that were her ticket out were artworks. I honestly don't know."

"Only a few more questions." Daniel gave her an apologetic smile. "We're almost done."

Claire straightened. "I don't mind. I'll help in any way I can."

"Okay then. Did Adèle ever mention a Jason or Jace?"

"No."

"Franz Roubaud?"

"No."

"The Oxus treasure?"

She blinked in surprise. "No."

Daniel glanced at the notes he'd made on his phone.

"That seems to be all the questions I have for you at the moment."

"Oh. Okay." She leaned forward. "I'll leave my phone on and will keep it with me all the time. If you need to know anything else, please phone me."

"Thank you. I will." Daniel paused. "You're an exceptional woman, Claire. I see why Adèle did so much to see you succeed. Two exceptional women, the both of you."

Claire's eyes filled with tears. She tried to speak, but couldn't. As silent tears ran down her cheeks, she nodded her thanks.

Daniel spoke with Fabien, then reassured Claire and Arnaud that he'd stay in touch. It took a few minutes to convince them to accept police protection until the case was solved. But they immediately agreed to keep the interview and all questions asked confidential. They understood that any leaked information could jeopardise the case and possibly put their lives in danger. A few more pleasantries and the call ended.

It was silent in my viewing room for a few seconds. My mind was racing with this new information. It was most frustrating to have so many unconnected bits of information. I put the photos from Adèle's basement back on the monitors and stared at them. What had I missed?

Was there any information, any indication who the dangerous man was? Had I missed any mention of her aliases? I clicked on one of the photos and methodically started going through them. I didn't know how long it would take me to analyse all this information. I barely heard Francine promising Manny she'd get all the dirt on Élodie and Janine, and the ensuing banter.

"Jen-girl, get your butt over here." Vinnie stood next to the round table and shook his index finger at the coffee and cookies in the centre of the table. "I didn't make you fresh coffee for it to get cold."

I glanced at the clock on my computer. I'd lost myself in the photos for more than four hours. It had been longer than that since I'd eaten and the thought of refreshments made my stomach rumble. I got up and walked to the table. Everyone else was already seated and Manny was sipping his milky tea. He appeared to be in slightly better humour.

"Can anyone tell me how this new information helps us understand what happened to Adèle and the other victims?" Manny put his mug on the table and took another cookie from the heaped plate. Vinnie's oat cookies were my favourites.

"Well, I'm having one hell of a time trying to get anything on Élodie and Janine. Adèle hid those two aliases as well as she hid her sister." Francine lifted her tablet. "So far, I managed to get their national IDs. They're both registered residents of Strasbourg with a really good backstory. Whoever sold Adèle the IDs did a great job. Élodie is self-employed as a manicurist and earns just enough to survive, as per her tax returns. I am yet to find a bank account."

"But that's where we'll see a shit-ton of money." Vinnie pushed a cookie into his mouth.

"Most likely." Francine's frustration at her lack of

significant progress was evident. "Janine is a virtual assistant who works freelance for entrepreneurs."

"Both professions hard to trace," Colin said. "Did you ask Da—"

"No, Mister Smarty-pants." Francine rolled her eyes. "I actually asked Pink to dig deep to give me anything he could on these two. I've also been snooping around Adèle's business. She registered her online shop for selling cosmetics just like Claire told us. Everything the sister said was true, including the outrageous prices Adèle charged for the perfumes. A bottle of Armani perfume that usually retails for around a thousand euros goes for nine to twelve thousand euros on her online shop."

"Bloody hell." Manny jerked. "Who on God's green earth would buy perfume for a thousand euros?"

Francine shrugged. "I do. And you told me last night..."

"Enough!" Manny glared as Francine giggled.

Colin shook his head at them. "It's such a simple, but elegant plan. Adèle didn't even need to launder her money after the fact. These sales were all legit."

"And she paid her taxes," Francine said. "She had a successful online business that wouldn't attract too much attention. I don't know if her accountant was in on this as well, but it wouldn't have been too difficult to keep him or her in the dark. Everyone would just have thought that Adèle was crazy selling perfumes at such prices and her customers even more insane paying those prices."

"What about her web traffic?" Colin asked.

"Minimal." Francine shrugged. "That's no surprise. She

didn't advertise anywhere and no one in their right minds would spend time on this site with these prices. Not if they were really shopping for perfume. I must admit that I'm surprised her website isn't on the dark web. Here, we can trace traffic and the IP addresses of people who visited her site."

"What I would like to know is where Iran comes in." Vinnie leaned back in his chair. "I mean, I know that Adèle got the wine from Iran and the wine had the heroin, but who is her connection in Iran?"

"And is this only about drugs?" Colin raised his index finger. "Not that I'm saying drugs aren't bad enough. But is this a security threat? We all know that Iran has all kinds of nuclear issues with the world."

"Holy hell." Manny looked at me. "Found anything new in those photos, Doc?"

"A lot, but I'm not willing to speculate." I wasn't. I needed more time. It felt like there were small streams of water in my brain and they were about to converge into a river. I was waiting for that moment when all the seemingly disconnected elements flowed into a motivation for these crimes.

"Dan and I checked the security cameras in Jace's building." Vinnie straightened when we all looked at him. "We used the metadata…" He sighed when Francine faked a coughing fit. "Franny helped us by giving the metadata from Jace's smart glasses. We used the time-stamps to search for anything or anyone suspicious on the security feeds, but nothing."

"So he came up through the basement like we thought," Colin said.

Francine turned the conversation to outrageous theories and I lost interest. I got up and returned to my viewing room. Something about the photos was niggling in the back of my head. I sat down and cleared the monitors. I'd been through all the photos the crime scene technicians had taken of the house.

It was the photos of the organisational chart that had my interest. There was a lot to study and try to understand. I opened the photos of her chart on my monitors. A photo of the wine bottle in Adèle's basement was in a prominent place next to the chart photos and deserved attention, but first I needed to understand the code Adèle had used when making her chart.

I adjusted my keyboard so it was perfectly aligned to the edge of my desk and narrowed my eyes at the monitors. After all the distractions yesterday and this morning, I was pleased to return to the chart. I zoomed in on the photos of the other wine bottles Adèle had pinned next to the chart.

"What do you make of the labels?" Colin was sitting next to me. Every now and then he entered a search for something on his laptop, but so far neither of us had uncovered any significant information.

I zoomed in even more on the bottles. "The resolution is not good enough to see the detail of the labels." I turned to him. "The label on the bottle we found in her house had a watermark. I can't see if there's a watermark on these bottles."

"Huh." He leaned back in his chair and looked at the ceiling. "I didn't think much of the watermark. Do you think there's something to it?" He looked at me and smiled. "Don't answer that. I know we'll have to see the bottles to determine that."

I looked at the photos on the monitor next to the wine bottles and zoomed in on the photo with the best quality. The mystery man Adèle had secretly photographed in a few places was standing at a pedestrian crossing talking on his phone. It was summer and he was wearing a fitted black shirt hanging over tailored khaki trousers.

His bearing was that of a confident man, his spine straight, his shoulders back. My eyes were drawn to his hand holding the phone to his ear. Stretching from his wrist and disappearing between his middle and ring finger was a birthmark. The brown colour of the oval-shaped mark blended in well with his skin. None of the photos gave an indication of his race, so his tanned skin could be from the sun or heritage.

I shook my head in frustration and moved my attention to the monitor next to the photos of the man. These were the handwritten notes that appeared to be receipts of some kind. As I zoomed in, the elevator opened and Daniel walked into the team room, nodded at Manny and joined him at his desk.

Vinnie walked into my viewing room and sat down in the chair on my other side. The chair Manny usually occupied. "Whaddup?"

"Bored?" Colin asked.

"Nope." He stretched out his legs and crossed his feet at the ankles. "You two just looked like you need my expertise." He ignored Colin's snort and looked at the monitors. "What are we looking at?"

"Photos of the chart in Adèle's basement."

"Ah." He frowned and pointed at the monitor with the handwritten slips. "What's that?"

"I don't know." And it was most vexing. "These appear to be receipts, but it's not clear for what."

I zoomed in on the top receipt until it filled the monitor. There was only one word. The rest were numbers. The four numbers at the top of the receipt could easily indicate a date—day and month. Below that a word was written in Arabic. The handwriting was strong and slanted to the right. I was confident that a man had written these notes. Under the word were two strings of numbers. There was no punctuation separating the numbers to indicate whether these were phone numbers, IP addresses, GPS co-ordinates or something else.

"Well, fuck me." Vinnie's soft curse took my attention away from the monitor. He was leaning forward, his elbows resting on his knees. His eyebrows were high on his forehead and a small smile pulled at the corners of his mouth. "I know what this is."

"Then don't play games." Manny walked into my room and glared at Vinnie. "Tell us what this is."

Vinnie turned his back on Manny to face me. "These are Hassan's hawala slips."

Chapter NINE

"WHO'S HASSAN AND what the hell is lalala?"

Colin shook his head and looked at Manny. "Hawala is a very old manner of transferring cash. It started as far back as the eighth century between Arabic and Muslim traders as protection against theft. It's an informal system operated by hawaladers—money brokers. And even though hawala follows Islamic traditions, its use is most definitely not limited to Muslims."

"I heard it described as the 'working man's Bitcoin'." Francine walked into my viewing room and stood next to Vinnie. Daniel walked past them and walked straight to the back of my room. I was grateful.

"Hawala was the first manner in which money changed hands without changing hands," Colin said.

"Huh." Manny scratched his stubbled jaw. "I've heard of that. It has been used by terrorists to get funding from Western countries to their home turf."

"It's still being used," Daniel said. "A lot. It is estimated that around four hundred million dollars is moved through the system each year."

"Holy mother of all." Manny looked at Colin. "Explain the system. Without a history lesson and poetry."

"You're such an arsehole." Colin exhaled loudly. "You want to send money to Vinnie who is in Russia."

"No, I don't." Manny scowled.

Colin ignored him. "But you can't or don't want to use banks or any financial transfer institutions. So you come to me, a hawala broker, and give me the one million dollars."

"Yeah, baby." Vinnie's smile widened when Manny's scowl deepened.

"Along with the money, you give me a password." Colin waited until Manny nodded impatiently. "I call my counterpart Francine who runs her hawala brokerage in Moscow. I give her the amount and password. In the meantime, you've called Vin and given him the password and Francine's address. He goes to Francine, gives the password and she gives him his million dollars. Both Francine and I will take a small commission which is usually less than the banks charge."

"And now my man owes Franny a million bucks," Vinnie said.

"Since hawala is entirely based on an honour system, she knows I'm good for it." Colin smiled at Francine. "I'll settle the debt at a later date or it will balance out through hawala payments coming from her side and paid out by me."

"Hassan would die before he reneges on a debt." Vinnie crossed his arms, all humour gone from his face. "He told me his business is built entirely on trust and the use of his huge network of connections."

Colin nodded. "The vast majority of people using the system are hardworking civilians sending money to their relatives. In some parts of the world, it's really the only way to transfer money legitimately. Even aid organisations use it because it's the only functioning institution in certain areas. And it's fast."

"It's not quite as anonymous as cryptocurrency, but it's definitely one of the safest ways to move money across borders." Francine was standing next to Daniel, her tablet in her hand.

"It makes sense that this would be the way Adèle paid for her drugs and stolen art." Colin turned back towards the monitor and stared at the enlarged photo. "Not that we can tell anything from these."

"Who's Hassan?" I asked Vinnie.

"I've known him for many years and he has the deep respect of the Arabic and Indian communities."

"Then don't just sit there." Manny fists tightened until his knuckles turned white. "Get us a meeting with this criminal."

Vinnie's *risorius* muscles pulled his lips into a sneer. "And this is why I think you should stay the fuck away from Hassan. He's a good man. People trust him. Much more than they trust the police. With all the hate against immigrants, they will lose faith in Hassan if you go in there guns blazing."

Manny's face turned red, the vein on his forehead becoming more pronounced. His lips thinned and he inhaled sharply. Colin got up. "Dan can come with us while you cool down."

"Now you're talking." Vinnie gave Manny an insincere

smile and took his phone from his pocket. He got up and walked into the team room.

Manny glared at his back, then turned his anger on Colin. "I hold you personally responsible."

Colin laughed. "For what? It's not my fault you're such an arse."

"Doc?" Manny focused on me.

"Yes?"

He threw his hands in the air. "Bloody hell."

Daniel laughed. "I'll make sure the interview with Hassan is on the up and up, Manny."

"You bloody better." Manny stomped out of the room. Francine followed, teasing him about sexy angry men.

It exhausted me, so I looked back at the photos, but ten minutes later I was in Colin's SUV, my analysis of Adèle's charts yet again interrupted. Daniel and Vinnie were sitting in the back and Colin was navigating the large vehicle around a parked delivery truck. For a moment, I allowed myself to think about the senselessness of driving large vehicles in narrow European streets. But my mind was gripped by the many mysteries surrounding Adèle's business.

I hoped Hassan would be able to give us more context to the receipts we found in Adèle's basement. Vinnie had been completely truthful when he'd said Hassan was a 'good guy', but I'd seen the deception when Vinnie had avoided giving Daniel a forthright answer to the question of the lawfulness of all Hassan's dealings.

Colin turned the SUV into a street off the main road.

We were in a district known for large outlet stores. My eyes widened when he parked in front of a Persian carpet store. I'd been so absorbed in my concern about Manny and thinking about the case, I had not listened to the directions Vinnie had been giving Colin.

We got out of the SUV and I looked at the other cars parked in front of the store, all high-end vehicles. Daniel was staring at a red sports car. "Who drives a Ferrari when it's minus five and the roads are full of snow and ice?"

"People with money, dude." Vinnie pulled the zipper of his thick jacket all the way to his chin. "Come on. Hassan is waiting for us."

I followed the men into the warm store and blinked. In my travels, I'd been in a few Persian carpet stores and most times had left as soon as I'd entered. The chaos of the rugs piled on top of the other without any regard for lining up the edges had been too much for my mind. This large store was a surprise.

It looked more like a gallery exhibition than a rug store. Dark wooden floors gave the store an upmarket feel, the hidden ceiling lights adding to the impression. Strategically placed spotlights were aimed at the exquisite rugs hanging against the walls like paintings. Lining the walls were neat piles of rugs, organised according to colour and size. Even the price tags hanging off the sides of the rugs were aligned. This was a place where I could spend time.

"Vinnie!" A rotund man rushed from the back of the store, his arms open. "You rascal!"

"Hassan." Vinnie's smile was genuine and wide.

As Hassan neared us, I noticed that he favoured his right leg and had dark rings under his eyes. His joy to see Vinnie lifted his cheeks and crinkled the corners of his eyes in a true smile. Vinnie walked into Hassan's open arms and lifted him off the floor in a strong embrace.

Hassan's laugh sounded through the large space and he slapped Vinnie on the shoulder. "Put me down, you big child."

Vinnie lowered Hassan gently and turned to us. "Hassan, these are my very good friends. The pretty boy is Colin, the cop is Daniel and this is my best friend Doctor Genevieve Lenard."

"Welcome! Welcome!" Hassan shook Colin's hand, then Daniel's. "A cop?" He narrowed his eyes, not letting go of Daniel's hand. "You bringing trouble to my house?"

"No, sir." Daniel lowered his head not to tower over Hassan as much. "We're hoping you can help us."

Hassan stared at him for a few seconds before another genuine smile deepened the wrinkles in his face. He let go of Daniel's hand and turned to the back of the store. "Ali! Bring us tea. A lot of tea."

"Sure, boss." A lanky man in his late twenties jumped up from a heavy wooden desk and hurried to the left of the store.

Hassan turned to me. "I hope you will enjoy my tea, Doctor. It's Moroccan mint tea, specially imported."

"I—"

"We would love to try it." Colin took my hand and squeezed.

I supposed now was one of those times when polite lies were socially important. Academically, I understood the concept of diplomacy and its social importance. Rationally, I considered these lies to be silly and not relevant to our reason for being here. But I'd learned that my rational approach didn't build easy rapport with strangers. Not like Colin and Daniel were currently doing.

"Follow me. We'll go to my office and you can tell me how you think I can help you." Hassan limped to the right side of the store and we followed. He opened an ornate wooden door next to a particularly beautiful rug.

I stopped. This rug had swirling motifs and minuscule lines that defined the contrast between the vibrant array of colours. At the centre of this Persian rug, the lines exploded in a familiar pattern, one that always soothed my mind.

"A woman with superb taste." Hassan sighed happily. "This is a late twentieth-century Persian Tabriz rug. Personally, I love the kaleidoscope effect."

I found it calming. "It's beautiful."

"Indeed." Hassan took a step back to make space for his young assistant carrying a heavily laden tray into the office. "Our tea is ready. Shall we?"

I nodded and followed him into his office. Again I was surprised. It was in complete contrast to the traditional and classical feel of the store. Bleached wooden floors, a glass and chrome desk and two modern cream leather sofas created a loft interior finish. The seating area was arranged on a large Persian carpet, so light in colour it looked like it had been left in the desert sun for years. The only bold flash of colour was an abstract painting of geometric shapes on the wall behind his desk.

Hassan waved us to the sofas as his assistant placed the tray on the glass coffee table in the centre. He sat down in the only wingback chair and made a show of pouring tea from a beaten silver teapot into the glass cups. He waited until Vinnie, Colin and Daniel took their tea, then raised an eyebrow and looked at me. "You're rejecting my hospitality?"

"No. I'm merely not accepting the tea. It should not be viewed as a personal affront." I so deeply loathed the rituals of social niceties.

"Personal affront." Hassan stared at me for a few seconds then turned to Vinnie. "These people are your friends?"

Vinnie nodded. "And I trust them with my life."

"Even the cop?" Hassan's *risorius* muscle contracted slightly to form a small sneer as he glanced at Daniel.

"These are people who care deeply about those who can't protect themselves." Vinnie's micro-expressions and his tone indicated that there was history behind his statement. "These are good people, Hassan. We're not looking to jam you up."

Hassan stared at Vinnie, then turned to me. "How can I trust you won't jam me up if you won't show me enough respect to drink my tea?"

"I don't have any jam." I knew this was some euphemism, but I didn't care to figure out its ridiculousness. Nor did I feel the need to justify myself. "You're not showing me respect by accepting my decision to forego the tea you offered."

Hassan blinked a few times, then leaned back in his chair. "You know, I never thought about it like that. Huh." He turned to Vinnie. "You keep strange company, Vinnie."

"Good company." Vinnie winked at me. "Jen-girl here is the best in the world when it comes to reading people's body language. She uses her superpowers to help people."

Hassan glanced at me, his expression softening slightly. "So what do you need from me?"

Colin got up and showed the screen of his smartphone to Hassan. "We think this might be yours."

His eyes widened in a typical display of recognition, but he quickly schooled his features. He made a show of narrowing his eyes as he took the phone from Colin. He stared at it for six seconds before looking at Vinnie. His reluctance to admit to anything and assist us was clear on his face.

I thought about his nonverbal cues and the show of pride he'd exhibited when talking about helping people. I moved to the edge of the sofa. "Somebody is killing young people."

"Genevieve." Daniel's soft warning was accompanied by an expression I'd come to recognise when he was trying to convey censure.

I ignored him and turned back to Hassan. "We found those receipts in the home of the first victim. The other victim is part of a small community for people usually on the fringes of society. They did nothing to deserve the brutality they suffered before they were murdered."

"We fear for the lives of the other people in this community." Colin took my hand. "That's why we're here. We're trying to prevent anyone else from being murdered."

"The motherfucker tortured them, Hassan." Vinnie's soft words didn't hide his anger.

Hassan swallowed and closed his eyes. When he opened them, he pointed at Daniel. "What about him?"

"Dan is good people."

"I'm not here for any other reason than to find this killer and stop him." Daniel looked straight at Hassan. "Anything else happening in this space is for another day."

Hassan looked down at the phone in his hand. He shook his head, sadness pulling the corners of his mouth down. "Ellie is dead?"

"Élodie?" Daniel had been quick to remember Adèle's pseudonym for her drug business. "Yes."

"What a loss." Hassan's grief was genuine. "She was such a smart young woman."

"How long did you know her?" Colin asked.

"Do you mean how long did I do business with her?" Hassan pushed himself out of his chair and walked to a wooden filing cabinet, the same bleached colour as the floors. It took him less than twenty seconds to find what he was looking for. He walked back with a blue folder and handed it to Daniel. "She first came to me about four years ago."

"To send money?" Daniel looked up from the folder, one eyebrow raised.

Hassan smiled. "Look, I knew she wasn't sending money to family or friends. That girl was as Arabic as Vinnie."

"It says here the first time you sent money for her was four years and five months ago."

"Sounds about right." He reached for his cup of tea and took a sip. "I never asked who she was sending it to. It was enough money to make me wonder, but in the beginning not enough to make me worried."

"And then she started sending a lot." Daniel blinked at the folder. "Three hundred thousand euros?"

"You'll see that's only the last six months or so." Hassan put his cup back on the coffee table. "By then, Ellie had been here once a month, every month and I'd grown to like her. She was funny and had wonderful positive energy. She was also very respectful of my culture." He looked at me. "She always drank my tea."

I studied his expression. "You were suspicious of something."

"I was." He nodded. "A few months ago, she sent money to Brussels. The first and only time she sent money in the EU."

"Brussels." Colin looked at me. "Belgium. Johan Klein."

The artist who'd painted the Roubaud painting in Jace's flat.

Hassan was watching us closely. "This is bad. Really bad, right?"

"You know or suspect something." I nodded when I registered his expression. "What do you suspect?"

He put his cup on the coffee table, his lips pulled in a tight line. "After the first three hundred thousand, she kept sending similar amounts, but not once a month. It became more infrequent and didn't have a pattern. Not like the monthly amounts she'd sent before. Then last month she sent—"

Daniel whistled softly. "Nine hundred and seventy-five thousand euros."

"I wanted to ask her, but she begged me not to. She looked scared and excited. Like something good was going to happen, but with a lot of risk." He pressed his lips tightly together. "But this made me very suspicious. I did a bit of research and discovered that she sent this money the day after a big heist in Iran. Thieves raided a museum of our cultural heritage and sold it to Ellie. That was it. I was going to tell her that I wouldn't send any more money for her again. Not for stolen art."

"But drugs are okay?"

Hassan ignored Daniel, but I'd seen his micro-expression of distaste. I wondered what motivation was strong enough for a successful businessman who was proud of helping his people to be a part—albeit indirectly—of drug trafficking. Especially if he viewed it with such contempt.

"Well, then." Daniel smiled. "Can you at least tell us to whom or where she sent the money? The receipts we found don't have any of that information."

"I don't know the recipient." Hassan pointed at the file. "The only information I have in there is how much was sent and to which hawala broker. The senders and receivers can keep their identities secret if they choose."

"I suppose the broker is one of the numbers on the receipt." I had looked at each one and hadn't seen any names, only numbers.

"Correct." Hassan glanced at the folder. "I don't have to look to know that she sent the money to Tehran."

"Iran." Colin narrowed his eyes. "Vin didn't tell us. Are you from Iran?"

Memories immediately softened Hassan's expression. "I was born in Shiraz."

"Ah, the city with the most amazing museum." Colin looked at me. "The Pars Museum is an octagonal building where royal guests were hosted during the"—he looked back at Hassan—"the Zand dynasty, right?"

Hassan's pleasure at Colin's knowledge was evident in his genuine smile. "Indeed. It also has a display of almost thirty handwritten Qurans and many magnificent paintings by our most famous Persian artists."

"And it's been mostly untouched." Colin's lips tightened. "Your country has suffered so much art looting already."

"It's a travesty." Hassan's gnarled index finger tapped hard on his knee. "We're losing our history. Just last year three heritage workers were shot by these... these thugs. The heritage workers were investigating reports of looting at a heritage site when they were ambushed. Horrid. Just horrid."

Colin and Hassan continued talking about the many artefacts that had been stolen during the numerous wars and invasions. I wasn't paying close attention.

Iran. Not only did the bottles of wine originate from this country with such complicated political relationships with the West, now we knew that Adèle had been sending large amounts of cash there. I didn't discount Hassan's suspicion that she had bought the stolen art from the most recent heist, but we didn't have concrete evidence that tied her to that crime.

We did, however, have her photos with numerous other artefacts found in the self-storage locker. This new information was yet another new connection that tied Adèle's and Jace's murders to Iran.

How it was linked, I didn't know. Not yet.

"Hassan, you're the man." Vinnie got up and I realised that the men had concluded their conversation. I considered whether there was anything else I wanted to ask Hassan, but there was nothing. I followed them out of the modern office into the elegant showroom.

Hassan stopped next to the rug I'd admired and looked at me. "Where can I deliver this?"

"I haven't bought it." How was it possible that I'd miscommunicated that?

"I know." He smiled. "But I decided that I like you and since you're Vinnie's friend, I want to give this to you."

I didn't know how to respond. I'd looked at the carpet because its design was soothing to my mind. I had not once considered buying it.

"Breathe, love." Colin took my hand in his and squeezed. He looked at Hassan. "We deeply appreciate your generosity, Hassan, but we can't possibly take such a beautiful work of art without giving you something for it. Clearly you have an important business here and giving away your profit would be too much to accept."

Hassan stared at Colin. It was clear that he viewed Colin's intervention as a polite rejection.

"I need time." I was not like Francine who constantly bought things on impulse. "This will bring a significant change in my space and I need to consider it before I buy this."

"And we *will* buy this," Colin added.

"At a discount." Hassan's facial muscles relaxed and he smiled. "A huge discount. You will only pay seventy-seven euros for it."

I frowned. "That's a peculiar amount."

"It was my grandmother's favourite number and you remind me a lot of her." He put his palm on the Persian Tabriz rug. "She had one very similar to this in her bedroom. Much smaller, but she loved it. She said the shapes made her smile."

I realised that this rug was more symbolic to Hassan than just another carpet in his store. We said our goodbyes and left. I had many questions about this case, but it took ten minutes into our trip to the team room before I stopped obsessing about whether I wanted to purchase the rug and where I would put it.

Chapter TEN

"WHAT'S UP WITH Nix, Jen-girl?" Vinnie pushed between the two front seats of Colin's SUV and looked at me.

I pushed myself against the door and frowned. "What do you mean?"

"I mean she didn't laugh at my joke last night. That's not normal."

"Could it be that your joke wasn't funny?" Colin turned into the main road that would take us back to the team room.

"Dude!" Vinnie slapped Colin's upper arm. "My jokes are always funny. So this is the one I told Nikki." He took a dramatic pause. "Archaeologist—someone whose career lies in ruins." He chuckled. "Huh? Huh? Funny, right?"

Colin and Daniel laughed. I didn't.

Vinnie's pleasure in Colin's reaction fell away when he looked at me. "Why aren't you laughing?"

"I don't find it funny." It was obvious.

"It's funny, Vin." Colin glanced at Vinnie. "Why do you think something is wrong with Nikki?"

"Can't put my finger on it. She just seemed distracted."

"She's starting a new job." I'd had a few conversations with

Nikki about her nervousness about her fulltime employ-
ment. "She's concerned that she won't meet her boss'
expectations."

"Well, that's just dumb." Vinnie huffed and shook his
head. "She's a genius at restoring those old paintings."

"She's not a genius." I enjoyed Nikki's above-average
intelligence, but she definitely didn't qualify as a genius.

Vinnie snorted. "I miss Rox. She would know what's up
with Nikki."

"Is she enjoying her conference?" Colin asked.

"Yes, but she said she misses us. Me the most."

"Of course."

Vinnie turned back to me and I pushed harder against
the door. "Do you think there's something between Pink
and Nix?"

"What something?"

"Something romantic-like." Vinnie frowned and rubbed
the long scar that ran down the left side of his face. "Pink
has been helping her a lot with Eric and they're always
chatting."

I didn't know how to answer this. The only way I felt
comfortable in my friendships was by analysing my
friends' nonverbal cues. I knew most people didn't like
the idea of being exposed and vulnerable to analysis, so I
almost never shared my insights. It would be similar to
betraying their trust. I didn't know how to be diplomatic,
how to be deceptive, so I searched for an appropriate
answer. "Nikki trusts Pink. They trust each other."

"Yeah, but do they like each other?" He drew out the

word 'like', wiggling his eyebrows.

I pointed at his eyebrows. "What does that mean?"

He laughed. "Are they in love?"

"Maybe you should ask Jenny what the body language of love is." Colin winked at me.

"Huh." Vinnie nodded slowly. "So? How would you know people are in love?"

I felt much more comfortable answering this. "Nonverbal cues of romantic interest usually include lowered voices, giggling, gazing at each other with the eyelids lowered and smiles that seem to hide some secret."

"That sounds like flirting to me."

"It's more than superficial flirting." I thought of Francine and how she flirted with the male waiters in every restaurant we visited. Her flirting was a sexy form of friendliness, but without any nonverbal cues inviting further action. "Romantic flirting has the definite message of expecting more from the interaction."

"Roxy flirts with me." Vinnie's smile was sweet.

"Yes." I looked at Colin. "I don't flirt."

"No, you don't." He winked at me and returned his attention to the traffic in front of us. "And I'm really glad you don't."

"Oh." The sound of a superhero cartoon jingle from my handbag interrupted me before I could ask him why he felt that way. Daniel's phone pinged and he took it from his pocket as I took my phone from its usual place in my bag and glared at Colin. "Stop changing my ringtones." I swiped to answer the call. "You're on speaker."

"Hi, Genevieve." The smile in Pink's voice made me realise my social blunder.

"Hi, Pink." I hated the politeness always needed with neurotypicals, but understood and respected the need for it. "I'm with Colin, Daniel and Vinnie and you're on speaker."

"Where are you guys?"

"In the car, about five minutes from the team room." Colin manoeuvred around a car looking for parking. "Why?"

"Turn around." The tension in his voice brought tightness to my chest. "Meet me at Robertsau forest."

"Did you find more victims?" I irrationally hoped my assumption wasn't correct.

"Yes." He paused when Vinnie swore colourfully. "Two bodies were found this morning by tourists who came for an early walk. I've asked the first responders and crime scene techs not to touch anything until you get here."

"On our way." Colin glanced in the rear view mirror, then his side mirror before making an illegal U-turn.

I ended the call, grabbed the sides of my seat and tried to control my breathing. Colin turned on his hazard lights and rushed through the late-morning traffic at a most alarming speed. Experience had taught me that Colin was a competent driver and his advanced driving skills had not once caused an accident. It didn't make me enjoy the speedy journey to Robertsau forest.

After the fifth time I gasped and strengthened my hold on the passenger seat, I decided it would be more prudent to look out of the window than to watch Colin's driving. I thought about Adèle and her beautiful house as we passed the turn-off to her neighbourhood. The forest wasn't too far from her house and I wondered if she'd spent any time there. Or had her focus been solely on her work and providing for Claire?

Pink had sent the exact GPS coordinates of the crime scene. It was close to the Rhine River. The nature reserve stretched across the border to Germany, the larger area on the French side of the river. Located to the north of Strasbourg, it was as popular as the Neuhof forest in the south for locals and tourists to spend their leisure time. In some places it looked like a virgin forest because of the creepers and there were many paths to choose from when hiking, cycling or even horse riding.

By the time Colin parked his SUV next to the familiar GIPN truck, my fingers were stiff from clutching the sides of my seat. I inhaled slowly and deeply while wiggling my fingers and trying to relax my shoulder muscles. The start of my day might have been routine, but getting out of the SUV in the middle of the Robertsau forest instead of sitting in front of my monitors most definitely was not.

I made a point of visiting this nature reserve at least once every summer. It was a wonderful place for a long walk in nature. Weekends saw a lot of families and cyclists, which made the paths crowded and took all enjoyment from time in nature. I preferred to spend a weekday walking a pre-planned route, stopping only to take photos when I noticed something uncommonly symmetrical in the flora.

In the colder seasons, the forest lost its attraction for most people. A few brave hikers would visit on weekend days, but weekdays left the reserve empty. With the exception of today.

Apart from Colin's SUV and the GIPN truck, two police patrol cars, one Ford and a Seat were parked in a haphazard manner. People were milling around and three officers were standing next to one of the patrol cars, chatting.

Pink walked to us, his expression serious. "You made good time."

Colin nodded and looked past the vehicles into the forest. "What have we got?"

"A man and a woman in their late twenties." The corners of Pink's mouth turned down. "They were viciously tortured. Then the bastard dumped them."

"The old man is here." Vinnie nodded towards Manny's old sedan stopping next to Colin's SUV.

As if in silent agreement, no one spoke while we waited for Manny to join us. He took longer than necessary to turn off the car and get out. I frowned. When he eventually got out, he kept his back turned on us. I narrowed my eyes— the tightness in his shoulders worried me. But when he turned I gasped and took Colin's hand.

It was there for only a second, but the raw grief that had been etched on his face had been unlike anything I'd ever observed in his nonverbal cues. The look he gave me as he walked towards us was one I was much more familiar with. It was a warning. The almost imperceptible shake of his head made me blink. He didn't want me to ask what was causing him such emotional pain.

"Dan, everyone." Manny nodded. "Where are they?"

Pink pointed to our left. "Deeper into the forest. See the tourists over there?" He pointed at a man dressed in jeans and a thick blue winter jacket leaning against a patrol van while listening to three young women talking to a police officer. The women were dressed in winter hiking outfits that would protect them from temperatures much lower than this. Yet two of them were rubbing their arms as if they were cold.

"They the ones who found the bodies?" Colin asked.

"Yes." Pink turned back to us. "The man found the bodies first. He was looking for signs of life when the ladies saw them as well and hurried over. Good thing too. The man had left his smartphone in his car, wanting a pure forest bath. All three of the women had their phones. They called it in."

I tried. I really did. But my mind wouldn't allow me to focus on the more relevant information. "What is a forest bath?"

"It's actually called forest bathing." Vinnie leaned back when we all turned to him in surprise. "What? Roxy told me all about this. It's a Japanese thing. The idea is to consciously walk in the forest and take in the atmosphere and let it heal you."

"Ridiculous." Manny sliced his hand through the air. "I

don't have time for such nonsense. Take us to the scene."

"Sure." Daniel's eyebrows rose at Manny's harsh tone, but he turned and followed Pink to the copse of trees on our left.

"It's a bit off the hiking paths, but not so far out that you'll need snow shoes," Pink said over his shoulder.

"Is it too much to hope for footprints in the snow?" Colin asked.

Pink nodded. "Between the tourists and the first responders, the snow is pretty trampled. There's no way we'll get any useful impressions now. The killer's prints have been stomped over a million times already."

"Impossible." I simply couldn't stop myself. "It would take the sixteen people I counted here a minimum of nine hours each to take a million steps."

"Of course." Pink laughed. "I must have been channelling Francine or Nikki with that exaggeration."

"Definitely Franny." Vinnie tilted his head as he stared at Manny's stiff gait. "What crawled up your butt, old man? You and Franny had a little tiff?"

Colin smiled at Vinnie's unsuccessful attempt at a British accent.

"Did the bodies have any ID on them?" Manny ignored Vinnie and followed Daniel deeper into the trees.

Apart from the gross exaggeration, Pink had been correct about the trampled snow. We were off the designated path, but the snow between the trees here was flattened, shoeprints visible everywhere. About twenty metres in front of us, two police officers stood guard. Both rested their gloved hands on their belts, their postures relaxed, but alert.

It was easy to spot the bodies behind them. Like Jace, they weren't dressed in outdoor wear. Both of them were wearing jeans. The man had on a long-sleeved red t-shirt and the woman was wearing a green and orange sweater. Their feet were bare.

"No ID." Pink's answer was soft, his eyes on the two bodies. "No bags, phones, nothing in their pockets."

Colin squeezed my hand. "You're ready for this?"

I didn't take my eyes off the two young people as we walked closer. "No. I'm never ready to see murder victims."

"But you'll be okay." Vinnie poked me in the shoulder. "You always are, Jen-girl."

"Stop dilly-dallying and get your arses over here." Manny was leaning over the young man. He straightened and looked at me. "It's vicious, Doc."

I nodded stiffly and focused my mind on Mozart's Overture from *The Marriage of Figaro*—one of my favourite works. Letting go of Colin's hand, I walked closer and stumbled to a stop when I saw the young man's hand lying on the snow. Every finger on his hand had been broken. In more than one place. His hand was swollen and deeply discoloured, which told me he'd been alive for some time after this had been done to him.

I inhaled deeply and took another step closer. In contrast to Jace's crime scene, there wasn't a lot of blood in the snow. I was irrationally grateful for that. The contrast of the small amount of blood on the snow surrounding the bodies was already jarring.

I looked at the man's face and gasped. "He's unrecognisable."

"It looks like the bastard broke every bone in his face." Colin's tone was tight with tension.

"Fuck!" Vinnie went down on his haunches next to the woman. "That motherfucker sliced her face up." He pointed at the top of her sweater. "And stabbed her in the chest."

"The paramedics that got here said she received dozens of shallow stab wounds in her breasts." Pink swallowed. "The killer never went deep enough to kill her."

"Just to torture her." Manny's facial muscles contracted with anger. "We need to find this bloody killer and put a stop to this."

"We need more data." A lot more. I couldn't see us catching this ruthless killer with the frustrating lack of a connection between all the clues we had at the moment. "Having their identities would be a good start."

Manny pointed at Colin. "Take photos and let Francine show Caelan. He might be able to identify them."

"I don't think that's a good idea, Millard." Colin ignored Manny's lowered brow. "There's no way these people's best friends or parents would be able to recognise them at the moment. Showing photos of brutally tortured dead people to Caelan is not going to help us and will not help him."

"I don't want to help that little shit. I want him to man

up, identify these people so we can stop this from happening to anyone else."

"Dude." Vinnie stood up and frowned at Manny. "Chill."

Manny swung around and glared at Vinnie. "Don't you bloody call me 'dude'. Instead of wasting time standing around here, why don't you hit up your criminal buddies and find out if any of your friends have a friend who does this kind of thing for pleasure."

"Whoa." Vinnie leaned back, stared at Manny for a second, then looked at me. "I guess I have some phone calls to make."

Colin watched Vinnie walk back to the vehicles, then turned to Manny. "That was not necessary."

"Back off, Frey." Manny pushed his hands in his coat pockets. "Doc? Do *you* at least have something useful?"

I took my time to study Manny. His expression revealed that he regretted his outburst and dreaded my response. It was truly difficult for me not to confront him with whatever was causing his emotional pain, but I recalled all the conversations Phillip and Colin had had with me about appropriate timing. I shook my head. "The bodies alone don't give me any new information. We need to know who they are and how they fit into the victimology of Jace and Adèle."

"If it's not going to piss you off too much, Frey, I'll ask Caelan about the other players in his geocaching gifted club."

I stepped away from Colin and made sure my look at Manny conveyed my censure. "Your sarcasm isn't helpful."

"I think it's a good idea to get names from Caelan." Daniel stepped forward to obscure Manny's view of Colin. Always the mediator. "I'll put a rush on the medical examiner to give us everything he can so we can try to ID these two."

"How long have the bodies been out here?" Colin asked.

"I have no idea." Daniel raised his shoulders.

"It snowed lightly early this morning." I pointed at a bush close to us. "There's a light dusting of snow there. But there's nothing on the bodies."

"Could the snow have melted from their body heat?" Colin shook his head even before he finished his question. "No. They were dead before they got here. So they must've been dumped within the last four hours."

"I'll get an exact time from the weather guys to find out when it snowed," Daniel said. "And hopefully, the medical examiner will be able to give us an exact time of death."

I doubted the medical examiner would be able to give a precise time for these people's deaths. "An estimate is more likely."

Daniel smiled at me. "Then we'd better tell the crime scene techs and the guys from the medical examiner's office the scene is theirs."

I was grateful to turn away from the awful carnage on the snow. I took two steps towards the cars, then stopped. "I want to speak to the tourists."

"Sure." Pink nodded. "They have been very co-operative."

I thought about it some more. As we walked back to the parking area, I moved away from Colin to walk next to

Manny. "Are you able to give a professional interview?"

He stopped. "What the bloody hell does that mean, missy?"

"It means that I know you are dealing with emotional pain, but I would prefer if—like usual—you spoke to the tourists and I observed their body language." I pointed at his scowl and flared nostrils. "But if you are this easily riled, it might be counterproductive and I won't get an accurate reading from their reactions."

"Bloody fucking hell." Manny pushed both fists against his eyes for a few seconds. Then he glanced at Daniel and Colin continuing along the path without us. The narrowing of his eyes made me wonder if he realised they were giving him time to compose himself. He inhaled deeply, rolling his neck on his shoulders. "I'm good. Let's do this."

I didn't believe that he was 'good', but I trusted that he would conduct the interview with the tourists in his usual professional manner. We walked in silence until we reached the others. Vinnie was out of earshot, talking on his phone. Colin, Pink and Daniel were leaning against the GIPN truck, but straightened when we got close. None of them said anything about Manny's behaviour.

We walked over to the tourists still standing next to the patrol car, Daniel and Pink leading the way. We were about fifteen metres from them when Manny held out his hand to the side. I stopped and looked at him. He turned around to face away from the tourists and closed his eyes. I waited.

Manny took fifteen slow breaths before he opened his eyes and looked at me. "You need to pay extra attention, Doc."

"I always pay full attention." The intensity of my focus on others often caused them discomfort. I stopped this line of thinking and studied Manny's face. This was not what he'd meant. He was doubting his own focus. "I understand."

He grunted, inhaled deeply and turned around. "Let's do this."

I relaxed considerably when Manny's posture changed. He hunched his shoulders and slowed his gait, his facial muscles less tense. We neared the small group and I turned my attention to them. Pink was introducing Colin and Daniel to the tourists and the police officer was taking a step back, allowing Daniel to take the lead. I was surprised to hear British accents all around.

"And this is Doctor Genevieve Lenard." Daniel gestured towards me, then pointed at Manny.

"I'm Manny Millard." Manny followed his interruption by stepping forward and shaking their hands.

The three women were in their forties and were spending a week away from their families and jobs in Oxford. Nina Gray was a mid-level manager at a public relations consulting firm. Her long, dark hair was covered by a fashionable turquoise knitted cap. The rest of her outfit seemed to have been ordered from an outdoor sports catalogue and was much more sensible than the pretty cap.

Rose Wright was the shortest of the three women and

owned her own small children's clothing company.

"And my name is Joan Hazard." The third woman's smile lifted her freckled cheeks. "I know, I know. Not quite the surname you want when you're adventurous."

"Are you adventurous?" Manny's smile was small, but inviting.

"Is she ever." Nina rolled her eyes. "She's the one who made us come out here before I've had enough cake and coffee."

"We all wanted to come." Rose's soft voice was controlled, her arms wrapped tightly around her torso. "So far the week has been wonderful. We're doing things we wouldn't do back home because we're too busy or lazy. We decided to come to Strasbourg for the bridges, cathedral and fine art museums. And when Joanie suggested the nature reserve, we thought it would be wonderful to be out in the crisp morning air."

"It's crisp, all right." Manny snorted and the women smiled. Rose relaxed a bit, her hands no longer clutching her coat. Manny turned to the male tourist. "So Pierre, what brought you here this morning?"

"The same as them." Pierre Bruel nodded towards the woman. He was in his forties, well-groomed and spoke with quiet confidence. Like the women, he was dressed warmly, his knitted cap pulled low over his brow and his scarf high against his jaw. "I'm here for a conference and decided to do some forest bathing before our workshops start today." He glanced at his watch and smiled. "Yeah, I think I'm going to miss the first few."

"I can't place your accent." Manny slumped lower into his coat. "Where are you from?"

Pierre's smile lifted his cheeks, but didn't cause small wrinkles in the corners of his eyes. "I was born in Belgium, spent my first five years there before we moved to England. I'm currently living in Reading. I work for an international IT company there. I suppose my formative years and my mother being Flemish still has an effect on my accent."

"Makes perfect sense." Manny's faked friendliness was convincing. "Reading, huh? There are some beautiful woods around for forest bathing."

"My favourite is Fobney Island Nature Reserve." Pierre paused until he noticed Manny's positive reaction. "I wanted to come to this forest because I heard it was famous for horse riding paths."

"Oh, you got the wrong forest." Daniel smiled. "You're most likely thinking of the Neuhof forest to the south of Strasbourg."

"Seriously?" Pierre's disappointment was the first genuine reaction he'd shown. "Dammit."

Manny chuckled. "You still have time to explore, right?"

"Right." Pierre appeared distracted for a moment. On a quick inhale, he smiled. "I'm here for another three days, so there's indeed still time for that."

"I'm sure you've told the officers more than once, but could you please indulge me by telling once again how you found the bodies?" Daniel first looked at Pierre, then at the women.

"Oh, those poor people." Nina glanced towards the crime scene and crossed her arms. "It's just awful."

"I got here around nine." Pierre nodded as if agreeing with himself. "Yes, the news was just starting on the radio when I pulled into the parking area. I got out, locked my phone in the boot and went in that direction." He pointed to the crime scene. "I hadn't walked three minutes when the colours caught my eye. One of the things I love about forest bathing in winter is how monochromatic everything is. Just the snow, the bark and green leaves. Nothing else to distract my mind."

"What did you do when you saw the bodies?" Daniel asked.

"Oh, I didn't know they were bodies at first." He rubbed the back of his neck. "I thought someone had dumped some camping gear or rubbish or something there. But as soon as I was close enough, I saw they were people. It was horrible."

"We arrived after Pierre," Rose said softly. "His car was already parked and we were glad that there weren't more people. We wanted a true nature experience."

"We went in the same direction and saw Pierre staring at the people." Joan cleared her throat and closed her eyes. "The bodies."

"I didn't know what to do." Pierre hunched his shoulders. "I could see they were dead."

"We didn't know what he was looking at, so we walked there." Nina blushed. "I might've screamed when I saw those poor people."

"She did." Pierre's smile was wide. And genuine. "Gave me the fright of my life."

"I immediately called 112." Joan straightened a bit. "I make a point of knowing the emergency numbers in every place I visit."

"Wise." Manny nodded slowly. "I can't imagine how difficult it must've been for you to see all of that."

"Terrible." Pierre shook his head, his sigh deep.

"I..." Rose swallowed. "I think I'm going to have nightmares about this."

"It's okay, lovey." Nina stepped closer and put her arm around Rose's shoulders. "We'll find a way to cope with this. We're hardy like that."

"Did you see anyone else?" Manny asked.

"No one." Pierre looked at the women. They nodded. He stared into the forest. "It's so quiet and white here that it would've been easy to see someone else."

Manny was quick to hide his scepticism. A few days ago, Vinnie and Pink had been in a deep discussion about camouflage in numerous environments. Manny had pretended to read a book, but I'd seen his attention drifting to their conversation.

He looked at me, one eyebrow lifted. I exhaled sharply. He wanted me to give him a verdict on the short interview we'd just had. Experience had taught me that he would be most displeased if my opinion was frank and therefore obvious. I thought about my wording for a few seconds, then looked at Pierre. "Where's your car?"

Manny gave me a sideways glance before dropping his

shoulders a bit more. He made a point of looking at Daniel as if the latter was annoying him before facing the tourists. "This is so daft. The Frenchies have a million silly rules. If you guys don't let us look in your cars, they're going to kick up all kinds of fuss because we didn't dot our i's and cross our t's. So to speak."

"No problem." Joan took a set of keys from her jacket pocket and pointed at the only red vehicle. "It's a rental and it's in my name. You can record everything if that would help. I don't mind."

"Oh, that's darling of you." Manny took the keys and handed it to Daniel. "I'll make sure they don't scratch the car."

She shrugged. "I have insurance."

"Pierre?" Manny turned to the IT specialist. "May we see your car?"

"Of course." The contractions of the *orbicularis oculi* muscles under his eyes were fleeting, but I'd noticed it. He was relieved. He took a key fob from his trouser pocket and handed it to Manny. "Also a rental. But I would appreciate it if you guys didn't scratch it."

"No problem." Manny walked to the gray car that would blend in on most of the roads in Europe. Ten minutes later, Manny handed Joan and Pierre their keys back. "The crime scene techs recorded everything just in case we're called to the carpet. Now we can show them we were diligent and you guys are only guilty of witnessing something extremely horrible."

"If you could go with these officers, they'll take your

statements and you'll be free to go." Daniel smiled at Pierre. "And hopefully, you'll get to visit the Neuhof forest."

Pierre's smile was relieved. "Thanks. Yes, I will definitely make a point of getting there. Something good has to come out of this experience."

Two officers led the tourists away and we walked back to our vehicles. Vinnie was leaning against Manny's sedan, still talking on his phone. We stopped next to Colin's SUV and Manny held up his hand while he made sure the tourists were occupied and out of earshot. "What did you see, Doc?"

"Inconsistencies." I winced. "The problem is that it's not really suspicious to show a few inconsistent nonverbal cues under circumstances such as these."

"What did you see?" Manny lowered his brow and stared at me.

"The women's body language didn't raise any alarms with me." I glanced at Pierre talking into a camera while an officer recorded him. "Pierre showed relief that could've been because he wasn't caught in a crime or because this traumatic event is over." I paused, recalling his micro-expressions. "He tried hard and mostly succeeded in controlling his responses and nonverbal cues, but a few times it was too calculated. I can give you exact examples. Should I tell you all of them?"

"Dear God, no." Manny scratched his chin and looked at Daniel. "Your guys found nothing suspicious in his rental?"

Daniel shook his head. "No evidence of blood. It's

clean inside, the boot is empty and clean."

"Hmm." Manny thought about this for a few seconds. "Can you get someone to tail Pierre? Someone who will not be made?"

Daniel nodded. "I'll organise it."

"I would really like to get out of this cold." Colin stomped his designer boots. "I wasn't really thinking I had to hike through the snow when I got dressed this morning. My feet feel like they're dying."

Something Colin had said triggered an extremely negative emotion in Manny. His lips thinned and his hands fisted in his coat pockets.

"Okay, old man." Vinnie walked closer and bumped fists with Daniel while the latter talked on his phone. "I've got ears and eyes all over the place looking for gossip about this kind of MO."

"And what?" Manny swung his angry gaze from Colin to Vinnie. "You want a pat on the back?"

Vinnie's eyes widened, then he smiled maliciously, turned his back on Manny and said over his shoulder, "Yes, please."

"Bugger off, criminal." Manny stomped over to his sedan and opened the door. He paused and looked at me. "See you in the team room. Don't make me wait."

He got in his car, started it and on high revolutions left the parking area. Vinnie stared at Manny's car until it was out of sight and looked at me. "What the fuck, Jen-girl?"

I took a step back. This was a completely new situation for me.

"Let it go for now, Vin." Colin took my hand and squeezed. "We'll talk about Millard later. Let's just go to the team room."

"No way, dude." Vinnie put his fists on his hips. "That old man better have a fucking good reason lashing out at me like that. I'm so pissed at him right now. I think it's better if I hang back with Dan."

"I won't be long." Daniel finished his call and nodded towards the tourists. "As soon as they're done, Pink and I will come in too. The crime scene techs are going to be busy here for some time still and I agree with you." He looked at Colin. "It's freezing out here."

Colin nodded and opened the passenger door for me. "See you guys at the team room then."

He got in and started the car without speaking to me. I quietly stared out of the window until we reached the city centre. This time I didn't even notice Colin's driving or how many cars were on the road with us. My mind was on a loop, trying to find a logical way of dealing with this new situation. When we drove past the European Parliament, I twisted in my seat to face Colin. "I don't know what to do."

He glanced at me. "About Millard?"

"Yes."

"Hmm." He overtook a truck with ease and glanced at me again. "What did you see? No. You know what? Don't tell me. Millard knows you saw whatever is eating at him. I bet he's hoping like hell you won't tell me or anyone else."

"So what do I do?" Friendship was still a relatively new concept to me. Before Colin had entered my life, I had never had friends before. As a child, I'd been too isolated and socially inept to make friends. Phillip had been my boss for a long time before I learned how to relate to him on a deeper level. Colin, Vinnie and Francine had taught me most of the friendship skills I had. Still neurotypical friendships remained mostly a mystery to me.

Colin thought about his answer for a short while. "If you were in Millard's shoes and he in yours, what would you like for him to do?"

"A hypothetical situation?" I considered such an event. "I would prefer for him to let me deal with my emotions and share it with the others when or if I'm ready."

"Then do that for him. Trust Millard to work through his own feelings and talk to us when he's ready."

"You're saying 'when', not 'if'."

He snorted. "Yeah. It might be the optimist in me, but I'm thinking that despite his British reticence, Millard knows we care and want to be there for him."

"Vinnie is angry." It had been evident in all his non-verbal cues.

"Vin will be fine." Colin slowed down and glanced in the rear view mirror. "He knows Millard is picking the strongest of us to dump his sadness on. This is new for us too. Vin obviously needs to calm down so he won't punch Millard when the idiot lashes out again. But he'll handle it. Don't worry."

That was just it. I *was* worried. I didn't know what was going on with Manny, only that something had happened after we'd left to meet with Hassan and it was causing him tremendous emotional anguish. Moreover, I was deeply concerned that his way of dealing with his pain by taking it out on Vinnie might damage their relationship.

It was ridiculous how irrational my thinking was at the moment. I felt responsible for maintaining the emotional equilibrium of the group. I shook my head at myself in disgust and turned back to look out of the window. Colin was right. I needed to trust Manny to know how to work through his own pain. And I needed to trust Vinnie to manage whatever abuse Manny was going to aim at him.

Despite this new development, I no longer longed for the days when my life was void of friends and the wealth of emotions and experience they brought into my life. I couldn't imagine what it would be like to lose one of them. I wondered if Caelan was coping with the loss of his friend. Did the intensity of the emotions he was experiencing confuse him or had he learned how to understand and deal with it?

I wasn't able to ease Caelan's grieving, but I could do everything in my power to find out who had killed Jace and stop that person. My mind was already cataloguing every bit of evidence we'd gathered so far and prioritising which I should peruse next.

Colin's phone rang. He glanced at the screen clearly displayed where the phone was in its holder on the dashboard. He smiled at me. "It's Johan Klein."

Chapter ELEVEN

"JOHAN, I'M GLAD to hear from you." Colin's accent shocked me and I glared at him. He was speaking with a heavy Scottish accent. He winked at me, then turned his attention back to the road. "How are you?"

"I'm well, Isaac. Just a bit surprised to hear from you."

Johan Klein was speaking to one of Colin's aliases. Isaac Watts was known for the hundreds of hymns he wrote in seventeenth-century England, not for the poems or the textbook on logic he wrote. I disliked it immensely when Colin went under a false name. Deception was not a strong point for me and having to remember all his different aliases was exhausting. He enjoyed it.

"Well, the other day I saw a painting that came from your talented hands." Colin's tone was calm and respectful.

"You flatter me. What did you see? Where?"

"It was a stunning Roubaud."

"Hmm." His reply was quiet and he paused before continuing. "Yeah, that."

Colin lifted one eyebrow and glanced at me. "Tell me more about this Roubaud."

"Why?" The suspicion in Johan's tone was so obvious that even I picked up on it.

"Come on, Johan. You know that I can't resist finding out about something when I'm intrigued."

"Word is that you're turning people in."

Colin snorted. "Turning people in? What does that mean?"

"That you're working for the cops now. You're ratting your friends out."

I frowned at Colin's phone and tilted my head in an irrational attempt to hear better. I was concerned. Even though Colin didn't actively work at maintaining his reputation as a notorious thief, he'd been excessively careful not to let anyone find out he was indeed working for Interpol as well as our team.

Colin didn't appear worried though. He uttered a sound of derision. "Who said what to you?"

"Nobody said anything specific. It's just that a few of the forgers you were in contact with are now in jail."

"For forgery?"

"Uh… no." Friendliness returned to his voice. "They were arrested for murder, grand larceny and fraud."

"Things you know I have zero interest in. I only care about art."

"That you do." The smile that accompanied his words hinted at history between him and Colin. I thought about this for three seconds and decided I didn't care. I wanted to find this killer who tortured people before throwing them away like trash.

"So tell me more about this Roubaud." Colin glanced in the rear view mirror and frowned before he turned into a side street. "You know I want all the juicy gossip."

"Like a dog with a bone." Johan sighed. "Fine. I painted that Roubaud on request for a client. A paying client."

"I know you don't do illegal stuff, Johan. Just borderline." Colin chuckled. "That's why I like you. You skirt the edges all the time."

"Yeah, but I don't know if I skirted too close to the edge with this Roubaud."

"Why?"

"I don't know." It was quiet for a few seconds. "I had a bad feeling about this from the start. The client was very specific about the painting she wanted. There was something off about the whole deal."

"She?" Colin looked in the rear view mirror again and frowned.

"Yes. Élodie Baille. A soft-spoken young lady. She didn't know very much about art, but she seemed cultured enough. Her English was quite good, but then we spoke French because she was more comfortable with that."

"Did she say why she specifically wanted a Roubaud?"

"It was a private joke, she'd said. Didn't tell me what the joke was."

"Huh. Did you meet this Élodie?"

"No, we did everything online. She insisted I use a courier to deliver the painting."

"Do you remember the courier's name?"

"Yes. It was banal. Easy Post. No creativity at all when

they thought up that name."

"How did she pay you?"

There was a long silence. "What's going on, Isaac? You're asking a lot of questions here."

"It's something bad." Colin glanced in the rear view mirror and his eyes narrowed. "So? How did Élodie pay you?"

"In cash. You know, this is another reason I didn't like this deal. She paid promptly, didn't quarrel about the price, but…"

"Yes?"

"I don't want to sound like one of those anti-immigrant people, but the guy who brought the cash was Arabic. He looked okay and was very nice. But now you're asking all these questions and… well, I don't know. I'm thinking that I should stay far away from Ms Baille."

When Colin looked in the rear view mirror again, his expression sent a rush of adrenaline into my system. He entered the main road we'd just come from and pushed himself against the seat. "Johan, I'll have to call you back in a bit."

"Oh. Okay." Johan cleared his throat. "Listen, I'll be unplugged for the rest of today. Phone me tomorrow."

"Will do." Colin was no longer paying attention to the conversation. Instead he looked at the side mirrors before ending the call. Immediately, he tapped on the phone to start another call.

I looked behind us, but didn't see anything out of the ordinary. Except that we'd turned around and were returning to the forest. The road we were on was always busy. It only emptied when one got closer to the forest. As I turned back to ask Colin why we were going back, his call went through.

"Dude! Whaddap!" Vinnie sounded happier than after the confrontation with Manny.

"Vin, we're being followed."

"The fuck?" Vinnie paused then shouted to get Daniel's attention, his voice muffled, but loud enough to make me wince. "Where are you? We're coming to you."

"I'm on my way back to the Robertsau forest. We crossed the bridge and are just about to go past the turnoff to Adèle's house." Colin glanced in the rear view mirror again. "Two SUVs, both with tinted windows. I can't see how many inside."

A door slammed and the sound of an engine starting came over the phone. "You think they know you're onto them? Did they do anything when you turned around?"

"No. They just continued following us at a distance."

"Jen-girl, you there?"

My voice croaked when I answered and I cleared my throat. "I'm here."

"You doing okay?"

"I'm well." I was also extremely worried and was trying to see these vehicles Colin had spotted. I couldn't. There were too many other cars on the road to be sure which ones were following us.

"Dude, bring them all the way here. Dan is on the horn to the old man. We'll get Franny to track as much as she can on the city cameras as well."

"I'll keep this line open for now, but I'll let Jenny speak to Francine. You deal with Millard."

"Oh, boy." Vinnie's resigned sigh would've been amusing had it not been for the deep concern etched into Colin's expression.

"You're worried." I felt silly stating the obvious.

"I am." He nodded. "I have something very precious in the car with me that I want to keep safe."

I frowned. "What?"

Colin's smile was immediate and relieved some of the tension. "Not a what, a who." He glanced at me. "You."

"Oh." I shook my head to change the topic. "I can't see the SUVs following us."

"They're keeping a really good distance and they're not making it obvious." He looked at the rear view mirror again. "The first one is the silver SUV behind the small blue Toyota. The second is four cars behind him. A charcoal colour."

I looked again and saw the silver SUV. But I couldn't see the darker-coloured vehicle. I turned back in my seat and looked at Colin. Really looked. His eyebrows were drawn in and down, the corners of his mouth also turned down, his lips tight.

Colin's past and his many aliases had helped him develop exceptional control over his emotions, especially allowing his thoughts and emotions to show through nonverbal cues. To see him so obviously concerned brought pure panic to my mind. Darkness seeped into my peripheral vision and my breathing shallowed.

"Jenny!" Colin's sharp tone brought me back from giving in to the safety of that darkness. "Love, I need you to phone Francine."

I couldn't. I wanted to, but I was frozen. I hadn't given in to the looming shutdown, but my mind didn't allow my body to react to Colin's request. I couldn't even speak.

I pushed Mozart's Horn Concerto No. 1 in D major into my mind and thought about Jace. He had overcome so much more than I had. My ability to verbalise my thoughts had always been a way for me to maintain control over my life and mind. He'd never had that. Yet he'd achieved so much. I focused harder on the Allegro playing in my mind. If Jace could venture out into the world without the ability to talk then I could regain control over my hands and phone Francine.

It wasn't that simple. Colin spoke gently to me, encouraging me, but I felt powerless. Knowing that he needed my help to keep us safe exacerbated my panic. It was the dramatic Queen of the Night aria of Mozart's *Die Zauberflöte* that jerked me out of this new kind of shutdown.

Immediately, I knew where it came from and I took my phone from its place in my handbag. This might be the only time I wasn't irritated with Colin for changing the ringtones on my phone. I swiped the screen to put her on speakerphone. "Francine."

"Hey, girlfriend. Are you okay?"

"No." I cleared my throat and rolled my shoulders to get rid of the lingering effects of feeling trapped in my own body.

"What can I do?" She paused for a second. "Colin? Are you listening?"

"Yes, you're on speakerphone." Colin raised his voice slightly, but didn't turn towards my phone. I rested it in the palm of my hand and held it closer to him. "Can you get eyes on our location?"

"I got your GPS location from your phone the moment Dan called Manny. But you are fast on your way out of the range of the city cameras." The sound of keystrokes in the background was non-stop. "You thinking I can get a lock on the idiots following you? Hack their cars?"

Colin huffed a laugh. "Um, no. I wasn't thinking that, but if you can do it, great. I was hoping for IDs on those guys. Car registration or something that can help us know who we're dealin—"

"Woohoo! Gotcha!" Francine's loud exclamation interrupted Colin and startled me. "Dammit. I won't be able to hack them. These are rental cars, but"—her voice drifted off and the clicking of keystrokes increased—"yup, they've disabled all ways to track them or connect to them remotely. No Bluetooth, wifi or anything like that."

"Where's Millard?"

"He ran out as soon as Dan called. Ooh! This is interesting."

Colin glanced in the rear view mirror again, his eyes widening slightly. "It will have to wait. Can you hack the traffic lights of anything that will give us a chance to catch them?"

"No." Immediately I shook my head. "No. No. I don't

want to catch anyone."

"You don't have to, Genevieve." Daniel's confident tone coming through Colin's phone calmed me. "We're just about finished setting up fifty metres before the entrance to the forest parking area. Colin, bring them in. We'll close behind you and lock them in."

"We also cleared all oncoming traffic," Vinnie said. "As soon as you pass that little condo village and the bend that takes you on the straight stretch before the parking area, drop your foot on the gas and let them race on behind you."

I gripped the sides of my seat. I didn't like this plan. I didn't like breaking the speed limit. And I really didn't like racing away from unknown assailants.

Colin glanced at my hands. "Should I play Mozart?"

"No. Wagner's *Ride of the Valkyries* is more appropriate."

Colin let out a surprised laugh. "Did you just make a joke?"

"No." I frowned when my answer made him and the others laugh. It did lift some of the tension in my muscles and I listened as Vinnie and Daniel talked in the background about their plan.

We drove past the last upmarket two-storied condo buildings and entered the long bend to the left that took us over a small bridge. Ahead of us, the road straightened and Colin accelerated like Vinnie had suggested. "Vin. Dan. I'm coming in."

I couldn't help the keening sound that escaped my mouth. I pulled my knees up and hugged them tightly to my chest, biting down on my lips to avoid another keen from filling the car.

"They still tailing you?" Vinnie asked.

Colin looked at the side mirrors. "Yes. And they're also speeding up. They know I'm onto them."

"We see you, dude. Come straight through."

I could see them. Two GIPN trucks were parked diagonally across the road, leaving a small space in the middle. Colin was aiming for that space. Another keen left my mouth and I felt my muscles lock into place. We raced past a small entrance road to the forest, too fast to confirm that I had indeed seen another GIPN truck parked there.

I didn't want to be in this car. I didn't want to see that small space coming closer and closer at a speed that could mean our deaths if Colin merely clipped one of the trucks. Yet I couldn't close my eyes.

I exhaled on another keen as we went between the two trucks without incident. The moment we cleared the narrow space, Colin slammed on the brakes and with the handbrake turned our vehicle on squealing tyres until we stopped, facing the opposite direction.

There was no longer a space between the trucks. The two large GIPN vehicles blocked the whole road. The road had no shoulder or even space for our pursuers to pass the trucks without risking major damage to their vehicles. I couldn't see past the large vehicles onto the road, but knew that the SUVs had to be very close.

I saw the silver SUV when it left the road and went

onto the rough embankment leading down to the forest. It made it past the left side of the trucks, but hit a log or a rock or something that sent the front end into the air. As if in slow motion, the vehicle became fully airborne, twisting on its way back as gravity won.

It landed with a deafening crunch on the front and continued to flip. Over and over and over until it came to a shuddering halt against a tree.

And exploded.

The shockwaves from the explosion reached our SUV and gently rocked it. I tightened my hold around my knees as Colin uttered a barely audible, "Oh, shit."

At that moment, the darker SUV came roaring past the other side of the two GIPN trucks, through the billowing smoke and right past my window. I thought of trying to catch a glimpse of the driver, but my eyes were glued to the muzzle flashes coming from the gun aimed at me.

"Jenny!" Colin grabbed my arm, pulled me down and threw himself on top of me as tiny pieces of glass rained down on us.

It was over so quick that the silence that followed felt deafening, the sound of the departing SUV soon gone.

Then chaos erupted.

"Jen-girl! Motherfuckers! Jen-girl! Dude!"

"I'm okay, Vin." Colin got up and pulled me too as well. He stared at me, his facial muscles tight with concern. "Jenny?"

I couldn't speak. This was even worse than before. My muscles were completely frozen. I could barely breathe.

"Love, I'm going to make sure you're okay." Colin unlocked his seatbelt, then mine and searched my body for any injuries. My eyes didn't even want to cooperate and follow him as he lifted my boots and touched my legs. All the while, he talked quietly to me, assuring me that we were safe. Once he was satisfied that I was unharmed, he straightened and looked past me. "She's okay. But she'll need a moment."

"She doesn't get a bloody moment. Get out of my way!" Manny's harsh tone was followed by my car door being jerked open. "Missy! Look at me! You don't get to hide. Tell me you're okay!"

"Millard." The gentleness in Colin's tone brought a familiar tightness to my chest.

"Bugger off, Frey!" Manny gripped my shoulders, something he never did. He shook me. "Tell me you're okay. Missy!"

I couldn't. I wanted to. I wanted to reassure him so the stark fear I saw in his eyes would go away. But my mind didn't allow that. Instead it pushed me deeper into the darkness until I could no longer hear Colin's soothing words trying to calm Manny.

Chapter TWELVE

THE FIRST THING I became aware of was the discomfort in my arms and legs. I was still clutching my knees to my chest, my arm muscles quivering with the effort. It took mentally writing the first two lines of Mozart's Violin Sonata No. 17 in C major before I could open my eyes.

I was still in the passenger seat of Colin's SUV and we were driving. The window on my side was gone, cold air coming into the car, yet I was warm. I looked down and saw a GIPN blanket wrapped around me. The floorboard was covered in small pieces of glass. I swallowed and looked out of the open window.

The streets looked familiar and I soon realised we were about five minutes away from the team room. On a deep inhale I lowered my legs and winced. The blood circulation had been hampered by my position and now that the flow was restored, pins and needles caused me great discomfort.

Colin glanced at me once, then longer and smiled. His facial muscles revealed true pleasure. "Hey, you."

"Hey." I rubbed my calves. "How long?"

"Almost an hour. How are the legs?"

"Uncomfortable." I sat up. "Is Manny well?"

"No." His smile dimmed. "He had a really hard time with you not responding to him. And I thought Vin was going to punch him."

"It's not good."

"No, it's not." He turned into a street that ran parallel to one of the beautiful canals. "Dan phoned Francine, who got Manny to go back to the team room before something happened that we'd all regret."

"I don't know what to do." The absurdity of it irritated me, yet the urge to do something to restore Manny's usual grumpy mood overrode logic.

"Yeah. None of us know how to handle this situation. Vin just wants to punch him. I would really like to do that too, but I think Millard needs to talk. He needs to tell us what is going on so we can help or butt out." He smiled. "So we can mind our own business."

"'Butt out' is nonsensical. I've heard Vinnie use it and it simply doesn't make sense."

Colin laughed. "I can agree with that. Yet we use it all the time."

"I don't."

He smiled at me and returned his attention to the road. We were close to the street leading to our team room. "Millard needs to get himself together though. This chase changed things for us on this case."

"What changed?" This was why I hated my shutdowns. Most often it happened during a crucial moment when important information was revealed. I usually felt like I had a lot of catching up to do after a shutdown. It was most frustrating.

Colin parked his SUV in the designated spot for our building and turned to me. "Are you okay to get out?"

I wiggled my toes and moved my arms before I reached for the door handle. "I'm well."

"Okay then." He opened his door and joined me on the pavement, then took my hand as we walked to the entrance of Phillip's building. The small elevator in the back of the foyer was the only way to reach our team room from the street.

Colin entered the code into the keypad and the door slid open. I could no longer wait. "What changed? Why is this case different now?"

"Francine was able to trace the company who rented the two SUVs that followed us to Iran."

"Is that what she found interesting when she spoke to us?" There were a few other things she'd said that I wanted to follow up on, but I decided to take it one revelation at a time.

"Yes." He leaned against the side of the elevator, watching the numbers change as we went to the top floor. "So my question is how does Iran fit into this? Are we talking a national involvement or is it only private citizens who are somehow involved in this wine-drug smuggling thing and torturing the young people?"

I realised his question was rhetorical and didn't answer. It reflected much of what I was thinking.

The elevator stopped and the doors opened to a busy

team room. Francine was at her computer, furiously typing away. Pink sat next to her, his hands moving fast on his tablet as he swiped and tapped. Manny was at his desk glaring at his computer and Vinnie was in the kitchen area, putting more mugs on a tray.

He turned when we entered and smiled. "You're just in time for coffee and pastries. I think we all need some comfort food. Except maybe the old man. He needs a personality transplant."

Francine jumped up and rushed over to me. "Hey, girlfriend. Are you okay?"

"I'm well."

"You better be." Manny walked over and glared at me. "You shaved a good ten years off my life, missy."

"I don't know what that means."

Francine put her arm through Manny's and leaned her head on his shoulder. "It means Manny cares for you and was extremely worried when you guys were being followed."

Manny shook her loose and walked over to the round table. "Sit. We need to talk."

"Did you find anything else on these guys?" Colin asked Francine as we walked to the table.

"Nada." She looked at me. "I'm really glad you're okay."

I nodded and sat down. Vinnie put the tray down on the table and placed the two plates heaped with pastries in front of me. "You get first choice, Jen-girl."

"Where's my tea?" Manny scowled at the tray.

"If you want tea, you can make it yourself. Or you can drink coffee like the rest of us." Vinnie sat down hard in his seat and raised both eyebrows at Manny. "Or you wanna take this outside?"

It was Manny's lack of response that really had me worried. He took a mug of coffee, added milk and sugar and slumped into his chair.

I took one of my favourite pastries and put it on a small plate. The one thing I didn't like about these delicacies was the mess they left behind. That was why I'd taken to eating them with a cake fork—one that Vinnie had supplied for me. He smiled and winked when I looked at him. "Enjoy."

"Thank you." I looked at Daniel, who reached for the second plate of pastries. "Was there any salvageable evidence from the SUV that exploded?"

"Nope," Vinnie answered before Daniel could. "Everything and everyone burned to a crisp."

"All the evidence is gone. We have to wait for the car to cool down before the techs can look at the engine for VIN numbers and the like, but I doubt we'll find anything useful."

"All their electronics are gone too." Pink sighed heavily as he stirred the sugar into his coffee. "I saw the casings of at least two smartphones, but they're completely destroyed. We won't get anything from that car. The back of it is completely gone. There had to have been some incendiary device or substance to make it blow up like that."

"Let me just pile on to this good news report." Francine's expression revealed her sarcasm. "I have nothing on the

Iranian company. I looked, but man, it's hard to find anything understandable from that country. Their government databases are hard to hack and then there is of course the language thing." She held up her manicured finger. "But fear not, I have guys on it. We'll find out who they were."

I resisted the urge to ask her about the 'guys' helping her. Francine frequently used her network of hacker contacts to help her find intel. For my own peace of mind, I'd found it best not to ask details about favours being exchanged and other borderline illegal activities happening in pursuit of information we needed.

Daniel's phone pinged and he took it from one of the many pockets in his uniform. His eyebrows rose slightly before lowering into a frown. "We still don't have an ID on the two victims in the Robertsau forest. The crime scene techs are doing everything they can, but there's nothing to give us a lead. No one has reported them missing and they're not showing up in any databases."

"That's just wrong." Francine rubbed her arms as if she was cold. "Those young people should not be anonymous. Someone knew them, laughed with them, loved them."

"We'll get their names, Franny." Vinnie pushed a plate of pastries towards Francine. "We'll honour them."

"Ask Caelan." I blinked when everyone turned to look at me.

Manny's brow lowered and he inhaled deeply. "I almost forgot about him. Get that little bugger in here."

Francine blew Manny a kiss and swiped the screen of

her phone. A short conversation later, she smiled at him. "Caelan is with Phillip. They'll be here in five minutes."

I thought of what Pink had said about the burned-out SUV. "How many people's remains were in the SUV?"

"The crime scene guys have to confirm, but we all agreed that we could see three people." It was fleeting, but Daniel's micro-expression revealed the horror of what he'd seen. "They're completely burned."

"What are you thinking, Doc?"

"Adèle had photos of a man as part of the chart. Somehow he plays an important part in that business organisation." I sighed. "He has a visible birthmark on his right hand."

"Ah, and you thought that he might've been one of the dudes in the SUV." Vinnie nodded. "Yeah, we won't be able to tell now. Not from that birthmark on his hand. All gone."

"Their hands were the first we checked once the fire was out." Daniel swallowed. "We were hoping to get fingerprints."

The elevator doors pinged. "Doctor Lenard! I'm here."

"I see that." I wondered why Caelan so often felt the need to state the obvious.

"How can I help?" He sat down next to Francine. "I want to help. Tell me what I can do."

Colin put his hand on my arm and I looked at him. He shook his head slightly before looking at Caelan. "We need your help, but this will not be easy."

Caelan looked at my shoulder. "What happened?"

"Two more people died." I considered trying to be more sensitive with my words, but then stayed with what I knew Caelan would understand. "They were tortured like Jace and Adèle. And discarded in the forest."

"Tortured. The Andes Mountains are the longest continental mountain range in the world." He took his backpack from his shoulder, reached inside and came out with two stress balls. We all watched as he squeezed them five times slowly while watching his hands. Then he looked up, again at my shoulder. "Okay. How can I help?"

"Give me a minute." Francine lifted her tablet and turned it so Caelan wouldn't be able to see the screen. "I'm just cleaning up the photos a bit."

"It's not necessary." Caelan squeezed the stress balls harder.

"Oh, it is, superman," Vinnie said. "Let Franny do her magic. Then you can see if you know them."

"You don't know who they are?"

"No, we don't." Daniel's tone was gentle. "And it will definitely help us if we have their names."

"Done." Francine turned her tablet, but then pulled it away again, looking at Caelan. "I cleaned it up as best I could, but you'll still see they were badly beaten up."

Caelan nodded and squeezed the balls a few times. "Okay. Show me."

Francine tilted her tablet towards Caelan, the *frontalis* muscle raising her inner eyebrows in concern.

"The Sargasso Sea is the only sea without any coasts."

Caelan closed his eyes tightly, his hands frantically squeezing the balls. "The Pacific Ocean basin is home to seventy-five percent of the world's volcanoes. I know them. It's Camille Vastine and Martin Gayot. They're also members of the geocaching group. That's Camille's favourite sweater. She always wore it."

Pink was already putting the names into his tablet when Vinnie knocked on the table close to Caelan. "You really are a superman, dude."

"Did you know them well?" Daniel asked.

"No. Jace met up with them a few times. I didn't want to. I don't like meeting new people. Jace did. He wore his glasses so I could watch them when they met for coffee. They were nice to Jace. They were nice. Mexico has more pyramids than Egypt."

"And they were part of the geocaching group," Colin said.

"Yes. Jace and I were the best team. Especially when it came to the caches that weren't easy to find. Camille and Martin were also good. Very good. They were second best. Now there's no one left. Only me."

I thought about Camille's and Martin's connection to Jace and Adèle. "Did Camille and Martin go to Self-Storage Solutions to look for that cache with the 'e'?"

Caelan nodded. "They got there forty minutes after Jace."

"Oh, my God." Francine's eyes were wide. "I see where you're going with this. I mean, we already think the killer saw the security footage from the warehouse. That must be how he knew Jace took the crates. But this must also be how he knew to look for Camille and Martin."

"We need to get the names of the other people in your group." Manny straightened. "Do you have a list?"

"What group?" Caelan glanced at Manny's shoulder.

"Your geocaching group."

"I can't give you their names." He shook his head repeatedly. "They'll never trust me again."

"Then they are not as smart as they think." I hoped logic would convince Caelan. "You'll be saving their lives by giving us their names."

He thought about this for a few seconds, nodded and started rattling off names.

"Whoa, there." Daniel chuckled. "Give us a moment to make notes."

Caelan repeated the names he'd already given, slower and waiting for Daniel to nod before he gave the next one. Pink put them all in his tablet.

"Do you want everyone in France or only the people in Strasbourg?" Caelan asked after he'd given the nineteenth name.

"Only Strasbourg." Daniel looked at Pink and Francine. "Did you find any other crimes with the same MO in other cities?"

"Nope." Francine winked at him. "How did you know I looked?"

"You always do." He smiled at her, then looked at Manny. "I'll mobilise teams to get these people to safety. It might take a while though."

"Good luck with that." Manny didn't look sincere. "I'll stay here and keep this lot safe."

Vinnie snorted and Manny's head jerked up. His eyes narrowed and he inhaled sharply, but a foreign notification tone caught his attention. Caelan took his phone from his trouser pocket and swiped the screen. "Russia spans eleven time zones. Australia is wider than the moon."

"For the love of all that is holy." Manny slumped deeper into his chair. "Now what?"

"The countdown finished." Caelan turned his smartphone so we could see his screen. On it was the interface for the application he used for the geocaching. Large red numbers were in the centre of the screen.

"Do you know what that is?" Colin asked.

Caelan turned his smartphone back and looked at the screen. "It's a GPS location. Jace gave me a GPS location."

Chapter THIRTEEN

"HOLY HELL!" MANNY squinted at the monitors in front of us. "Is that—"

"We're in Jace's basement." Vinnie's voice was clear over the speakers. He had joined Daniel's GIPN team to go to the GPS location Caelan had received. Phillip had taken Caelan to his office when it had become clear that the young man wasn't coping with this new information. He was missing his friend and the GPS location caused him great distress.

It had also caused a few minutes of intense debate until everyone agreed that Daniel would ask the other GIPN teams to get all the members of Caelan's geocaching group to safety. Daniel, Pink and Vinnie had left immediately after they'd assured me that I could receive live streaming when they found and entered the location.

I watched as Vinnie followed Daniel into the dim space, their guns swinging from side to side, their nonverbal cues clearly communicating their readiness to take action if needed. Three seconds later, the tension in Daniel's muscles decreased and he lowered his rifle. "All clear."

"Well? Let's see what's in that bloody basement." Manny

had received a call just after Vinnie had left. He'd been in an even more disagreeable mood since. Behind the posturing, his grief was clear. I didn't know what to do.

So I returned my focus to the monitors and gripped Colin's hand. He was quiet next to me.

"I count eight crates." Vinnie pointed at the wooden crates in the centre of the room. They were in the same place they had been on Jace's video.

"And we know that Jace took eight." Daniel swung his assault rifle over his shoulder and rested his hand on his holstered handgun. "We have these eight, but where are the four crates that Adèle took?"

His question was in the forefront of my mind. But I had many other questions too. "Are all the wine bottles still in the crates?"

Vinnie moved towards the crates, but Daniel held out his hand to stop him. "I think we need to get the bomb squad in here first before we open anything. Just to be safe."

"That's going to take forever." Manny hunched his shoulders.

"Unfortunately, yes." Daniel glanced at Vinnie's button camera, which made it appear as if he was looking at us. "We'll try to make this as quick as possible though."

"I want the bottles." I saw Daniel reacting with a slight frown and collected my thoughts to be clearer. "I want to study all the bottles. I think their labels might give us important information."

"I don't think I can get you the bottles very soon,

Genevieve." Daniel turned to look at the crates. "If these bottles contain liquid heroin like the one we found in Adèle's house, we won't be able to handle them without all of them first being processed. Will photos do?"

I considered this. "The photos will have to be of the highest quality. I need to see every detail of the labels."

"I'll do that as soon as the bomb squad clears the room." Daniel tilted his head and thought about this some more. "I might get our hazmat team in here as well. I've heard of cops dying from overdoses when they handled confiscated drugs. Rather safe than sorry."

Manny scowled. "How long is this drama going to take? We need those labels, Daniel."

Daniel's eyebrows rose slightly, but it was Vinnie who answered. "Back off, old man. Go drink some milky tea or something. Just get off this fucking line and let us do our jobs."

"Us? Our? What, you think you're bloody law now?"

I leaned away from Manny. The anger in his voice was most disturbing.

"Vin, get the photos to us as soon as you guys can. I'll handle things here." Colin leaned forward and disconnected the streaming. Then he turned to Manny. "You need to get yourself together, Millard."

Manny got up and walked away without a word. His shoulders were tight, his gait stilted. I knew this was not physical, but it truly felt like my heart was hurting when I watched him walk to the elevator.

"Give him time." Francine walked into my viewing room

and sat in the chair Manny had vacated. "He'll come around."

"He's pushing all Vin's buttons, Francine." Colin shook his head. "I've never seen him like this."

Francine rubbed her hands as if she had just put on hand lotion. Self-soothing. "Thank you for not asking what this is all about."

"I reckon Millard will tell us when he's ready." Colin sighed. "But it better be before Vin decides to punch his lights out."

Francine snorted. "Or before *I* punch his lights out."

Since there was nothing I could do to ease Manny's turmoil, I turned back to my monitors. I didn't know how long I was going to have to wait for the photos of the labels, so I decided to make use of the time. I opened the folder with the photos of Adèle's basement. I'd been through these photos so many times, I immediately chose the ones I knew gave me the best view of the chart she'd hidden. I used all fifteen monitors to display the photos.

"What are we looking at, girlfriend?"

I frowned in annoyance. "Photos of Adèle's basement."

She giggled. "Sorry. Yes, I know we're looking at those photos. What I meant was, why are we looking at it again?"

"Because something is wrong."

"What's wrong, Doc?" Manny was standing in the doorway, his nonverbal cues more composed. He nodded at Colin, then leaned against the door where Vinnie usually stood.

I frowned at the monitors. "I don't know what's wrong."

"What's your gut telling you?"

I sighed. I found it vexing when neurotypical people diminished years of experience, expert knowledge and finely tuned intuition and called it a 'gut feeling'. I looked at all the photos from top left to bottom right. "There is something not quite right about this business model."

Manny grunted and breathed loudly through his nose. "Okay, why don't you explain to me what you see, Doc?"

"This is without a doubt the organisational chart for a company. See this central square?" I pointed at the monitor in front of me, the photo focused on the large green square. "This is the nucleus of the business. Everything else revolves around this. We assumed the FF stands for Freedom Fragrances—the name of Adèle's company." I continued pointing. "Here you can see the business branching in two distinct directions. To the left are the squares showing what I assume to be her distribution plan."

"Have you managed to decode her descriptions?"

"No." That was most frustrating. "I've come to the conclusion that she used phrases and words that were known only to her." Again I pointed at a monitor. "See this square? She wrote 'round cheeks in rainbow village'."

"What the hell?"

"Yeah." Colin shifted in his chair. "I also had a look at this and all of it is like this. She used descriptions that will help her remember. But we have no idea what the name of this rainbow village is."

"It could be a small area in the city known for gay clubs." Francine shrugged. "Or it could be one of those quaint pedestrian streets with colourful umbrellas over the entire street."

"Speculating would be a waste of time." I'd determined that very early. "We have no idea what Adèle's frame of reference was."

"Hmm." Manny scratched his chin. "You said the business branches in two directions. Explain more about the first."

"The distribution." I didn't like all this speculation. "I'm working on a supposition here since all of these squares refer to a person and a place. They are also not connected to each other, but all have their separate connections to the green square."

"And the second branch?"

"I'm not a hundred percent sure what that is." Even though I'd spent countless hours looking at the photos and mentally writing Mozart to help me.

"Just tell me what you think, Doc."

"This might be her supplier." I pointed at the three photos of the man. "And I think he is very important to her business model."

"Ah, so he's the guy with the birthmark." Manny stepped into the room and stopped behind Francine. He leaned a bit forward to look at the monitors with the photos. "Can't see his face on any of these."

"I don't know if Adèle did this on purpose." I had thought about this a lot. "If she had been following him and taking these surveillance photos, surely she would've had an opportunity to take a better photo."

"She had photos of this man and of the men who'd bought the Iranian artefacts." Manny pushed his hands into his trouser pockets. "Why would she have photos of these people and only descriptions of the other people?"

"I don't know."

"I know you don't know, Doc. It's rhetorical."

"Oh. There's also no clear indication who she used as a courier." I'd spent an entire hour searching the photos with only that in mind.

"We have nothing." Manny rubbed his hands over his face. "We have so much, yet we have nothing."

"We have the wine bottles."

"And just what do you think you're going to find on those labels, Doc?"

"I'm not sure." Yet there was a niggling in the back of my head. Usually this meant that my subconscious had made some connection that had not yet filtered through to my thinking brain. "But I need to study all the labels. I think it will give us valuable information."

"It bloody better." He walked back to the door and leaned against it. "I've been trying to track down the vineyard that sent those bottles. The Iranians have not been helpful at all."

"See!" Francine threw both her hands in the air. "I told you how hard it is to find out anything about Iranian companies."

Manny raised his eyes to the ceiling and sighed heavily.

"At least I wasn't trying to hack anything. I went through legal and also diplomatic channels to establish whether this company, this vineyard even exists. But everywhere I turn, I'm being stonewalled." He glared down at me. "I'm being blocked from finding out anything or pushing for any information."

A notification sound came from Francine's tablet. "Ooh! The first photos are coming through."

I straightened in my chair and opened my inbox. There were already three emails from Pink with attachments. I downloaded all the photos and replaced Adèle's chart with labels of the wine bottles. I ignored Manny's insistent questions whether I was seeing something helpful. Instead I started mentally playing Mozart's Piano Quartet No. 1 in G minor, leaned back in my chair and studied the photos.

Two hours later, I was still looking at the photos. Pink had taken a photo of each of the ninety-six bottles and sent them all to me. The last one had come through seven minutes ago. It had taken them a long time to have the premises cleared by the bomb squad as well as the hazardous materials team. Even though I'd been impatient, I appreciated the importance of keeping everyone safe.

"Do you people know what the time is?" Phillip walked into my viewing room and looked at me, then at Colin and back at me.

I nodded. "It's twelve minutes to eight."

"And?" His expression was familiar.

"I'm in danger of hyper-focusing."

His smile was warm. "Vinnie phoned me. He knew you would be captivated by the photos they'd sent, so he asked me to get you to go home."

"Has he made dinner?" Colin asked.

"Yes." Phillip opened the bottom drawer of one of the antique-looking cabinets at the back of my room and took my handbag from it. He held it out to me. "Time to go."

I glanced back at the monitors in front of me. Today had been extremely taxing. Seeing the brutality that Camille Vastine and Martin Gayot had suffered and then being chased by two vehicles that we still hadn't identified had put immense strain on my mind. Taking a break and spending time with Eric might very well be what my mind needed to bring to the fore the connection I felt lingering.

It took less than ten minutes to close down our computers and get Francine to join us. Manny gave us a feeble reason for not coming for dinner, but I could see his lie. The tension around his mouth and eyes led me to believe that he needed a short while on his own, without observant and concerned glances aimed his way.

Dinner was uneventful and quick. Vinnie wanted to join Pink and Daniel making sure all the members of the geocaching community were safe. He also wanted to check on Jace. No sooner had Nikki taken Eric to bed and Phillip had gone home than I sat down at the table with my laptop.

"Working?" Francine sat down next to me, holding a refilled glass of red wine.

I opened the folder with photos of the labels and

clicked on the first one. "There is something here."

"Okey-dokey." She interlaced her fingers and stretched them out in front of her, then shook out her hands. "Let's make these photos our bitches."

I looked at her. "I don't know what that means."

She laughed and lifted her tablet from the table. "It means we two ladies are going to figure this out."

We didn't. Hours later, I had looked at each photo, but had not yet made the connection.

"I'm hungry." Francine stretched her arms high above her head and yawned loudly. "Vinnie's fettuccini is all burned up now." She looked at her empty wine glass. "And I need more wine."

"Alcohol produces detectable impairments in memory after only a few drinks."

"Hah. Yeah, but it does taste good." She got up and sighed. "I suppose I'll make us some coffee then."

I returned my attention to the labels. The photos Pink had sent were of superb quality. I could see the smallest detail, including the lines in the background that formed a watermark. I enjoyed working at home, but at this moment, I wished I was in my viewing room. Being able to put fifteen different labels next to each other would've helped me get a better visual perspective. I flipped through the photos again, each time zooming in on the background.

"The men need to get back now." Francine put a steaming coffee mug next to my left hand. "Including your man."

I frowned. Colin wasn't with Vinnie and the others.

He'd made sure that Daniel ordered a second patrol car to protect our building. Then he'd kissed me on the forehead and told me he'd be back soon. I'd known not to ask. Colin was doing something that was in the gray area of legal.

"You're no fun, girlfriend. You're not even chatting to me tonight."

"I never chat."

She lifted her coffee mug as if to toast me. "Very true."

"The chart doesn't reflect Adèle's business."

"Huh?" She put down her mug and looked at my computer monitor. "You're looking at the labels. Does that have anything to do with Adèle's chart?"

I thought about it. "I don't know yet."

She picked up the mug again and sat back in her chair. "Well, the labels are not helping us at all. There's nothing funky on them. They all have the same wording, same name, same logo, same everything."

"They're not exactly the same." I split the monitor and put two photos next to each other, both zoomed to see the background better. "The watermark is different on this one than on the other."

"What?" She drew out the word as she moved closer to me. Then she looked at me until I nodded, allowing her to pull my laptop closer. She studied the monitor. "Huh. What do you know? They really look very much the same, but the lines are a bit off."

I pulled my computer back and zoomed in even more. "The lines are not solid. If we magnify it, you'll see that they are broken. The difference between the labels are the breaks in the lines."

"You think it's code? Like Morse code or something?"

"It's not Morse code." I'd already eliminated that option. "But it means something. There are nineteen different labels with different broken lines. All ninety-six bottles have one of the nineteen labels."

She closed her eyes, then opened them again. "Well, my brain is fried. I'll look at it tomorrow. If Manny doesn't come—"

The sound of keys turning in the front door caught her attention. Her eyes widened and a smile lifted her cheeks as Vinnie stormed into my apartment.

"Fuck you, old man!" He looked at Francine, who was now standing, her smile gone, her expression concerned. Then he looked at me, his anger not diminishing at all. "I can't deal with this asswipe. Do something."

Manny stomped into my apartment, his shoulders hunched, his lips thinned. Behind him Pink and Daniel followed, both men looking uncomfortable.

Francine walked to Manny and pulled him towards the sitting area. "What's cookin', good-lookin'?"

Manny grunted, but allowed Francine to drag him to the sofa under the window. He sat down hard, his lips thinned. Francine glanced at me, her eyebrows drawn tightly together.

"I'm going to my room. If you guys want food, there's the kitchen." Vinnie glared at Pink. "Just clean the fuck up after yourself."

"Once, Vin. Only once did I leave three crumbs on your precious kitchen counter." Pink chuckled, his attempt at humour failing.

Vinnie sneered and walked to the connected apartment, the side he shared with Pink and Nikki. Pink shrugged and walked into the kitchen. He opened the refrigerator and took ingredients to make sandwiches.

I looked at Daniel as he sat down next to me. "Are all the young people safe?"

"Yes." He rubbed his neck and winced. "It's been a long day, but we have everyone on the list Caelan gave to us. They are all in safe houses, under police protection for the night."

"What about tomorrow?"

He smiled. "Tomorrow too. They will be protected until we stop this killer." He looked at the photos on my laptop monitor. "Did you have any luck with the photos?"

"Nothing actionable." I briefed him on the broken lines that made up the watermarks and the nineteen different labels.

"What do you think it means?"

"I don't know yet." I zoomed out until I could see the entire bottle. "Are all the bottles filled with liquid heroin?"

"So far the lab has tested more than half the bottles and yes, they are all filled with thousands of euros' worth of heroin." He shook his head. "The potential street value in each of these bottles is staggering. I wonder if Jace knew what he'd stumbled onto."

Once again, the sound of keys in the front door drew

our attention. Manny got up and reached for his gun holstered under his arm.

The door opened and he dropped his hand, but his expression hardened. "Where the bleeding hell have you been?"

Colin winced, then sighed. The relaxed triumph that I'd seen on his face when he'd first opened the door was replaced with resignation. "Good evening, Millard."

"What the blazes have you been up to, Frey?" Manny walked closer and glared at Colin's black outfit, his flexible sneakers and the black gloves still covering his hands. "And what the bleeding hell do you have in those bags?"

Colin walked to the table, put the two large sports bags on the floor and leaned over to kiss me. He nodded at Daniel and turned back to Manny, pointing to the bags. "In there you will find a few artefacts that are reportedly part of the Oxus treasure. There are also two small paintings, a marble statue and three beautiful bronze works that I'm sure the British Museum would love to have back. They were quite worried when they received an anonymous call and then discovered a few of their prize artefacts on display had been replaced by brilliant 3D facsimiles."

Manny's eyes were wide and his nostrils flared. "What have you done?"

"I visited a few old friends." Colin was enjoying this. He had broken the law and now he was flaunting it in front of Manny. And Manny wasn't handling this well. At all. Colin smirked. "Remember those four men I identified in the photos? Well, I visited them while they were sleeping and took the things that didn't belong to them."

"Fucking hell, Frey!" Manny walked to the front door, turned around and walked back, his scowl deepening as he neared. He shook his index finger at Colin, then walked away again.

"Colin." Daniel frowned at the sports bags. "Are you sure all these are stolen?"

"Oh, yes." Colin went down on his haunches and unzipped one bag. With his gloved hand, he carefully took out a bubble-wrapped shape, no bigger than the palm of his hand. "I made sure these babies will get back to their homes unharmed."

Francine joined us as we watched Colin unwrap the shape until he held a small statue of a gold fish in his hands. "This, my lovely family, is the gold fish vessel that should be on show at the moment with all his mates from the Oxus treasure."

"All of them stolen?" Daniel asked again.

This time Colin wasn't glib. "One hundred percent sure. You can take the bags as is and log them in as evidence. The moment the museums find out you have this, they will put in their claims. That is, if the insurance companies don't get wind of it first."

"I think I'll do just that." Daniel reached into a side pocket in his uniform trousers and came out with two latex gloves. Manny joined us, but didn't say anything. Once Daniel covered his hands, he took the statue from Colin and rewrapped it. "Nothing that will point back to you?"

"I'll pretend you didn't just say that." Colin got up and winked at him. "This is all yours."

"I can't believe you people! If no one is going to ask for the deets, I will." Francine pushed past Manny and poked Colin in the chest with her nail. "Tell me everything. All the dirty little details."

"Don't." Daniel got up. "Let me take this and leave. I want deniability."

"Spoilsport." Francine smiled at Daniel and watched as he walked to the door. The moment the door closed behind him, she turned back to Colin. "So?"

The effort it was costing Manny not to give in to his anger was visible. At least to me. I watched as he controlled his breathing, his fingers tightening in fists and relaxing, only to tighten once again until his knuckles were white. He was looking at Colin, waiting for him to reply to Francine.

"I don't just know who these men are, I also know where all of them live." Colin didn't look at Manny. "So I broke into their homes once they were asleep and I took the things they illegally bought. Mayer, Riner and Picon were average break-ins. I'd been there before, so I knew where to look and found the artefacts very quickly."

Francine narrowed her eyes. "What was the other guy's name? Damian?"

"Yes. Damian Leveaux." Colin's triumphant smile returned. "He had the jackpot."

"You found something more than only the Oxus artefacts." I could see it clearly on his face.

"The bastard had three different statues and seventeen coins. Seventeen." His lips thinned. "Good thing I'd been in Leveaux's house before. He might have a state-of-the-art safe, but the idiot was never smart. He didn't change the code since the last time I reappropriated art from him."

"And, of course, he will never report it." Pink put a large plate of sandwiches on the table and sat down. He waved at the plate. "Help yourselves."

We didn't.

"And?" Francine gestured impatiently.

"I found his black book." This time Colin's smile had a hint of malice in it.

"Did you take it?" Francine asked.

"No. That would give him grounds to report or find me. That really is his property." He smiled at Francine and took his phone from his trouser pocket. "But I took photos. Many, many photos." He looked at Manny. "There's enough evidence for you to close your case on him."

"Frey." Manny glared at Colin's phone. "How do you know we're investigating him?"

"Who is this 'we'?" I knew Manny frequently visited the Interpol offices, but I didn't know he worked cases separately from the ones we did.

"Millard here runs an elite task force over at Interpol as well." Colin raised both eyebrows, his posture challenging.

"Handsome?" Francine took a step away from Manny. "Is that true?"

The tension around Manny's mouth and eyes increased, his face turning red. "It's not related to anything we do here."

"Like hell it isn't." Colin stared at Manny. "Are you going to tell them or must I?"

"Frey." Manny pressed his fists against his eyes. When he lowered his hands, he looked exhausted. "Later. Let's deal with that crap later. Tell me what else you found."

Colin looked at Manny through narrowed eyes for a few seconds before nodding once. "Okay. I found entries in his black book about his dealings with Élodie."

"Adèle's criminal pseudonym." Francine was still looking at Manny, a frown pulling her eyebrows together. She turned to Colin. "What did you see?"

Colin swiped the screen of his phone and turned it so I could see. The handwriting was too small on the screen to read. I looked at Colin and he smiled. "He detailed the whole deal he did with Élodie. Adèle. The payment, the shipment, everything."

"Let me guess." Francine tapped her chin in fake contemplation. "He paid her using some hawala broker."

Colin nodded. "He glued the hawala slip in the book as well."

"The courier?" I asked.

Colin's smile was wide. "Easy Post."

"Them again," Manny said.

"Oh, yeah. Again. And again." Colin put his phone back in his trouser pocket. "When I saw the name, I remembered that Johan told me Adèle had insisted he used Easy Post to send the Roubaud he'd painted for her."

Manny turned to Francine. "I want everything on Easy Post."

"And I want a unicorn." She lowered her chin and stared at him. "And I want to know about this super-secret task force."

"You might get that unicorn first, Franny." Vinnie walked to the table, more relaxed than before. He was wearing sweatpants and a sleeveless t-shirt. His pyjamas. "But I would also like to know about this task force."

"Later." Manny rubbed one eye, which drew my attention to the dark rings under his eyes.

"Let's do this tomorrow." I surprised myself by suggesting a break.

"It is tomorrow, love." Colin smiled. "But I agree. We can all do with a few hours' rest." He looked at Manny. "To get our heads a bit more level."

"Bugger off." Manny turned towards the door. "Eight o'clock tomorrow morning in the team room. I want everything on Easy Post."

Francine followed him to the door and waved at us before she also put on her outerwear and left with Manny. Vinnie sat down at the table and took one of Pink's sandwiches. "That old man better deal with his shit."

"Be patient, Vin." Something in Colin's tone caught my attention.

I turned to him, but stopped when he shook his head at me. "Let's go to sleep, love. We'll deal with everything tomorrow."

It was clear that he wasn't going to tell me what he knew, but I could see that he'd discovered something about Manny that worried him.

I didn't know if I was going to get any sleep tonight. My mind was obsessed with those photos of the labels. And my concern for Manny had deepened even more.

Chapter FOURTEEN

"SPEAK." MANNY KNOCKED on the round table in the team room. We'd sat down a few minutes ago and Francine was telling yet another joke, Daniel and Vinnie already laughing as she came close to the punchline. Manny knocked on the table again. "Bloody hell! Tell me about Easy Post."

"Pharmacy!" Francine burst out laughing as Vinnie and Daniel joined her.

Colin was also smiling. I didn't understand the joke. And I didn't care.

Manny's lips thinned and colour moved from his collar into his face. He inhaled deeply, but stopped when Francine turned to him, the wrinkles at the corners of her eyes evidence of her genuine smile. "I found quite a lot of intel for you, handsome."

"Don't make me ask again." Manny took the mug of milky tea he had made for himself this morning.

Francine picked her tablet up from the table. "Easy Post was established nine years ago. There are only two branches—one in Paris and one here in Strasbourg. First impressions are that it is a small business and the info on their website confirms it. Their website also claims that they act as couriers for a high-end clientele and ensure full confidentiality and complete safety of each and every parcel entrusted to them. But guess what?"

Manny just glared at her.

"Spoilsport. I found out who established Easy Post and has been the sole owner ever since." She pointed dramatically at me. When I didn't respond, she shook her hand even more.

I sighed. "Gilles Mahout founded Easy Post."

"Gilles Mahout?" Manny sat up. "The manager from Adèle's self-storage place?"

"The one and only. I have no idea why he managed Self-Storage Solutions when he owned Easy Post." Francine leaned back in her chair as if she'd completed her briefing.

There was more. "Francine and I looked at his phone records. He made a lot of calls to a number that wasn't registered to any account."

"Of course we couldn't get a name from a burner phone." Francine smiled. "But then I worked my cell phone tower kung fu. Almost all those calls bounced off a tower three hundred and seventy metres from Adèle's house."

"How many phone calls?" Manny asked.

"Two or three a week."

"They were in this together. Hellfire." Manny turned to Daniel who joined our meeting this morning at Vinnie's request. "Have you found that little weasel yet?"

"No." Daniel reached into his top pocket and took out

his phone. "I'll send Pink word that finding Gilles is now a priority."

"Top priority." Manny turned back to Francine. "Has he been using Easy Post for smuggling all along?"

"I can't say for sure." She winked at me. I had helped her for an hour and a half this morning finding information on Easy Post. I had also refused to allow her to speculate on anything we couldn't confirm. She pointed at her tablet. "Everything Genevieve and I found seemed to be on the up and up. All their business dealings. I had a look at their finances and that also looked clean." She paused. "Just like Adèle's."

"What are you saying?" Manny frowned.

Francine touched her sculpted eyebrow and once again I noticed the fatigue pulling at the muscles around her eyes. She might have mastered the art of using make-up to its fullest advantage, but she couldn't hide the micro-expressions revealing that she hadn't slept much last night. If she'd slept at all. She flicked her hair over her shoulder and smiled. "Yup, just like Adèle. According to Easy Post's finances and their tax records, they are the most profitable courier since the first caveman ran to the neighbouring tribe with a gift for a girl."

I frowned at the irrelevance of her analogy. "If we work on the assumption that Gilles used Easy Post to smuggle drugs and art, he was smart to keep his business dealings subtle."

"Oh, the man was low-key, all right." Francine winked at me. "He only had the two outlets—the one in Paris and the one here in Strasbourg—and never lived it up. He didn't buy sporty cars or crazy houses. I still have to get into his finances and I'm really curious about it. I would love to know what he did with all his money."

"Most likely put it somewhere abroad where it's not traceable and is waiting for the perfect moment to retire." Vinnie grunted. "Huh. Now is the perfect time for him to go to some island and access his offshore accounts."

"We've had all airports on full alert the moment we discovered he went missing," Daniel said.

"Oh, my dear law-abiding Danny." Francine fluttered her eyes at him. "All he has to do is drive across one of France's many borders, get to a small airport and start his onward journey from there. Or get to a port and take a nice cruise to a Caribbean island with friendly bankers."

She was right. I had considered these possibilities the moment we'd discovered Gilles had been deeply entrenched in Adèle's drug-dealing business. His business accounts had revealed thousands of parcels, packages and letters being shipped between Paris and Strasbourg, but seldom outside of Europe. A lot of shipments were received from abroad at both outlets, but we couldn't find much detail on the content of the shipments. I had posited that since Gilles had been in the shipping business— presumably the illegal shipping business as well—for over a decade, he would have expert knowledge on how to enter and exit a country unnoticed.

"I want Gilles." Manny was looking at Daniel, his eyebrows drawn low.

Daniel nodded, but paused when my phone started ringing. I stared at it where it was lying on the table in front of me. I very seldom received phone calls. Only the people in this room called me and occasionally the president's wife. I lifted the phone. It wasn't Isabelle.

I swiped the screen. "Caelan, why are you phoning me?"

"Mongolia is the least densely populated country on Earth! Over eight hundred and twenty languages are spoken in Papua New Guinea!" His voice had reached a keening tone and I moved the phone away from my ear. I thought about it and then put him on speakerphone.

I was about to respond by telling him to calm down, but then thought about Caelan's coping mechanisms. "Which country produces more of the world's oxygen than any other?"

"Russia." He inhaled and exhaled loudly. "Siberia is home to approximately twenty-five percent of the world's forests."

"What is the densest substance on Earth?"

"Osmium." He sounded more in control, his voice not quivering as much. We listened to him breathe three times.

"Caelan, bud." Colin leaned closer to my phone. "Where are you?"

"Chanceux Café. The cops following me are drinking coffee by the window. They think I'm crazy. I'm sitting at my own table. Alone. The others are sitting at the back table. The Atlantic Ocean is the saltiest of them all."

Colin glanced at me. "Do you want us to come to you?"

"Yes. Every part of the yew tree is poisonous, except its berries."

"Bloody hell." Manny leaned away from my phone and shook his head.

Vinnie gave Manny an extremely hostile glance before moving closer to my phone. "Okay, superman. We'll be there in seven minutes."

"Lightning strikes the earth over eight point six million times per day." Caelan gave another three facts before Colin swiped the screen on my phone to end the call.

"What on earth set him off?" Francine's concern made her look even more tired.

I didn't answer. Depending on the day, it could be the smallest change in a routine or even just a thought that could trigger a shutdown. I knew. I fought this daily.

Four minutes later, I was in the passenger seat of Vinnie's SUV, Vinnie in the backseat. Colin had organised for his SUV to be repaired and Vinnie had happily given Colin his keys. We had barely left the parking space when Vinnie leaned in between the two front seats. I moved closer to the door.

"I'm gonna kill the old man." Even though his expression confirmed his anger, I knew his words were not to be taken literally. He was frustrated with Manny's behaviour.

"He's hurting, Vin." Colin glanced at me, then winced. He knew I'd seen his micro-expressions. He knew the reason for Manny's emotional pain. "Like I said last night, it's not my place to say anything, love."

Colin sped down the street towards the café I'd been to only twice. Both times with Francine.

"What are you talking about, dude?" Vinnie looked at Colin's reflection in the rear-view mirror, inhaled sharply then leaned even closer to look directly at Colin. "You know what's going on!"

"Vin, give Millard space. He'll talk when he's ready."

"Bastard doesn't deserve our compassion." Vinnie threw himself back on his seat. "He's being a complete asswipe."

"We're here." Colin parked in front of the café in the street. The cars legally parked wouldn't be able to leave, but I assumed Colin didn't care about that at the moment. He put on the hazard lights and turned to me. "Ready?"

I nodded and got out, pulling my coat tightly around me. It was colder than yesterday. I hoped this cold spell would end soon. Just as I met Colin on the pavement, Vinnie's phone rang. He looked at the screen. "Gotta take this. One of my contacts getting back to me."

"Meet us inside." Colin took my hand.

We walked to the café and Colin held the door open for me to enter. The smell of coffee immediately surrounded us as well as the typical buzz found in cafés. People were chatting, cutlery clanging against sturdy plates and mugs, the coffee machine's hissing completing the aural stimulation. At times I enjoyed it, but the second time Francine and I had been here, I'd left after only thirteen minutes. The noise had been too much for me that day.

I took off my coat and looked for Caelan. Colin was

also looking, but as always he looked for more than the obvious. At first I had found it disconcerting that he and Vinnie both would scan a venue before deeming it safe to enter. The way Vinnie looked at everything and everyone was an observable search for possible threats to our safety. But Colin's narrowed gaze was different. I'd once asked him if he was looking for valuables to steal. He'd laughed, but had never answered me.

"There he is." Caelan was sitting at a small round table, partially hidden behind a large pillar, another pillar on his other side. The pillars as well as all the walls looked like they were in ruins, plaster only covering parts of them and the exposed brickwork damaged. Francine had called it boho-loft-industrial chic. I didn't know what that meant.

All I cared about was the way Caelan was rocking slightly, clutching his stress balls. We weaved through a few tables, nobody stopping their conversations or work on computers to look at us. Only one more table separated us from Caelan when Colin's hand tightened around mine. It was so slight that I might not have felt it had I worn my gloves.

I glanced at him and immediately all my muscles tensed. He shook his head. "Pretend that everything is okay, love."

"What isn't okay?" I gripped his hand tighter and started looking around the café. The two officers who'd been assigned to keep Caelan safe were sitting at a small table closer to the door. I hadn't seen them when we'd entered. They had empty plates and oversized mugs in front of them, their body language completely relaxed. I wondered if they'd even noticed Caelan's distress.

"Hey, bud." Colin pulled me to Caelan's table and pulled an unused chair closer for me to sit down. He removed Caelan's coat from the other chair and sat down as well. "We need your help now more than ever."

He took his phone from his trouser pocket and started texting. We were sitting so close, it was easy to see he was addressing Vinnie. I didn't care to read the message. I looked at Caelan. "What is triggering you?"

"The men in black. The Earth's inner core is about the same temperature as the sun." He put both stress balls on the table and started tapping his thighs. "They're bad men."

I studied him. I'd seen Caelan in many phases of his shutdowns. This was just another one. He was not suffering a psychotic break. That meant we had to take what he'd said literally. I turned to look for men dressed in black, but Colin stopped me. "Don't look around. Just pretend like everything is okay."

"This is the second time you've said this. What do you mean?"

"There are three men sitting close to the door I think leads to the kitchen."

"The toilets." Caelan opened and closed his hands, then reached for his stress balls and squeezed them slowly. "That door goes to the toilets."

"You saw them, right?" Colin leaned towards Caelan. "This is why you're worried."

Caelan nodded. Then couldn't stop. I looked at Colin, finding it impossibly hard not to turn around and search for these men. "Why did you notice them?"

"With the exception of the cops dressed like cops, everyone else in here is either a hipster, a student or a worker on a quick break. Those three are wearing black suits, their hairstyles are definitely not from France and they look way too alert and interested in other people."

"I need to see them."

"Hmm." Colin frowned. "Move your chair closer to Caelan. That will put you behind the pillar and you will be able to observe them without them noticing."

I didn't even try to be covert. I moved my chair and ignored the increased tension at being this close to Caelan. I needed to see these people.

Colin reached across and put his palm flat on the table in front of Caelan. "I know you're worried, but Vin is going to get Daniel and Manny to come and help us."

"Who are they?" I leaned back and searched the area Colin had indicated. There, against the back wall, sat three men at a table as small as Caelan's. They did indeed look out of place with their military-neat hairstyles. They were shockingly unsuccessful in their attempts to manipulate their nonverbal cues into appearing relaxed. All of their feet were flat on the ground, their legs not trapped under the table, enabling them to move at a moment's notice. Their gazes roved over the café the entire time.

"I don't know who they are." Caelan squeezed his stress balls, then stopped rocking. "But I saw them on the app."

"Explain that, please." Colin's tone was calm, his body language communicating that he was having a relaxed conversation with a friend.

"I was at home." Caelan nodded towards the officers. "They were sitting outside my apartment and I was safe. And bored. So I went to the app to see what was happening. Everyone was talking about the cops taking them to safety."

"How did you see that?" Colin asked. "Do you have some kind of social networking place online?"

"Kind of. It's an app within the app. It's not as good as Facebook or Instagram, but it's better for us. We don't see stupid news or ads. We just chat there and we upload photos of our cache hunts, parties, dinners and other things. It's really—"

"The men." I could see that he was losing focus. "Tell us how you recognised the men."

"Oh, yes." He breathed deeply three times. "There were a lot of photos uploaded last night of the police taking people to safer places or the police sitting outside people's flats. There's even one where they insisted the police stayed inside. They had dinner together."

"The men," I reminded him.

"Yes. I looked at all the photos, then realised there was a stranger in two of the photos. Two photos in different places and uploaded by different members. They both live here in Strasbourg, but I don't think they've ever met. Julie is like me. She stays at home. She took a photo from her window, showing the cops sitting in their car outside her apartment building." He swallowed and looked towards the back wall. "The big guy was standing on the corner of the street."

It was easy to know who he was referring to. Two of the three men were very average in build and height. The third was taller than his colleagues by at least twenty centimetres. His uncomfortable-looking slump didn't succeed in making him look more relaxed or shorter. Instead it brought more attention to his muscular shoulders that didn't allow him to hunch over much.

Colin's phone buzzed and he looked at the screen. "Vin contacted Daniel, who's bringing Millard and the rest of the GIPN team. They'll be here in eight minutes."

I blinked a few times. There were only two empty tables in the whole café. The way the men were positioning their bodies alerted me to the fact that they were very likely carrying firearms under their jackets. If there were to be a firefight in this establishment, many people could be injured. Or worse.

"We should talk to them first." I couldn't believe I had just suggested such an outrageous and risky move.

"I can phone Vin now and you can talk to him." Colin lifted his phone.

I shook my head. "No. I don't want to talk to Vinnie." On the one hand I regretted my impulsive suggestion. But the more I thought about it, the more convinced I was that this would be the best move. "You and I should go and talk to the three men."

Colin's eyebrows shot up. "Seriously?"

"Yes."

He sat back in his chair and looked up at the ceiling. "You know, that's actually not such a bad idea." He lowered his gaze to look at me. "But first study them and be very sure that they're not going to do something stupid."

"Like kill you." Caelan squeezed his stress balls. "I don't want you to die."

"I don't want to die either." I really didn't. Just the thought of putting myself in harm's way like this already brought the blackness of a shutdown into my peripheral vision. I pushed Mozart's Symphony in A minor into my mind, leaned closer to Caelan to hide more of myself behind the pillar and studied the men.

They weren't talking much. Just a few quietly spoken words and then they continued observing the patrons of the café. I almost smiled when it became very obvious that their interest was completely focused on our table. I knew this because ours was the only table they didn't look at. Their studied avoidance was almost comical. It made me wonder about their training.

The tall man lowered his eyes when he spoke to the man with the acne-scarred skin and wire-rimmed glasses. The third man leaned a bit closer to listen to the taller man, his nonverbal cues also submissive to the man with the glasses. He didn't look at them, but it was clear that he was listening intently. When he answered, it was with the kind of authority that confirmed my impression that he was their leader.

The other two nodded and resumed their attempt at appearing relaxed while watching everyone. A few times their eyes rested on the two officers who were now sharing a joke. Each time, their eyes narrowed, but they didn't look concerned.

"Well?" Colin touched my forearm.

"They're ready to take action if needed, but there's no indication of aggression."

"Jenny?" He waited until I looked at him. "I don't like this idea."

"Neither do I." I thought back to the briefing this morning. "Manny will insist on coming in here with Daniel."

"And the idiot will get us all killed." Colin nodded and pushed himself up. He held out his hand to me. "Ready?"

"No." Caelan started rocking. "The Amazon rainforest is home to one third of the planet's land species. Don't go."

"We'll be okay, bud." Colin glanced at the cops, who hadn't even noticed us joining Caelan. "Stay right here. Vinnie and Daniel will be here soon. We'll make sure nothing bad happens."

"You can't give that guarantee." I hated it when neurotypicals lied in their attempt to calm or, even worse, placate others.

"I can." Colin pulled me up, his posture confident. "You and I make an incredible team and together we will make sure this situation doesn't escalate at all."

Chapter FIFTEEN

THEY NOTICED US the moment we stepped out from
behind the pillar. The tall man straightened, his unsuccessful
attempt at a slump forgotten as his eyes narrowed,
watching us approach. I resisted reaching for Colin's hand,
knowing that this would create the impression of
weakness. Instead I pushed Mozart's Fugue in G minor
into my mind, hoping the organ music would keep me
calm for the risk we were now taking.

The third man had a mole above his left eyebrow. It
moved when his eyebrows drew together in a deep frown.
He too straightened in his chair, his hand touching the
bulge under his jacket as if to reassure himself his weapon
was still there. The only one who didn't react outwardly
was the leader.

Colin had his phone out and swiped the screen a few
times before tilting it so I could see. He had phoned
Francine, but had muted the call. She could hear us, but no
sound would come from the speakers on Colin's phone.
He put his phone in the pocket of his designer shirt, the
screen and therefore the microphone pointing away from
him. He never put anything in the pockets of his shirts.

He'd told me a few times that it was the habit of a pen-pusher and he was definitely not one.

We were now two tables away from the men and I forced my mind away from the safety of thinking about metaphors used for office workers. It was imperative that I observed these men. I didn't want to miss any micro-expression or cue that could indicate actions that could put our lives and the lives of the café's patrons in danger.

The table next to the three men were unoccupied and Colin walked straight there and took the two chairs. One he put close to the leader and the other closer to the tall man. The position of the chairs would place us effectively between the men and the rest of the café. We would be blocking their path. I mentally turned up the volume of the fugue.

"Gentlemen." Colin sat on the chair by the tall man and waved at the other chair. "Sit down, love. We're going to have a little chat."

"Go away." The tall man pulled his shoulders back, his arms moving away from his torso—all indicators of aggression. Colin reacted by stretching his legs out in front of him and crossing his feet. With this position of comfort, he'd just conveyed that he was not feeling threatened. And that he was confident. Colin was an accomplished liar.

The leader pushed his glasses up on his nose. He first looked at me when I sat down next to him, then at Colin. He waved a dismissing hand at the tall man. "It's okay. Let them join us. Why not?"

The leader's accented English was less telling than the tall man's, but it made me take a second look at their features. All three men had dark hair, olive skin and facial structures that most commonly were associated with one area. "You're from Iran."

"We're visiting your beautiful city and enjoying the café culture everyone writes about."

The leader's non-answer and body language almost brought a smile to my face. "You're an inept liar."

Colin cleared his throat and I winced. I supposed it would be safer for me to keep my observations to myself. I bit down on my lips to prevent myself from saying anything that might provoke hostility. But the leader's reaction wasn't hostile. His smile was genuine. "We really *are* enjoying the beauty of your city."

Colin stared at him for a few seconds. After so many years with him, I could see his mind absorbing all the important information and working on the best way to approach this man. Before he could say anything, all three Iranian men's eyes left us to look at the front of the café.

I was sitting sideways, so only had to turn my head to see Vinnie, Daniel, Manny and the rest of the GIPN team clearing the café. With the exception of one young woman, everyone remained calm and left quickly. She left quickly, but wasn't calm. She was clutching Pink's arm, asking a lot of questions in a low voice. The café-type music was loud enough to mask most of the activity and her questions, but her body language plainly communicated her fear. Most of the other people appeared excited by this event. Odd.

The third man straightened as well, no longer taking his cue from the leader. His hand drifted to his jacket's button and he opened it, obviously getting ready to go for his holstered weapon. I focused on my breathing and paid closer attention to his micro-expressions. He seemed to be in full control, but was alert and aware of the position of every officer in the café.

"Now that we're alone"—Colin waved his arm at the empty café—"you can tell us why you are here."

The leader looked pointedly at the empty mugs and plates on their table. "To have breakfast."

Colin's only reaction was to stare at him.

Movement in the centre of the café caught my eye and I turned to see Vinnie and Daniel walking to us. Manny was standing at the door, a scowl pulling his eyebrows low over his eyes. He had his handgun out, but pointed at the floor. Pink and two more GIPN team members were in the café as well, their assault weapons ready. It was unsettling to see such readiness for violence.

Daniel stopped behind my chair and briefly touched my shoulder with the tip of his finger. I was surprised that it comforted me.

Vinnie took his position behind Colin's chair and stared down at the tall man, who reacted by getting up. He pushed his jacket open to reveal his weapon, his hand ready to grab it. His nostrils flared and his mouth pulled into a vicious sneer. I leaned back in my chair, my eyes wide.

"Shahab, stand down." The authority behind the leader's

quietly spoken order was unmistakable. He waited until Shahab relaxed his posture, his hand moving away from his holster. When it became clear that the tall man was not going to sit down again, the leader looked at us. "We're amongst friends."

"You're not my friend." The words came out before I thought about it. "I don't even know your name."

Colin smiled and pointed at me. "What she said."

"Well, then." The leader shifted and put his palm against his chest. "I'm Amin Alidoosti, the overprotective one is Shahab Hatami and—"

"I'm Hamid Keramati," the third man said.

"And you all are…" Colin drew out the last word as if waiting for them to finish.

"From the Criminal Investigation Police of NAJA."

"What the fuck is NAJA?" Vinnie didn't take his eyes off Shahab, but his question was addressed to Amin.

"It's the Law Enforcement Force of the Islamic Republic of Iran." Daniel smiled when all eyes turned to him. "NAJA is short for all of that."

The changes in the posture of the three men were small, but immediate. People always reacted positively to being acknowledged. Even Shahab's shoulders lowered slightly and he shifted his weight to one leg, putting him in a more vulnerable position.

"How do you know who we are?" Hamid's curiosity was sincere, almost childlike.

Daniel pointed at his GIPN badge on his uniform. "We make an effort to know who our counterparts are all over the world. I know you guys have top investigators and your Special Unit is huge and is also highly trained like us. Then there is your NOPO unit, which deals a lot with anti-terror action."

This was why Daniel was the leader of the GIPN team. He was indeed highly trained to handle conflict, but my personal opinion was that his true skill was at de-escalating a situation. The more he talked about the different branches in Iran's law enforcement, the more the three men relaxed. Hamid's body language had changed from ready for action to awestruck. In less than five minutes, Daniel had built notable rapport with them.

Amin leaned forward, resting his elbows on his knees. "I heard one of your GIPN teams deals in a lot of art crimes."

"We do."

Amin's reaction to Daniel's answer was telling.

I nodded. "That's why you're here."

He glanced at me. "We received a tip that quite a few of our looted artefacts have surfaced here in Strasbourg."

"Hmm." Daniel tilted his head. "And of course you've notified your embassy and our headquarters of your presence here." He looked at the bulge under Shahab's arm. "And the weapons you carry are all legally obtained."

"Of course." Amin touched his neck. I was tempted to roll my eyes the way Nikki did when she considered something to be ridiculous. Evidently, Amin's team had not been trained in deception skills.

As I wondered if it would be appropriate to advise them to hone those skills, Colin got up. "Well then. This explains everything." His smile was convincing in his apology and slight embarrassment as he looked at the empty café. "Sorry for the welcome."

I was surprised at first. Why would Colin end this conversation? We could learn so much more. A quick glance at his face, then at Daniel's made it clear that they both had reservations about continuing.

"It definitely was overkill." Hamid got up and held out his hand to Daniel. "It was truly a pleasure to meet you."

Amin was the last to stand, his authority not undermined by his lowered position at all. I remained seated. If anything happened, I planned to grab the table next to us as a shield and hide behind it.

Amin also shook Daniel's hand. "If you can give me your business card, we can stay in touch. Maybe you can tell us if you hear anything about Iranian artefacts."

"We can definitely do that." Daniel shook Amin's hand, then gave him a business card. "Feel free to call me anytime."

Amin's micro-expressions showed that the leader of this small team had no such plans. Yet he nodded, his enthusiasm fake.

"They won't tell us anything, Amin." Shahab closed his jacket, his posture no longer aggressive, but definitely defiant. "These Europeans view everyone who is Arabic as immigrant rubbish terrorists."

"No, we don't." Vinnie stepped closer to Shahab and slapped him hard on the shoulder. "Only assholes who think they can come and—"

"Vin." Colin pulled Vinnie away and shook his head when Vinnie frowned at him. "We're all friends, remember?"

"Yeah." Vinnie nodded, his insincerity shockingly visible. "Right." Before Colin could stop him, Vinnie walked to Amin, holding out his hand. "Friends."

Amin clearly didn't know what to expect from this interaction, but shook Vinnie's hand. He wasn't able to hide his concerned frown when Vinnie put his hand on the leader's shoulder and squeezed hard. This was such odd behaviour for Vinnie, I was also frowning.

Then Amin pulled his shoulders back and stared at Vinnie's hand still resting there. "I suggest you give us space to leave before this new friendship becomes unfriendly."

Vinnie raised both his hands and stepped back. "Of course, friend. Please." He waved his hand dramatically towards the door. "Feel free to leave."

Shahab stared at Vinnie through narrowed eyes until Amin was a few steps away from us. He and Hamid stepped around the table and joined Amin, one on each side. Manny, Pink and the others held their positions and didn't raise their weapons, but their muscle tension increased, their eyes following the three men.

Halfway to the door, Amin turned around and looked at Colin. "You might want to tell your president that this will definitely become an unfriendly incident if we find out you have our artefacts and are not returning them to us."

Vinnie pretended to take a step forward and smiled

when Daniel put his hand out to stop him. He winked at Amin, his smile widening when the other man turned around and walked to the door. We watched in silence until the door closed behind them.

"Should we put a shadow on them?" Pink asked as he walked towards us.

"My first answer is 'yes'." Daniel thought about this for a second. "No. I don't think that's a good idea. If they make us, it might get very ugly. I'm glad Colin stopped the interview. Politically, this is too sensitive. We need to get the brass involved."

"What the bleeding hell is wrong with you?" Manny stormed towards us, shaking his finger at Vinnie. "Have you completely lost your frigging marbles?"

"There's a—"

"I don't want to hear it!" Manny walked away, then turned around and came back. His face was turning red, his anger unlike I'd seen in a long time. "If this becomes a diplomatic incident between Iran and France, it will all fall on you."

Not giving anyone the opportunity to respond, Manny turned around and left the café. I glanced at the others to see that I was not the only one shocked by Manny's uncharacteristic behaviour.

Vinnie shrugged, then smiled. "That asswipe is going to eat crow." His smile widened. "And then I'm going to kill him."

I knew he didn't mean this literally, but it was still disturbing to hear these words leave his mouth. Vinnie winked at me, then announced that he'd see us in the team room. He fist-bumped all the GIPN team members on the way out.

Colin pulled his chair closer to mine and sat down, but looked at Daniel. "Where's Caelan? Is he okay?"

"He's not okay, no. I got one of my guys to take him to Phillip."

Colin took both my hands in his and studied my face. "Are you okay?"

"No." I got up, but didn't pull my hands from his. "I want to go to my viewing room."

I needed the safety of that space and the familiarity of my work. I also needed to lose myself in work for a while. This had been a very disconcerting experience. I wanted to find out what that connection was that kept evading me.

Chapter SIXTEEN

BACK AT OUR team room, Daniel took the elevator ahead of us. I seldom entered the small space with more than one person if there was no rush. I appreciated that Vinnie and Daniel had chosen the size of the elevator for security reasons, but being in too close physical proximity to other people caused most distressing anxiety.

Colin was lost in his own thoughts and we didn't speak. The elevator returned and I was prioritising the list of things I wanted to research as we entered. I wanted to get back to the photos of the wine labels. And Adèle's chart.

The elevator doors opened to the team room and I gasped at the scene that greeted us.

Vinnie and Manny were standing toe to toe, their bodies nearly touching. Manny was shouting at Vinnie about Hassan, Iran, Amin and terrorists. None of it made sense. Daniel was standing to the side, his muscle tension indicating he was ready to intervene at any moment. Francine was next to her desk, both her hands over her mouth, her *orbicularis oculi* muscles contracted in sadness.

"Good God." Colin let go of my hand and walked to Vinnie and Manny. "Less than ten minutes and we walk into this? What the hell, Millard?"

"Stay out of this, Frey!" Manny pushed his index finger into Vinnie's chest. "This is between me and this criminal."

It felt like the darkness that always came before a shutdown was pushing against the back of my eyes. I blinked a few times, but the pressure was still there. Manny's nonverbal cues were such as I'd never seen before. He was aggressive and seemed to wish for a physical altercation with Vinnie.

My large friend was angry. The long scar running down the side of his face was white against the colour flushing his cheeks. He looked down at Manny and I wondered if the latter even saw the sadness that juxtaposed Vinnie's anger.

I knew the feeling was not real, but it felt like someone was sucking the air out of my lungs. My chest felt hollow with despondency and it felt like my heart was bruised. "Pain never heals pain."

"Huh?" Vinnie glanced at me when my words came out hoarse.

I cleared my throat and looked at Manny and Vinnie. I couldn't speak again. The sadness of what they were doing overwhelmed me. Neurotypicals caused each other so much unnecessary hurt. Intentionally.

I shook my head and was jarred to feel the warmth of a tear running down my cheek. With a final look at them, I walked into my room and closed the door. It was the first time in very long that I'd done this to exclude them—not because I needed to focus, but because I didn't want them near me. I sat on my chair and glanced back into the room.

Vinnie was at the kitchen, his back towards me. Tension caused his movements to be stilted, his shoulders slightly raised. Manny hadn't moved. He was looking at me, his aggression replaced with regret. And shame. And he was letting me see it.

My head hurt. As did my heart. I didn't want to see those micro-expressions on his face. I didn't want the very people who had been my security, my stability for years causing me to feel so lost.

So I turned away from them, opened the folder with the photos of Adèle's chart and blocked everything outside my viewing room from my mind.

"Genevieve?" Phillip's deep voice pulled me out of the hyper-focused state I was in. I glanced at the clock on my computer and was disappointed that only an hour had passed. Irrationally, I'd hoped to hide longer so Vinnie and Manny had more time to sort things out.

I rolled my shoulders, then moved my head from side to side to relieve the stiffness that resulted from sitting in one position for too long. Finally, I turned to look at Phillip. He was sitting next to me, his body language relaxed, but his facial expression revealing his concern. "Are you well?"

I looked past him into the team room. My door was open.

Vinnie was nowhere to be seen; Manny was sitting at his desk, glaring at his computer, and Francine was at her desk looking at me. The moment my attention turned to her, she smiled at me. It was a small and sad smile, her usual boisterousness not evident.

I turned back to Phillip. "Physically, I'm fine. But the antagonism between them is distracting."

"And it's hurting you." Phillip sighed. "Caelan was in a bad state when the officers brought him here. We both decided he would be best off at home. Now I think it was a very good decision. The atmosphere here will trigger yet another shutdown. At least it seems like things have calmed down for now. I don't know where Daniel is, but Colin's taken Vinnie to go buy pastries or something. They should be back soon."

"Pastries won't solve the problem."

Phillip smiled. "No, but it might smooth things over a bit."

I doubted that. Manny's reaction to his own pain had changed the dynamics in our team. I didn't know what it would take to restore things to how it had been.

I blinked and leaned back in my chair. Maybe things would never return to how they had been. That was one of the many things in life I found extremely difficult to come to terms with. Events changed us. Whether for good or bad, it caused a change that aided in our development if we allowed it to.

I wondered how the event that was causing Manny such distress would change him. If it would be permanent. And whether the effect of his behaviour would be the cause for any permanent change in our team. That thought brought the tension back to my muscles. I didn't like change.

"Genevieve." Phillip's tone indicated that he'd called me a few times. I looked at him and leaned a bit back in surprise.

He had lost colour in his face. "Who is that?"

He was pointing at one of the photos that had surrounded Adèle's chart. It was one of the three photos of the man with the birthmark on his hand. In this photo, it was clearly visible as he held his phone to his ear. "I don't know who he is. All three photos we have of him obscure his face, so Francine wasn't able to run it through the facial recognition software."

"Don't bother." He pulled at his collar. "His name is François Dumaux."

It was the fact that he knew this man that disconcerted me as much as the emotions revealed when he spoke the name. "Who is he?"

"A ghost from the past." He closed his eyes, shook his head, then looked at me. "He's not literally a ghost. This is someone I knew a very long time ago."

"Tell us everything you know." Manny walked into my room and leaned against one of the filing cabinets in the back. "We could really do with a break in this case."

Phillip swivelled his chair to better face me and Manny at the same time. "He worked for me many years ago. Let me think... yes, he started with me when he left university in 1997."

"More than twenty years ago." Francine walked in and sat in the chair Colin usually used. She was swiping and tapping on her tablet screen. "Which university did he graduate from?"

"University of the Arts Utrecht."

"Holland?" Manny asked.

"The Netherlands." It annoyed me that so many people got this wrong. "The official name of the country is the Kingdom of the Netherlands. Holland is not the name of the country. There are two provinces named Noord-Holland and Zuid-Holland, but they're only part of the country. When people say Holland they mean the Netherlands."

"Holland?" Manny asked Phillip again, ignoring me.

His reaction brought me immediate comfort. This was the kind of rudeness I'd become accustomed to. Not the aggression and hostility from the last two days.

Phillip nodded. "Yes, he graduated—with honours, I might add—from the academy of arts. He specialised in art history and had the perfect character traits for working in this business. I hired him immediately after our first interview. He was such a bright and rising star."

"What happened?"

"Ooh." Francine's eyes were wide as she stared at her tablet. "François was a naughty, naughty boy."

"He'd been with me for three years when things went bad." The sadness of that memory deepened the lines around Phillip's mouth. "François came from a scandal-ridden family. They had a lot of old money, but his mother's gambling habits used it all up. They were left with nothing. There were also a lot of rumours about fraud, extortion, child abuse and a range of sexual scandals.

"François never talked about his family at all. In the three years I knew him, he never mentioned them once. He just pretended to be superior to everyone else, always with subtle references to places, events, brands and people only the upper class would carry knowledge of. There was always some form of duality to him."

"What does that mean?" Manny asked.

Phillip thought for a moment. "With others he was calculated, pretentious, even cruel at times. But for some reason, he was real with me. Honest. That had been the reason I'd hired him. His other side only surfaced after a few months with us.

"But he was good at his job. I had chosen well when I'd hired him. In those three years, he absorbed everything I taught him like a sponge. It was inspiring to watch him became better, sharper, more efficient every single day. He was hungry for more information, hungry to be the best insurance investigator in the art industry and hungry for more money."

"Let me guess." Manny raised one eyebrow. "He stole art or forged it or helped some criminal traffic it."

"The latter. And he used his exceptional computer skills to make it happen. Internet transactions were still in their infancy, with many ways to circumvent legal avenues. It was quite easy for him."

"Well, give me a hammer and call me Thor." Francine's mouth was slightly agape. "I think you guys need to see this." She swiped her tablet screen twice, then looked at the monitor next to the one displaying the photo of François talking on his phone. "This is the ID photo of François Dumaux."

"Holy bloody hell!" Manny walked closer and pointed at

the monitor. "That's Pierre."

He was right. The Dutch identity card Francine had put full screen on the monitor showed the man we'd interviewed in the Robertsau forest.

"Who's Pierre?" Phillip asked.

"That man"—I nodded towards the monitor—"was at the Robertsau forest where Camille Vastine and Martin Gayot were dumped. We spoke to him. He was wearing gloves, so I never got to see his hand or the birthmark. He was quite helpful when we interviewed him. He'd been the first one to find the bodies. The three tourists walked past him as he was looking at the bodies."

"He must have been the one to dump them there." Francine shivered. "Did he also kill them? Torture them?"

Nobody answered her. We were quiet for a few seconds.

"You cleared him, right?" Manny asked.

"I did." Francine frowned. "I checked all the witnesses. All the info the three woman gave checked out. Because Genevieve thought Pierre was off, I made double sure he checked out. He did. He's registered at the hotel he said he was staying at as well as the conference he was supposed to attend. Even his rental car is registered in the IT company's name."

"Did you check the IT company?" I asked.

Her lips thinned. "No."

"Dammit." Manny took his phone from his trouser pocket. "He played us. I was about to call off the team tailing him. Now I'm getting them to bring him in."

"You had him followed?" Phillip narrowed his eyes. "What made you suspect him?"

I thought back to our conversation with François AKA Pierre. "His nonverbal cues were inconsistent. At times his answers and gestures were calculated."

Phillip's smile was sad. "Those times, his answer came a millisecond slower than the other times, right?" He sighed when I nodded. "He did that often with his co-workers and with clients. If it hadn't been for the first interview and the private moments when he was real with me, I wouldn't have picked up on it."

"Well, Doc picked up on it." Manny's eyes widened slightly, indicating that Daniel had just answered his call. He grunted and left the viewing room, briefing Daniel on our discovery.

"Do you think François is capable of killing these young people?" Francine asked Phillip.

"I haven't seen François in fifteen years. After I discovered what he was doing and testified against him, he disappeared from my life."

Francine looked at her tablet. "He was sentenced to five years in prison. Not a long time for these allegations."

"He co-operated with the authorities so they could finally arrest the mafia boss who'd hired François to obtain the stolen artworks." His smile wasn't kind. "I don't know what he is like now, but the François I knew was highly intelligent, cunning and always looking for an easier way to do things and make money—which could have been a great asset if he'd used it in a legal manner."

"You didn't answer her question." I was curious if Phillip considered François to be capable of torture and murder.

He looked at me and shook his head. "The François I knew was also a coward. He had an insatiable appetite for money and power, but no appetite for violence. The moment the police threatened to put him in a prison with violent convicts, he became an instant encyclopaedia of criminal activity. I was really shocked at how much he knew then."

I thought about this. It was not often that people changed. Not their core characteristics. And the way Phillip was describing François led me to believe that it was very probable that he'd continued his life of crime even after his incarceration. I could think of no other logical reason for him to have given us a false name and nationality when we'd spoken to him.

"Daniel's team is bringing François in." Manny walked back into my office. "They're quite close and Daniel reckons they should be here in less than twenty minutes."

Phillip got up and pulled at the cuffs of his suit jacket. "You can interview him in one of our conference rooms."

Manny looked at me. For a moment, I had a glimpse at the vulnerability he experienced before his usual scowl pulled his brow down. "What do you think, Doc? Should you and Phillip be the ones to interview François? He might give away all his secrets without having to be threatened."

I considered this. "If he still has the same characteristics as when Phillip knew him, it would be best to have a law enforcement officer in there looking intimidating."

"Daniel can join us." Phillip tried, but wasn't successful in hiding his understanding of what Manny was doing.

It made me sad that Manny didn't feel confident in his abilities at present. Yet my respect grew for him. Most people allowed their pride to interfere, most often resulting in them doing more damage than good. Manny knew his strengths and weaknesses. At this moment, we were his strength.

I also got up. "Daniel would be a good choice. He's good at reading people and would know when to be subtle and when to push harder for answers."

"I'll brief Daniel on everything we know so far." Manny looked at Francine. "Anything else you find, send it to everyone's devices. There might be something that can help Daniel when they interview him."

"Will do." Francine's smile was soft. She also knew that Manny was willingly standing back because of his emotional state. I was proud of my best friend. Despite her many frivolous interests and ridiculous theories, she understood the importance of allowing Manny to work through his problem in his own way and time. But I could see the toll it was taking on her. Not only was she exhausted, she was also deeply worried about the man she loved.

Manny left my viewing room, already talking to Daniel on the phone. Phillip and I took the elevator down to the foyer and the other elevator to his office.

"Do you need Colin here?" He pressed the button for his floor and turned to me. "We can wait until he and Vinnie return."

"No. Colin's expertise is not needed for this interview."

Phillip's small smile indicated that he'd meant something else, but was nonetheless pleased with my answer. The elevator doors opened and we walked into the reception area. Tim looked up from his desk, saw Phillip's face and got up. "What's wrong?"

"Nothing we can't handle." It was clear that Phillip liked the young man. And that he appreciated the concern. "We are expecting a guest. Please show him to conference room two."

Tim's eyes widened. "A guest. Ah. Okay. Anything else?"

"Yes, treat him like an honoured guest."

"An honoured guest." Tim looked at me, curiosity on his face. "Anything else?"

"Yes." Phillip waited until Tim looked at him. "Everyone will be watching the interview room from Genevieve's place. Ask Francine to link you in as well."

His eyes widened in pleasure. "Thank you."

Phillip nodded and led me to his office. I knew it was probably nothing, but I simply had to clarify. "That building isn't mine. It's not my place. Colin bought it from a fund he, Vinnie and Francine set up many years ago."

"I know." Phillip leaned his hip against his desk. "In my mind, the team is yours, ergo the building and the floor where your team room and viewing room are also belongs to you. Not literally, of course."

"They're here, sir." Tim leaned around the doorframe, his eyes wide with excitement.

"Who are 'they'?" Was he referring to the GIPN team bringing in François or someone else?

"The team brought in two men. One is a François Dumaux and the other his lawyer."

"His lawyer." Phillip smiled. "This is going to be interesting."

Tim's excitement intensified. "I'm going to make coffee now."

"Good." Phillip looked at me. "Would you also like coffee?"

"No." My mind was too fragile with all the emotional strain to deal with the distraction of a cup of coffee while having to observe François' reactions. Few neurotypicals understood the irrational sense of responsibility to finish a cup of coffee to the last drop—a sense that chose the most inopportune times to surface.

In the three minutes we waited for Tim to deliver the coffee as well as for François and his lawyer to get comfortable, Phillip prepared himself mentally. I could see his facial muscles relaxing as he focused on his breathing. It was subtle, but it was there.

Then he inhaled deeply and looked at me. "Ready?"

"Yes." I'd been ready when we'd entered the reception area. He'd been the one who'd needed to prepare himself to face a person from his past. "You cared for him."

"I did." Phillip pulled his shoulders back. "It was at a time when I still longed to have my own family. For a very short time I dreamed that François could be like a son to me."

I saw his hesitation. "How soon after he started with you did you suspect something was wrong?"

"Nine months." He closed his eyes briefly. "I suppose it was sooner, but I only admitted it to myself after nine months."

"Why keep him working for you so long then?"

"He'd done nothing I could accuse him of. I couldn't find any evidence that he was involved in illegal activities."

"That doesn't really answer my question."

His smile was self-deprecating. "I was hoping he would become the man I knew he could be."

"That's the same thing so many woman say about their abusive husbands."

His eyebrows shot up. "I never thought about it like that. Ours was by no means an abusive relationship. Not at all. Manipulative, yes. François was the person who taught me the most about manipulation and deception."

This was important information for me. It helped me build a better profile of the man we were about to interview. It also revealed just how much Phillip had been affected by the younger man's betrayal of trust.

"Here you are." Daniel walked into the office. "How do you want to do the interview with François? Should I sit, stand, talk?"

"Stand." I thought about this some more. "By the door, but relaxed. When you have a better read on the situation, I trust you will know what to do then."

"Are you going to be doing the questioning?" he asked.

"No." Phillip straightened his already-straight tie. "I will. I know what buttons to push. If that's acceptable to you, Genevieve?"

"I'd prefer that."

"Then let's do this." Phillip led us to the conference room, his bearing confident and relaxed.

We entered the room just as François moved to another painting. He glanced over his shoulder and stiffened when he saw Phillip. "You."

"Good day, François."

There was an immediate shift in François' body language at the sound of Phillip's voice. His pupils dilated, his confident posture that bordered on arrogant as well as his features softened.

He was wearing high-quality wool trousers, a tailored shirt and designer shoes. He tugged at his sleeves in a manner similar to Phillip when he got ready to say something important.

François waved at the paintings lining three of the four walls in the conference room. The birthmark on his hand was clearly visible. "You've done well for yourself." He glanced at Daniel, then at me, some of his cunning returning. "You have all these... people working for you."

"We are here against my advice." The man sitting at the table put his cup in the saucer and looked at Phillip. "I've advised my client not to say anything."

"Yes." François' *zygomaticus major* muscle pulled the left corner of his mouth into a smirk. "I'm not saying a word."

Phillip watched as he walked back to the table and sat down next to his lawyer. Then he pulled out two chairs and waited until I was seated before he sat down. His smile was genuine as he looked at François. "You don't have to say anything. I'll just talk and you can listen." Phillip crossed his legs, which served to emphasise his relaxed confidence. "I'm surprised that you are condescending about these experts"—he tilted his head towards me—"when you've been working with low-class criminals yourself."

François flinched, all signs of deception gone. He looked at Phillip with raw emotion etched on his face. Longing, shame, regret and sadness warred for dominance. But it was fear that ruled his facial muscles.

I thought back to all the materials I'd studied, all the people I'd seen interviewed. Seldom had I seen someone as expressive as François was right now. What added to my surprise was how well he had disguised his nonverbal cues when we'd spoken to him in the Robertsau forest. His history with Phillip must've left him vulnerable on a level much deeper than even Phillip suspected. His reaction had been pure, confirming Phillip's statement.

"Oh, wait." Phillip's tone was as if he was having a relaxed conversation. "Are you working with or working for... common criminals? Aha. *For.*"

François' increased blinking had been telling when Phillip had paused. This was most fascinating to observe.

"You know, François, for all your sins, I can't quite imagine that you tortured and killed those young people.

Hmm. I see. You didn't." Phillip narrowed his eyes. "Do I see guilt though? I do. So you were the one who dumped their lifeless bodies in the forest. Ah. There's that guilt. Hmm. So you really stooped low. Lower than I thought possible. You're now cleaning up after brutal murderers."

François' brow lowered—not in anger, but in anguish. Colour crept up his neck and he shifted in his chair.

"Don't say anything." The lawyer put his hand on the table. "We should leave."

François shook his head like Francine did when she flicked her hair over her shoulder. "No, Adam. We should stay. I like hearing these fairy tales."

I frowned. Not because of François' obvious lie, but because of what I thought I'd seen. He looked at Phillip and there it was again. He was hoping to be caught out and arrested. The stark fear that flashed over his face had to be his motivation.

Phillip's calm demeanour didn't waver. "So? Are you running a major drug distribution point from Rotterdam? Aha. Yes. And whatever happened to your passion for art? That was the one thing that was always honest about you."

"It's still the only thing I care about." François shook off the lawyer's restraining hand on his shoulder. Phillip had touched a very deep and important point in François' life. He had been completely truthful when he'd spoken.

"Persian art?" Phillip smiled when François didn't answer, but his reaction provided full confirmation. "All those beautiful artefacts. Did these drug-dealing and murdering criminals... or is it one criminal? Aha. One.

Did he buy your help with artefacts?" Phillip sighed, his disappointment real. "Oh, François. You had so much potential."

Movement by the door caught my attention. Daniel put his phone back in his pocket and stepped closer to us. "Gilles Mahout is dead."

"What?" François jumped up from his chair, his eyes wide, his mouth slightly agape. "How?"

Daniel shrugged as if this was not important information. Or as if François' reaction telling us that he'd known Gilles wasn't significant. Daniel's bored expression was convincing. "We've been looking for him for days. We got a lead and it must've happened mere minutes before we got to him. He was still bleeding out." He shrugged again. "It happened about an hour ago."

"That's it." The lawyer also got up, this time not allowing François to shake off his hand. "We're leaving."

"But…"

"Not another word." The lawyer lowered his voice and widened his eyes until François nodded. He turned to Daniel. "Is my client under arrest?"

"No."

"Good, because you have nothing to justify an arrest." The lawyer gave François a warning look and waited until the latter nodded. "We're leaving."

"Don't go too far." Daniel stepped into the lawyer's path. "Make sure your client is available for further questioning."

The lawyer didn't answer Daniel, just stepped around

him and led François out of the room. When they reached the hallway, François looked back, the stark fear from before again contracting his facial muscles, his eyes pleading as he stared at Phillip.

The lawyer pulled him away, whispering furiously.

"Well, that was unusual." Daniel sat down.

"Is Gilles really dead?" Phillip asked.

"Yes." Daniel looked at me. "I knew breaking the news to François was a risk, but I also thought we might get a lot from his reaction."

"We did." I knew Francine had recorded this interview and I wanted to watch it again. This man was a fascinating study.

"We know that he knew Gilles and he knew Gilles' life was in danger." Phillip leaned back in his chair. "The question is whether he worked for or with Gilles."

Chapter SEVENTEEN

"AND?" MANNY WAS waiting for us when the elevator doors opened to the team room. He nodded once at Phillip, then looked back at me. "Is everything Phillip asked true?"

"Yes." I was tempted to expand on my answer since I found François such an interesting person to study, but Vinnie was standing by the round table, his arms crossed and his usual smile not present.

"Come. Eat." Vinnie waved at the table. "There's plenty."

My eyes widened when I looked at the plates covering the table. "Plenty is an understatement—something you almost never... no, I can't remember you understating anything."

His smile lifted his cheeks and he lowered his arms. "I might've gone a bit overboard."

"I'm not going to complain." Phillip walked to the table and immediately put three pastries on a small plate.

Daniel was already seated at the table. I sat down next to Colin and he kissed me on my cheek. "All well?"

I nodded and reached for a pastry—one that didn't make such a mess. It was only half past twelve, but my stomach reacted to the sight of the food as if I hadn't eaten all day. I also was very grateful for the coffee Vinnie had prepared. Even though I hadn't wanted any while talking to François, I needed the warmth as well as the caffeine.

Vinnie sat down, but kept a wary eye on Manny. The latter was speaking to Francine at her desk. The concern on her face had not lessened. Neither had the dark rings under her eyes. I was becoming worried about her too.

Colin's phone rang and he lifted it off the table. And smiled. He swiped the screen. "Johan, I didn't expect to hear from you again. Pardon? Wait, say that again." Colin lowered his phone and put it on speaker. He motioned with his hand for us to be quiet.

"People are dying, Isaac." Johan's clear English came through Colin's phone. "You didn't tell me Élodie was killed. And now I'm getting intel that people associated with Élodie are also being killed. Is that true?"

Colin raised his eyebrows. "Yes."

Manny and Francine joined us at the table, sitting down quietly. No one was eating or drinking, everyone too interested in what the man who'd reproduced the Roubaud had to say.

"Are you doing something to stop this? You know I only do art. I paint. I reproduce. I don't forge and I've worked hard to make sure everyone knows that I'm not in the business of crime. I don't want any connection to these murders."

Colin narrowed his eyes and tilted his head while listening to Johan. "What do you know?"

I wished I could see the man's face so I could better read the nuances of his communication. Colin had heard something in his voice or words I hadn't noticed.

For a few seconds there was no response. Then Johan cleared his throat. "Élodie provided me with paint. She was very specific about the paint she wanted me to use for the Roubaud. I'd told her that it was not ideal and it would affect the authenticity of the reproduction, but she wouldn't budge." He paused. "She also said she had a 3D-printed Pollock and loved it. But the person who did that one is no longer in the painting business. He's now only doing statues. Then she asked me if I could do these paintings with a 3D printer if she provided me with the equipment and paint. She was talking about producing large quantities. Not as forgeries, of course. All of them would be clear reproductions."

"Did you agree?" Colin asked.

"I told her I'd think about it. She never came back to me."

"Because she was killed."

"Yeah." His laugh didn't sound filled with humour. "My mind went crazy with conspiracy theories. I even thought she would ask me to put hidden messages in the paintings."

It happened so suddenly that I imagined the click in my head. That missing connection that had been lingering in the back of my mind rushed to the fore and took over. I barely heard Colin asking Johan a few more questions, but not getting any more useful answers. I wanted this inane conversation to end so I could rush to my viewing room to confirm my theory.

The moment Colin ended his call, I pushed my chair back and ran to my room. I ignored Manny's expletive, followed by a demand to know what I was doing.

I sat down and opened my best graphics software programme. I uploaded the photos of the labels on the wine bottles and chose the one we'd found in Adèle's basement. I zoomed in on the lines that formed the watermark.

Then I zoomed in more. And more. This programme allowed me to zoom in extensively provided that the photo was of great quality. The photos were.

I zoomed in until the lines changed shape.

"Oh, my God!" Francine sat down in Colin's chair and clapped her hands. "Micro-printing. How did you know?"

"I didn't." I'd suspected. "There was something not quite right about these lines."

"And when Johan talked about hidden messages, you made the connection." Colin kissed me on the top of my head before walking to the back of the room.

"What does it say, Doc?" Manny sat down next to me. "Iran, François and everything will have to wait for now. Let's see if this can bloody tell us why all these people are dead and why Iran sent people here to spy on Caelan."

"We don't know that." I hated it when anyone made statements that were gross assumptions.

"Just tell me what the hell is written there, missy."

I turned back to photo and tilted it until the writing was horizontal. "It's a name." I looked closer. "No, more than a name."

"A name and a place. Gerard Roux and Colmar." Francine pointed at the monitor. "See how his name and place are repeated to form the line?"

"Who the hell is this?"

"I need time." Did he not see the impossibility of me knowing who this man was? I wanted to know as well.

"Well, hurry up."

"I'll help, girlfriend." Francine took her tablet and started tapping and swiping. I was no longer amazed at the things she managed to achieve on that device. She'd upgraded it to the point where it no longer resembled the factory model.

It took us fourteen minutes to go through all the photos and confirm there were nineteen sets of names and places. Each of the nineteen different labels had only one set— name and place—that was repeated throughout each line. I sat back and looked at the list Francine had made, putting an ID photo of some sort next to each name.

"How many code names and places were on Adèle's chart?" Colin's quiet question brought an avalanche of revelations.

I opened the folder with the photos of Adèle's business organisational chart and looked at it with this newfound information. I gasped. "This wasn't *her* business model."

"Then whose bloody business is this, Doc?" Manny was still sitting next to me, Daniel was with Colin at the back of my room and Vinnie in his usual place by the door. I didn't see Phillip.

"I don't know." And I really didn't want to mention my suspicion.

"I'm thinking it is her drug supplier." Francine was twirling a strand of hair around her index finger while looking at the monitors. "Yes, I think that these names are the distributors linked to the big supplier in the green square."

"We have no evidence of this." That was why I didn't want to say anything. I did, however, feel even stronger about my theory now that Francine had said the same.

"Then what do you call that?" Francine zoomed in on one of the squares where Adèle had written, 'round face, rainbow village'. She highlighted a name and place on her list, an ID photo next to the name. "You cannot tell me that man doesn't have a face rounder than the moon. And rainbow village? You will not find a more colourful place in France than Colmar. Which is only sixty-four kilometres from Strasbourg, I might add. And see here?" She pointed at the column where she'd made notes about each person. "Ol' Gerard Roux has a criminal record. For what you may ask? Drug dealing, of course!" She threw her hands up in the air.

I ignored her theatrics. "We need to confirm more than just one description before making any statements as if they were facts."

"Ooh, let me do that." Her fingers were already moving over her tablet screen. "This is going to be such fun."

"So somebody sent these crates of liquid heroin in wine bottles with labels that have the information of people she"—Manny glared at Francine—"thinks are drug dealers."

"I'm right, handsome." Francine didn't stop working. "Just you wait and see. I'll confirm that each one of these people has some connection to the drug trade."

"Why the bleeding hell would someone send those names?" Manny pushed the heels of his hands against his eyes. "Why would Adèle steal those bottles? Bloody hell, people!" He lowered his hands, both curled into tight fists. He got up and looked at Daniel and Colin in the back of my room, then at Vinnie standing in the doorway. "Why the bloody hell are you just standing here? This is not good enough. We have nothing pointing to the killer. Nothing that gives us motive as to why those kids were so brutally killed. I thought you were all so good at what you do. Right now, you're not looking like the crack team everyone thinks you are."

"That's fucking it." Vinnie stalked into my room, his arms away from his torso. Before I could warn anyone of his intent, Vinnie pulled his fist back and punched Manny hard in the stomach. The air rushed out of Manny's lungs and he folded double, his arms around his torso. Blackness immediately entered my peripheral vision and I sat frozen in my chair. Vinnie leaned closer to Manny, his aggression bringing on even more blackness. "I don't care what the fuck is wrong with you, but you don't get to take it out on them." He bent even lower so he was eye level with Manny. "You wanna hurt someone? You wanna make someone pay for whatever is eating at you?" Vinnie tapped his cheek with the scar. "Punch me. Right here. I can take it. But you don't fucking hurt them."

"Bloody hell." Manny's voice was strained, his movements jerky as he put his hand out and lowered himself into his chair. His breathing stuttered as he rubbed his hands hard over his face before looking at Vinnie. "I..." His voice broke.

"You're screwing up, Millard." Colin's gentle tone softened the harsh words. He waited until Manny looked at him. "We're your family. Let us be there for you."

"And stop being such a stubborn idiot." The exhaustion and stress of the last few days now appeared much stronger on Francine's face. She swallowed and looked at me. "I've been telling him to share. But his stiff upper lip is making him an idiot."

I frowned and studied Manny. "His upper lip is quite normal."

There was a moment of silence before everyone laughed. Humour had not been my intention at all, but the break in hostility had the added benefit of the darkness receding.

I was still looking at Manny. If I wanted to do as he said and find the killer as well as motive, we needed to focus. And I knew my friends well enough to be convinced it would only happen if this situation was resolved.

I also desperately wanted the agony visible in Manny's nonverbal cues to disappear. So I took a deep breath and moved my chair closer. A frown pulled his eyebrows together as he watched me take another breath and move even closer. I was breaking my own rule of maintaining a personal space of fifty centimetres. I was sitting so close to Manny I could feel his body heat. "What happened?"

Manny stared at me. Then he looked down at the proximity of our chairs. The tension in his face softened. The sigh he uttered was heavy and defeated. "The idiots at Interpol decided I don't have enough work."

"You're being sarcastic."

Manny grunted. "They assigned an elite task force to me. They didn't want me to run it, just to oversee it. The only problem with this bloody task force was they were all green and arrogant. Yes, they were the top of their class, but all of them were green."

"Green means inexperienced," Colin said quietly and I nodded.

"I told the bosses I don't have time to babysit, but they wouldn't listen." Manny rubbed his hands over his face again.

It was quiet in my room. Vinnie hadn't moved far from Manny, but all his aggression was gone. Instead, compassion flooded his face. Francine was sitting behind me and I could hear her shallow breathing. She needed comforting as well.

"You said 'they were'." The tense had been telling.

Manny closed his eyes and nodded. When he opened his eyes, he looked at his hands. "The bosses wanted to send the team on an assignment. I told them these guys were not ready. I also recommended they were split up and put in more experienced teams so they could learn. But no. The bleeding idiot of a young leader convinced the bosses I'm too conservative."

"You are."

The corner of Manny's mouth lifted slightly, but he ignored Vinnie's teasing. "They sent the team in to extract someone they thought was the leader of a growing extremist group. I helped them plan the op, but they resisted running through it again and again. Twice was enough for these arrogant idiots."

I waited, but Manny didn't continue. His lips tightened even more and he didn't lift his eyes from his hands.

Colin took a step away from the cabinets. "Only two of the six team members came back alive. The extremist group was holed up on a farm in the south of France. Their security was better than the team had expected. They saw Millard's guys coming from a mile away. When I went hunting for those artefacts, I got in touch with my contacts at Interpol. They told me everything." He leaned towards Manny. "I'm sorry, Millard."

Manny nodded and straightened. "Now the bloody bosses want to blame the two survivors. They can't blame me, because my *conservative* recommendation is official through an email to all of them. Those kids were not ready. The two who made it out barely did so. Already they have to carry the weight of their decision to follow their leader and go against me. Blaming them is not going to solve anything."

Francine got up, pushed Vinnie out of the way and sat down on Manny's lap. She ignored his protests and cupped his cheeks in both her hands, forcing him to look at her. "I've told you before and I will tell you again and again. This is not on you."

"You think you could've done something different?" Colin's laugh held no humour. "I have first-hand experience of the authorities at Interpol overriding any logical reasoning and making you do what they think will make them look good. Fortunately for me—and for them—it worked out. No matter what you did or said, they would've sent those men out, Millard."

"Manny won't tell you, but he's fighting to keep the two survivors from being prosecuted." Francine didn't take her eyes off Manny, her affection for him impossible to miss.

"And you're grieving for them." I narrowed my eyes. "On your own."

Manny snorted. "And I'm screwing up even more."

"Aw, old man. We're family. We forgive you." Vinnie held out his arms. "Wanna hug?"

In a shockingly uncharacteristic move, Manny rolled his eyes like Nikki. "Bugger off, big guy." He pushed Francine from his lap. "Enough of all this drama. We have work to do."

Francine poked Manny in the shoulder. When he looked up at her, she widened her eyes and nodded towards us. I didn't know what message she was trying to convey, but Manny must've understood. He sighed heavily. "I was out of line. I apologise."

"Bloody hell!" Vinnie's fake British accent was jarring. "You can't do that! Don't apologise, good man. Now I can't punch you again."

Colin chuckled and Francine blew Vinnie a kiss. Manny just ignored him, but the smile pulling at the corners of his mouth gave me comfort. I moved my chair back and Manny's smile widened. "So, do we have any actionable intel, Doc?"

"Oh, thanks for asking." Vinnie's smile was genuine when Manny turned to glare at him. "As a matter of fact, I have intel. Before our run-in with our Iranian friends, I got a call from a CI. He told me three of his buds died in a car crash yesterday. These guys were into everything: guns, drugs, explosives, even wet work."

"They're assassins?" Daniel asked.

Vinnie nodded. "My CI said they were hired to scare some people off, but then they crashed their SUV. The dumb bastards had explosives with them for some other deal and—"

"It exploded on impact." Colin ran his fingers through his hair. "They were in the SUV that chased us."

"All the details matched," Vinnie said. "I asked, but my CI didn't know who hired these guys."

This was interesting information, but not useful. I studied Vinnie's expression. "You know something more important."

Manny scowled. "Speak."

"Remember this morning when you were being an asswipe?" Vinnie shrugged. "Well, you were being an asswipe because I was being an asswipe."

Manny only stared at Vinnie.

"Well, you see, I had this little plan." Vinnie walked back to the door, leaned against the frame and held out a small round device between his thumb and index finger.

"A button cam?" Colin's eyes widened, then he laughed. "You didn't."

"Oh, I did." Vinnie's chest puffed. "I swiped a couple from Franny's desk. When I was getting all touchy-feely with Shahab and Amin, I planted these babies on them."

Manny jumped up. "Holy hell! Do you know what you did?"

"Yeah." Vinnie smirked. "I found a way we can track these Iranian assholes and find out what they're up to."

"No." Manny put his hands on the top of his head. "You created an international incident."

"I don't think so, handsome." Francine was once again sitting next to me, busy on her tablet. She replaced photos on two monitors with maps of Strasbourg. "We've been able to track their movements."

"You're in on this too?"

Francine's look of innocence was outrageously fake. "Of course. You were being an idiot."

Manny closed his eyes and shook his head. "Bloody hell. What do you have?"

"We can't get audio and visual outside a radius of seventy metres, but we can track their location for up to fifteen kilometres."

"Did you make any recordings?" I would love to see the footage.

"I didn't place them well." Vinnie grimaced. "I had to do it quick and thought that any location might be better than nothing. So I put it under the collars of their jackets where they won't be seen quickly."

Francine nodded. "That and the fact that they're wearing their outdoor coats over their jackets pretty much eliminates all audio and visual."

"But you have their location?" Manny asked.

"Yes." Francine looked at the maps, her eyes suddenly widening in excitement. "Oh, my God! Look at that. We have him!"

"What do you have?" Manny sat down and stared at the monitor when Francine zoomed in on the map.

"One of the button cameras went to Adèle's house after they left the café." She looked at me. "They were there for almost an hour."

"Isn't it still a crime scene?" Manny looked at Daniel.

"It is. Let me check." He took his phone and swiped the screen. He lowered it towards us, the ringing clear over the speakerphone. It went unanswered. Daniel frowned. "Give me a second."

He left the room, none of us speaking.

"I have a bad feeling about this." Vinnie rubbed his chest.

Francine's phone pinged and she lifted it to read. "Well, now we definitely have to speak to the Iranians again."

"What do you have?"

"My contacts got back to me about the vineyard that sent the crates of extra-special wine." She paused dramatically. "Yeah, they're registered as a company that also does a lot of contract work for NAJA."

"The Iranian police." Manny slumped in his chair. "This is just getting worse."

"But this is interesting." Francine smiled at me. "The company's name is Fereydoon Farrukhi Industries."

I blinked. "FF. The two letters in the centre of Adèle's chart didn't stand for her business Freedom Fragrances."

"It stood for Fereydoon Farrukhi—the Iranian company." Vinnie scratched his head. "What was she doing with the business model for this company?"

"We have a problem." Daniel stood next to Vinnie, his face pale. "An officer told the officers stationed at Adèle's house that he was relieving them, so they left. He was wearing a uniform, spoke flawless French, but looked Arabic."

"Impersonating an officer?" Francine's eyebrows were high on her forehead. "That's already bad enough. But an Iranian cop posing as a French cop? Ooh. Really, really bad."

"Bloody hell." Manny's whisper was loud in my room. He pushed himself up. "I need to speak to the president."

Chapter EIGHTEEN

"AND I SUSPECT Adèle planned to put the heroin in the paint, then use a 3D printer to mass-produce these paintings and sell them to distributors." Colin sat back as he finished his part of the briefing.

President Raymond Godard's eyebrows rose. "Would that have worked?"

"Possibly." Colin thought about this. "She would've needed a great chemist to make sure the paint-drug mixture is correct and also the way they would extract the drug would have to be very precise."

Manny, Colin and I were in the president's residence here in Strasbourg, where he had also his office. It had a very similar design to the Salon Doré, or the Golden Room in the Élysée Palace in Paris, an office that had served as the personal study for many French presidents. The gilded filigree on the walls, doors, tables and chairs made the name of the room self-explanatory, as did the ceiling-to-floor golden curtains. Everything in this room was a work of art, including the chandelier above us and the beautiful ceiling.

We were seated on wingback chairs at a round table

next to the president's antique desk. It had been only two and half hours ago when Manny had called the president and had revealed our findings.

The president had assured us that Amin, Shahab and Hamid would be here when we arrived. They were currently waiting in the adjoining conference room with the Iranian ambassador. The president had insisted on first getting all the information before walking into a conversation that could have devastating political and economic repercussions for both countries.

He looked at Manny. "Tell me everything you found out about the men next door."

"We don't have much." Manny grunted in frustration. "They entered the country eleven days ago—a day before Adèle was murdered. They rented a charcoal-coloured SUV at the airport, using a credit card issued to a company registered in Iran."

"The same company that sent the wine?"

"No. This company is more transparent. They do all the arrangements for accommodation and transport for official trips by Iranian law enforcement officers."

"Was that SUV the one that was pursuing Colin and Genevieve?"

"We're not sure." Manny had uttered a few rude phrases in frustration when we'd not been able to find a lot more information. "The car that blew up was definitely not the one these guys rented. I got the Iranians' GPS information from the rental company. They'd successfully manipulated the car's system to show they were only at their hotel, at shopping malls and a few tourist sites. We were also not able to find much information on them personally. My sources tell me that it's most likely because they're not on anyone's watchlist."

"Well, why don't we go and speak to them and find out more." President Godard got up and we followed him to the door connecting his office to the conference room.

It wasn't a large room, but the high ceilings created the impression of space. The dark wood of the rectangular table in the centre of the room was highlighted by the bright white walls and classical décor.

The leader of the three men, Amin, was sitting at the table next to a middle-aged man. Both men got up when President Godard entered the room.

President Godard shook the older man's hand. "Ambassador Sirvan Kanian. Please forgive me for making you wait so long."

"Oh, it's no problem at all, President Godard." His smile was genuine. He liked the president. "You know how I always enjoy our meetings. But I must say that I'm slightly perplexed as to why we are here."

President Godard gestured at the chairs and we sat down. I studied the ambassador. The president had told us about this man. His Oxford education was evident in his accent as he spoke English. We were also told that he was highly intelligent and, despite being open to many trade and cultural agreements, he was still very conservative.

"We'll get to that in a second." President Godard introduced himself to Amin. "Where is the rest of your team?"

"They're waiting in the reception area." The ambassador answered before Amin could. "We thought it would be best for only their team leader to be here."

Amin's reaction to the ambassador's words was telling. I narrowed my eyes, determined to observe every micro-expression. "You suspect something."

Amin looked at me, trying to school his features into a more neutral expression. "Yes. I told you this morning we were here about the artefacts."

President Godard held out his hand to stop my response. "This is not what Doctor Lenard meant and you know it."

Ambassador Kanian looked at Amin. "What are they talking about?" He looked at the president. "Please explain what is going on here."

"We've had four brutal murders which are all connected to each other. More importantly, they are all connected to drugs being smuggled into France from Iran."

Amin closed his eyes, his expression resigned.

The ambassador's lips thinned and he straightened in his chair. "That is an outrage. You have to know that we have nothing to do with any of that. We fight so hard against all the drugs entering our country, yet it sometimes feels like a losing battle. Anything, we'll do anything to help."

I looked at Amin. "Tell us what you know."

"I really wished it wasn't true. I didn't want to find any evidence here to confirm my suspicions."

"Was this drug investigation your true mission?" the ambassador asked Amin.

"We were here for the artefacts too." He glanced at

Colin. "Apparently, some pieces have been found and will go back with us."

"The drugs?" President Godard asked.

Amin crossed his arms, then immediately uncrossed them. "My team is only one of many investigating crimes. But we were tasked with finding out who was looting our cultural heritage and selling it to the West. We don't mind that it's on display in museums, but at the end of the day these pieces belong to the people of Iran. It's our history." He took a calming breath. "The more we investigated the artefacts, the more evidence we found that connected recent exports of heroin to the art.

"I contacted the narcotics team about the drugs. They specialise in finding these dealers and stopping the in- and outflow of narcotics. They told me that they've been trying to shut down one specific syndicate, but the leader has been one step ahead of them all the time. Apparently, this syndicate is so good that we don't even know the names of the players."

"Why were you in the café?" Manny asked.

Amin glanced at the ambassador, who nodded. He then looked at Manny. "We received intel that the young man had knowledge of the artefacts and possibly the drugs."

"Who gave you that intel?" Colin didn't even attempt to disguise his scepticism.

Amin smiled. "You know I can't, and I won't, tell you that."

As he spoke, his smile disappeared, numerous micro-expressions moving over his face. He was busy piecing together the information he had with the questions we were asking and the result was causing him distress.

"Where did you go after you left the café this morning?" Manny's tone was no longer friendly.

Amin frowned and shifted in his chair. "We split up to cover more ground."

President Godard held out his hand to stop Amin's explanation. He looked at Ambassador Kanian. "My people were never informed you had an investigative team here, Sirvan."

"President Godard, please." The ambassador raised both his hands, palms out. "Don't even think this was espionage. This is not what was happening here."

Manny snorted. "What do you call Iranian detectives in France following a young French citizen to a café and surveilling him?"

Amin's face lost some of its colour. "We're not spies. We were just following up on a lead that might give us back our artefacts."

"Where did you go?" Manny asked again.

"After the café, I went to my hotel room to meet with a contact. And no, I won't tell you his name. He's a good man. He helps many of our people here in your city."

"Hassan? The hawala broker?" The risk I took to voice my suspicion was immediately rewarded.

Amin's eyes widened, then narrowed. "Don't make trouble for Hassan. He's a good man."

"We know," Colin said. "Where did you go after your meeting with Hassan?"

Amin looked up and left—recalling a memory. "I went to the ATM to get more cash. Then I went to the mall to buy my wife perfume. She has enough bottles to open a shop, but she wanted something from France."

Manny's phone rang. The ambassador frowned, the corners of his mouth pulling down. President Godard wasn't surprised when Manny answered the call and put the phone on the table. "You're on speakerphone."

"Hi, everyone." Francine's voice was clear. She was excited. "I've been listening to your conversation and Amin has been telling the truth."

Amin jumped out of his chair and looked around the room. "You've been listening? Wait. How do you know I've been telling the truth?"

Colin also got up and walked to Amin. He reached out, but didn't touch Amin's jacket. "May I?"

Amin frowned, looked at Colin's hand, then to the ambassador before nodding.

Colin lifted the jacket's lapel and took out the button camera.

"This is not acceptable." Ambassador Kanian pulled the cuffs of his suit jacket and pushed his shoulders back. "Actually, this is an outrageous invasion of privacy."

"Pah! I wouldn't be calling the kettle black here, Ambassador. That button camera just exonerated Amin."

"What do you mean?" Amin walked back to the table and sat down, staring at the phone.

"Hold your horses." Manny pulled his phone closer. "Did you alert Dan?"

"I did. They're on their way to pick up Shahab." She paused. "Well, that's a problem."

"What now?"

"Shahab's button camera just went dead."

"You planted one on Shahab as well?" Amin's brows pulled together in grave concern. He blinked a few times and I watched as he added yet another piece of information to his conclusions. He gasped and looked at Colin. "What did he do?"

"First problem is where he is." Manny looked at his phone. "Is he still in the building?"

"Uh, no," Francine said. "He left as soon as you guys went into the conference room."

"He suspected something." Colin sighed. "Can you track him on the city cameras?"

"I'm working on it." The sound of a mouse clicking and keyboard strokes came through the phone.

"Officer Shahab was the one who suggested they wait outside and only Officer Amin and I meet with you." The ambassador looked just as worried as Amin. "What did Officer Shahab do?"

"He went to the house of one of the victims," President Godard said. "Only our investigators know about that crime scene. And the killer."

"We think he killed all four of the victims." Colin paused. "After he tortured them for hours."

Amin put both his hands over his mouth, his eyes wide.

"What can we do?" Ambassador Kanian asked.

"Help us find Shahab." Manny glared at Amin.

He lowered his hands and put them palms down on the table. "I honestly don't know where he is." He shook his head. "It all makes sense now."

"What does?" Colin asked.

"The fact that we were always at least three steps behind the art looters and the drug traffickers." He fell back into his chair. "Shahab has been controlling the inflow of intel for years. He's been in this unit for eleven years and on my team for two. He knows every case and every lead."

Ambassador Kanian's mouth opened in shock. "We have to let the police chief know about this breach."

Amin nodded absently, then looked at Colin. "Does our damaged rental car have anything to do with this?"

"What damage?" Colin's tone was harsh. "When did this happen?"

"Yesterday. Shahab took the SUV to meet a friend for lunch."

"That was around the time we were being pursued by two SUVs."

"Two?" Amin shook his head vigorously. "No, we only rented one."

"How was it damaged?" the ambassador asked.

"Shahab came back and said that some hooligans had thrown rocks at the car and even burning rags when they saw he looked Arabic. They were shouting all kinds of racist slurs at him." He frowned. "There were really burn marks on the paint."

I swallowed. That moment when the SUV came racing through the explosion and the shots entered Colin's vehicle, the glass raining down on us—it all rushed back at me and brought tightness to my throat.

"Um, guys?" Francine's voice pulled me out of my spiralling thoughts. "Shahab's gone."

"What do you mean, he's gone?" Manny was almost shouting.

"I caught him on three city cameras leaving the president's residence, but then he went into a private parking area and disappeared."

"Cameras in the parking?" Colin asked.

"They're on a closed system."

"Get that intel." Manny got up. "Now."

"Oh, God." Francine's voice broke, sending a rush of adrenaline through my system. "Oh, no."

"Francine, what's wrong?" Manny's words were breathless, a flash of fear joining his concern.

Even Amin and the ambassador leaned closer to the phone.

"Caelan." Emotion made Francine's voice extremely unsteady. "Oh, Genevieve, our boy genius is missing."

Chapter NINETEEN

"WHERE THE BLOODY hell is he?" Manny's frustrated question came out loud enough to register as a shout. I looked into the team room to see him rubbing both his hands over his short hair. "It's been two bloody hours."

I cringed at Manny's use of words, truly hoping that Caelan had not bled at all during these two hours. I didn't know if Caelan was even able to cope with what was happening to him at the moment.

Daniel had been the one to discover Caelan was missing. He'd gone to Caelan's flat to check up on him and found it deserted. Caelan's backpack had been on the floor of his apartment, the contents all over the living room floor. Daniel had found Caelan's two stress balls still in the backpack and another four amongst the scattered contents. Caelan's phone was also on the floor, broken as if someone had stomped on it numerous times. We had no way to track Caelan. And he didn't have his stress balls to help him cope.

Using the same method as at Adèle's house, Shahab had been dressed as a police officer and had told the officers protecting Caelan he was there to relieve them. It had been past their shift-end, so they hadn't questioned Shahab or the fact that he'd come alone. They'd been too happy to go home.

We'd never heard the voice of Jace's killer because he was whispering. But we had heard his perfect French. When Colin and I had spoken to Shahab, he'd used English, so we wouldn't have made the connection just by listening to his voice.

"I've looked everywhere. After Shahab went into that parking structure, he just disappeared." Francine had not lifted her hands from her computer keyboard or tablet screen since we'd returned to the team room. "I can't even find him on any of the cameras around Caelan's flat. He had fifteen minutes to get from the president's residence to Caelan, but I don't see him anywhere. I looked at all the cameras along all the possible routes."

"He's most likely using a disguise," Colin said. "Already we know he's got a police uniform. In this cold weather all you need is an oversized winter coat and a cap to disappear in the crowd."

Colin was right. Francine also knew this, but it didn't ease the frustration and concern on her face.

The president had told us to do whatever we needed. When we'd left, he had been busy berating the Iranian ambassador and pushing for any more information they could give on Shahab. He'd phoned fifteen minutes ago to let us know he'd had to let the ambassador, Amin and Hamid go before it became an international incident. They'd not been able to tell him any added information on Shahab, and Hamid had not known about any of Shahab's activities.

I turned back to the monitors in front of me. There was nothing new I could learn from Adèle's chart, nor the photos of the labels. All the names and cities from the labels had been matched with descriptions from the chart. But without more context, any conclusions would be speculative.

I closed my eyes and mentally called up an empty music sheet. Instead of my usual speed of writing a Mozart composition, I took my time connecting the top two staves with a solid line. Then I took care to draw the G-clef, finding pleasure in the curls that formed such a beautiful symbol.

My eyes flew open and I turned to the team room. "Where's François?"

"What are you thinking, Doc?" Manny walked into my room as Francine lifted her phone and tapped the screen. She got up and joined us, her phone pressed against her ear.

I looked at Manny. "François had an undeniable connection to the murders as well as the drugs."

"Nothing that we could prove and then arrest him for." The corners of his mouth turned down.

"True." I thought back to François' nonverbal cues. "My observations confirm Phillip's conclusions that François didn't torture and kill Adèle, Jace, Camille Vastine and Martin Gayot."

"That animal Shahab did it." Vinnie was leaning against the doorframe, his arms crossed.

"If we're working on that assumption, then François is connected to Shahab." Colin was sitting next to me and had been either working on his computer or phoning contacts to find out if they knew anything about these men. "I see where Jenny's going with this. If we can't trace Caelan or Shahab, it might be worth a shot to look for François."

"His lawyer isn't answering his phone." Francine sat down on the chair Manny usually used and tapped her tablet screen. "But... Hmm... I'm hacking François' phone. Damn, it's turned off. But... yup, I have his location history." She tapped the screen a few times. "I'm putting the map on the monitors."

As I looked up, photos of Adèle's chart on four of the monitors were replaced by a map of Strasbourg. Red dots littered the centre of the city, a few red dots to the north and the west. They started disappearing.

"What's happening?" Vinnie asked.

"I'm changing the time to the last four hours." She tapped a few more times, then looked up. "There. These are all the towers his phone connected to since noon today."

I saw it immediately. "That's the route to the self-storage warehouse."

"Holy hell." Manny lifted his phone. "I'm phoning Daniel."

"I don't know what he'll be doing there," Vinnie said. "That place is locked up. All the tenants have been told it's an active crime scene. And it hasn't been released yet."

"Is it guarded?" Colin asked.

"No. Dan told me the crime scene techs went through all the lockers and found no more artefacts or drugs. The brass decided it would be a waste of resources to post officers there when the locks on the doors worked perfectly fine. But the same clever brass also determined it should stay a crime scene. Smart, right? Not."

Colin's eyes narrowed. "What kind of locks?"

"Keypad." Vinnie grunted. "Easy enough to bypass."

"Their system is ridiculously insecure." Francine pointed at the bottom right monitor. It was split into three windows, all showing the outside of the warehouse. The parking area was empty and there was no movement anywhere. "Too easy to hack."

"We'll talk about your illegal hacking later." Manny put his phone in his trouser pocket. "Daniel says they were called out to a robbery. They're wrapping up and will leave in about ten minutes."

I looked at the security footage and wondered if we would be able to see anything once it got dark. This time of the year, we only had another thirty minutes of daylight left. I remembered Pink's disgust at the lack of security and I inhaled sharply. "Adèle had cameras above her lockers."

"Of course! How could I forget about that?" Francine's fingers were flying over her tablet. "I'll put the live streaming on the monitors. This is one of the times I'm happy someone has bad security on their system. I still have access to Adèle's entire system, including her…"

Everyone in the room jerked and inhaled sharply when the monitor above the warehouse videos came to life.

"Oh, God." Francine wiped roughly at her eyes and leaned forward. "Caelan."

He was only partly in view of the camera placed above one of Adèle's lockers. His feet were out of the view of the camera, his legs stretched out in front of him. He was rocking and slapping his thighs, his mouth moving constantly.

"He's reciting his geographical facts." The anger in Vinnie's voice made me turn around and look at him. Every muscle in his face was pulled tight in fury. "I'm going to find this motherfucker who picks on those weaker than him and I'll show him—"

"Save that for later." Colin got up. "We can be at the warehouse in less than ten minutes."

"It will take Dan and his team at least thirty to get there." Manny scowled. "They're on the other side of the city."

"I'm going now." Vinnie's hand rested on his holstered gun. "Whether you're coming with me or not. I'm going there right now to bring Caelan home."

"Take a breath and be smart about this, big guy. We're going, but we need to do this right." Manny turned to me. "We might need you, Doc."

"Fuck no." Vinnie took a step towards me. "She's not going anywhere close to danger."

"Will you be able to calm Caelan down *and* protect him?" Colin took my hand and pulled me up to stand next to him. "Look, I don't like it either, but with you, Millard, me and the GIPN team there, Jenny will be safe. There will be too much happening for you to focus on Caelan."

"I'm good at calming him." Francine didn't take her eyes off the monitor. "But I'll be much more useful here."

Sometimes, it amused me to observe neurotypicals argue. Right now, it only irritated me. I pulled my hand from Colin's and walked to the filing cabinet to get my handbag. "This is my choice. I don't want to go. I don't want to be in a dangerous situation, but Colin is right. None of you understand Caelan as well as I do. I'll go."

"I'm streaming this to your phones." Francine now had the live footage split on four monitors. I jerked. Caelan's eyes were wide in fear, his slapping was increasing and would no doubt leave his thighs bruised. Darkness teased my peripheral vision, but I pushed back at it. I needed to stay at my best until Caelan was safe.

We didn't speak on the way to the elevator. This time I didn't say a word about the small space when all four of us squeezed in. It was an uncomfortable fit, but I pushed my face into Colin's chest and mentally pulled up that empty music sheet again. Now it was time for me to write Mozart's Symphony in C major. It always calmed me when I needed it.

I also didn't complain when Colin raced through the city, breaking countless traffic laws. I wasn't paying much attention in any case. I had my phone in my hands, watching the live video on Caelan. He hadn't changed his position once, his rocking and slapping increasing and becoming more erratic.

Only when we entered the warehouse area did Colin slow down. Clouds had gathered and shortened the daylight hours. It wasn't completely dark, but the shadows from the warehouses could provide plenty of cover for someone who didn't want to be noticed. I changed from mentally writing Mozart to playing the symphony in my mind. Loudly.

Colin parked next to a building and rested his arms on the steering wheel. "He's in there."

I looked at the neighbouring building, then at my phone screen. Caelan's movements were jerky. "He's becoming more unstable."

"Did you see anyone else walk past the camera?" Vinnie asked.

"No. Only Caelan."

"The GIPN team is still thirteen minutes out." Manny's tone was tight.

"We need to get that kid out." Vinnie opened the back door. "I'm not letting him sit there another minute."

"Oh, for the love of all that is holy." Manny opened his door and we followed suit. The cold air was harsh against my exposed skin and I pulled my scarf higher to cover more of my chin and cheeks.

"Ain't it grand we came in my SUV?" Vinnie opened the boot and I blinked a few times. I had been so absorbed in the video and in my concern for Caelan that I hadn't noticed that we'd taken Vinnie's vehicle. From the back of his car, he took a device the size of a camera and aimed it at the warehouse. His smile was wide and genuine. "Thermal imaging, baby."

I stepped behind him and Colin joined me, both of us watching the small square screen as Vinnie slowly moved it from right to left. I hadn't seen this model before. "How accurate is it?"

"Very. It will pick up heat signatures as small as a kitten within six hundred metres." Vinnie's muscle tension increased as first one, then a second red light entered the small screen. "Two people."

One was lower than the other and I assumed that had to be Caelan sitting on the floor. "Who's the other person?"

"No idea." Vinnie frowned at the screen. "He's not moving at all."

Caelan was. His rocking and slapping caused the lower red image to expand and retract.

"Check the rest of the warehouse," Manny said. "Twice."

Vinnie did that. "Still only these two."

Manny turned to fully stare at Vinnie. "We lead." Then he turned to me and Colin. "You follow. No heroics."

"I'm not a hero."

"Doc." Manny's lips thinned, then he looked at Colin. "You make sure she's out of the line of fire at all times."

Colin nodded once.

Vinnie reached into the back of his SUV again and came out holding a handgun. He held it out to Colin. "I know you hate this, dude. But let's just make sure we're covering all our bases here."

Colin sighed deeply before taking the pistol. He removed the magazine, put it back and cocked the gun. Despite his intense dislike for weapons, he was expertly trained. The way he held it in both hands, his arms slightly raised and the barrel of the gun pointed downward, showed his unconscious competence at handling the weapon. It brought an uncomfortable tightness around my throat. I swallowed.

Manny looked at each of us, then nodded to himself as if satisfied that we were prepared. I wasn't. Yet I followed him and Vinnie as they walked to the door thirty metres ahead of us.

Colin stepped next to me. "Put your hand on my belt and stay half a step to my left and behind me."

I did that and focused on the sound of the snow crunching under our feet. It was strangely quiet for this time on a weekday. It made me wonder what was in the other warehouses that didn't require or invite a lot of movement. All those thoughts stopped when we reached the red metal door.

I recognised it from Jace's video. Except this time the keypad was badly damaged. The door was ajar. Manny and Vinnie raised their weapons at the same time, their postures focused and ready for action. Vinnie tapped Manny's shoulder. Manny responded by opening the door.

Manny went in first, Vinnie right behind him. Colin waited two seconds before he followed. My hand tightened around his belt and I stayed half a step behind him the whole time. My movements were stiff and even the most untrained eye could easily observe the fear making my shoulders hunch and bringing my arms tightly against my torso.

The utter silence in the large space exacerbated my nervousness. As did the low lighting. We stopped in front of the aisle, Vinnie lifting his device again to ensure no one was there. Once satisfied, he and Manny still moved around the corner, their guns aimed into the aisle, Manny aiming high and Vinnie low as if they'd agreed on this before.

"Clear." Manny's whisper was so soft that I barely heard it, but it made me exhale a breath I didn't know I'd held.

The next aisle was about ten metres ahead, the light coming from it brighter than anywhere else in the warehouse. My muscle tension increased to the point where it felt as if my boots had turned into lead. Everything in my mind and body screamed at me not to move forward.

Then I heard Caelan's keening. It was soft, but nonstop. The closer we came to the aisle, the clearer it became, until I could hear that he wasn't keening. He was reciting geographical facts.

Manny and Vinnie stopped at the corner and Vinnie reached for his device again. The two red images filled the screen when he aimed it towards the aisle. Caelan was in there. With someone.

Vinnie touched Manny's shoulder. Leading the way with his gun, Manny leaned around the corner. First his body tension increased, then significantly decreased. He stepped into the aisle, not lowering his gun or level of focus. "Well, well, well."

"About twenty percent of all volcanoes are underwater!" Caelan's shout wasn't very loud, his voice sounding damaged. How long had he been reciting facts? And at what volume?

Vinnie followed Manny into the aisle, but held out his hand to stop Colin from following.

My breathing increased, as did my heart rate. I started feeling lightheaded and pushed Mozart's symphony back into my mind and concentrated on taking slower and deeper breaths. Four of these later, Manny's voice reached us. "Clear."

"An erupting volcano can trigger tsunamis, flash floods, earthquakes, mudflows and rock falls! Doctor Lenard! The word volcano originally comes from the name of the Roman god of fire, Vulcan!"

I followed Colin into the aisle, wondering why Caelan was reciting only facts about volcanoes. When in great distress, he usually recited facts at random. Then all these thoughts left my mind.

Caelan was on the floor as I'd seen him on the video. His eyes were wide open and had a wild look in them. I was amazed that he'd not given in to the shutdown that had to be pushing down on him with an incredible weight.

Vinnie was at the end of the aisle, his weapon still raised, but the barrel now also aimed at the floor. Manny was standing between us and Caelan.

"One in twenty people in the world live within danger range of an active volcano!" He flapped his hands in the air a few times, then slapped his thighs. "One thousand nine hundred volcanoes are considered active!"

My eyebrows shot up when I saw the thick rope around his ankle. His jeans had ridden up and the rope had chafed away his dark skin. It looked raw and very painful. I took my hand from Colin's belt and took a step to the side to see Caelan completely.

Immediately, and irrationally, I wished I hadn't done that. On a chair three metres from Caelan was a badly beaten man. The rope was tautly stretched between one leg of the chair and Caelan's leg. It seemed as if Caelan had moved away as far as he could from the man.

I swallowed and took one step closer. Then another. With every step, Caelan recited another fact, his movements becoming more agitated. I stopped.

"Seems like Shahab got to you before we could find you." Manny lowered his chin and stared at the man on the chair.

"There are no active volcanoes in Australia because it sits in the middle of a tectonic plate!"

It took another second for me to recognise the man on the chair. It was François. His hands were resting on his lap, all his fingers broken. His face had been beaten and was swollen so badly, it was hard to see any recognisable features. Or micro-expressions. The dominant expression on his face was pure physical agony.

He wasn't dead. He raised his head a little to look at Manny and smiled. His mouth was filled with blood and it looked like he was missing a few teeth. Because of his injuries, I couldn't determine the nature of his smile, but found it hard to imagine it could be genuine. Not when he had difficulty breathing, most likely because of broken ribs.

His legs looked unharmed, but I couldn't see through his trousers. His ankles were also bound to the legs of the chair and a rope around his waist seemed to both hold him upright and seated. His bulky winter jacket hid any injuries to his torso.

"Caelan, bud." Colin walked closer, but also stopped when Caelan flapped his hands again and viciously slapped his legs. Colin glanced at me.

"Doctor Lenard! Japan has ten percent of the world's active volcanoes! The eruption of Mount St. Helens in 1980 had five hundred times the power of an atomic bomb!"

I closed my eyes for a second and held my breath as I considered Caelan's facts. My eyes shot open and I shook my index finger at François' jacket.

"Jenny?" Colin looked from my finger to François. "What's wrong?"

"Volcanoes. Explosion." I shook my finger again. "There's a bomb under his jacket."

Chapter TWENTY

"BLOODY HELL!" MANNY leaned away from François, staring at his closed jacket. "Is that true?"

"What?" François' voice came out hoarse. "A bomb?" His voice rose in volume and pitch and he shifted. "Get it off me! Get it off me!"

"Don't fucking move." Vinnie stepped closer, put his hand on François' shoulder and pushed hard. "We don't know what will set it off. Stay as still as you can."

François froze, his eyes stretched as wide as they could with the swelling. "Get it off me."

"The oldest fossil was found in a rock almost three and a half billion years old from western Australia!" Caelan slapped his thighs, looking at Vinnie's hand on François' shoulder. "Mayflies live only twenty-four hours!"

"Wait." Colin raised one hand to stop Vinnie when he reached out to lower the zipper of François' jacket. He was frowning at François. "How can you not know there's a bomb strapped to your chest?"

"Oh, God!" A tear rolled down François' face. "I… I passed out. He must've put it on me while I was out."

"Who's he?" Manny asked.

"Shahab." François raised his hand to wipe at his cheek,

but moaned loudly. "He broke all my fingers. Every single one."

More tears rolled down his face. I didn't know what to think. His injuries and the swelling made it impossible to read his micro-expressions. Phillip had told us about the François he knew many years ago. Given the current situation, I doubted that he'd changed his character traits and stopped being manipulative.

But after our conversation with him in Phillip's conference room, I found it hard to imagine that he would choose this moment to be deceitful. His fear had been real then. It was real now.

"Where is Shahab?" Manny kept shifting his glare from François' face to his closed jacket.

"I don't know. I don't even know how I got here." He looked past us. "Where are we? The storage place? Oh, God. How did I get here?"

"A Great Basin bristlecone pine in California is more than five thousand years old!" Caelan was busy losing his voice, the words a rough whisper. "It's the oldest tree on Earth."

I looked at the rope around his ankle and stared at the broken skin, dripping blood onto the floor. "We need to get this rope off him."

Colin shook his head. "I think we first need to see what's under François' jacket."

"Carefully, big guy." Manny raised his gun, but kept it pointed at the floor. "I'll provide cover."

Vinnie nodded and holstered his gun. He frequently

boasted about the training he did with Daniel's team, especially the basic training in identifying improvised explosive devices.

I barely breathed as I watched him carefully lowering the zipper. The sound of the slide gliding over each tooth was exaggerated in my mind, making me wince with each movement. The progress was slow, but smooth and Vinnie gently disconnected the zipper at the bottom.

I held my breath as he lifted the two front panels of the blue winter jacket and opened them to reveal François' torso.

"Oh, God. Oh, God." François' voice trembled, tears streaming down his face. "Get this off me. Please, get this off me."

"Did you tell Dan to bring the bomb squad, old man? Because we're going to need them." Vinnie straightened to give us a full view of François' chest.

Darkness immediately crowded my peripheral vision and my breathing became erratic. A small box was strapped over François' heart. It was the size of a smartphone, but four or five times as thick. The rope that went over the box and around François' chest seemed to be the same rope that tied Caelan to the chair. It seemed like the lid was only a thin piece of black plastic that covered the box and was held in place by the rope.

"Dan is bringing the bomb squad." Manny leaned a bit forward and scowled. "Do you recognise it? Can you disable it?"

"It's small." Vinnie rested both hands on his hips, his

thumbs pointing to the front. He was thinking. "I can't see much. And I don't think I want to mess around with it. In our last training, we were shown a bomb the size of a matchbox that could take out three of these buildings. I have no idea what explosives are in here. It could be just for this dude or to destroy the entire building."

"Russia and the US are geographically only four kilometres apart, but there's a twenty-one-hour time difference between them!" Caelan's rocking increased.

I was fighting to not give in to my shutdown. I was also angry with myself. What had I been thinking to come here? I was in no position to be of any help to anyone. I didn't know anything about bomb disposal. And I wasn't capable of helping Caelan right now.

"I suggest we turn off our phones." Colin reached into his trouser pocket. "We don't know what will set it off."

My throat was instantly dry. My phone was in my handbag in Vinnie's SUV. I didn't know if I would've been able to turn it off in any case. I felt frozen.

"The book says we should all leave." Vinnie looked at Caelan and his top lip curled. "Not happening."

"I'm not leaving Caelan." Colin took a step closer to the young man still rocking. "Jenny?"

I shook my head. Even if I wanted to leave, I didn't think my feet would obey signals from my brain at the moment. Colin, Vinnie and Manny were calm and composed. I was not. My mind was reeling and it was clear to me that François was close to a breakdown as well.

"Bloody hell." Manny exhaled loudly. "But the moment

the bomb squad comes, we leave."

"We'll see about that," Vinnie said. "What about Caelan? The rope?"

"Yeah." Colin walked over to Caelan and went down on his haunches. "Caelan, bud. I'm going to untie you, okay?"

"Russia spans eleven time zones." Caelan nodded, then didn't stop. A tear ran down his cheek. "The length of a day on Earth is twenty-three hours and fifty-six minutes."

"I know it's hard, superman." Vinnie's tone was gentle. "But you're doing a great job."

"Uh, Vin." Colin prodded the rope. "This is a double fisherman's knot."

"Fuck."

"What's a bloody double fisherman's knot?" Manny took a step back to better see everyone.

"Something that I'm not going to be able to untie. Not tonight. These knots were designed to be nigh-on impossible to untie." Colin looked up at Vinnie. "You have your knife on you?"

"Of course." Vinnie reached into one of the side pockets of his combat trousers and handed Colin a red multi-purpose knife.

Colin sat down on the floor. "Caelan, bud. I'm going to cut through this. Then we'll have you out of here and safely at home with some white cookies and milk. Or Vin can make you some of his pasta with white beans and white cheese sauce. Would you like that?"

"China encompasses five time zones, even though the entire country only uses one!"

Colin opened the knife and cut at the length of rope not tied around Caelan's leg, but the part connected to the chair. He grunted and sat back. "Well, shit."

"Speak." Manny's scowl intensified.

"This rope has a wire core as well as thin wires threaded in the nylon."

Caelan recited another fact and I had to force myself to slow my breathing.

"Can you cut through it?" Manny asked.

Colin looked at Vinnie. "Did you bring your toolbox?"

"Yeah, but Pink borrowed my wire cutter yesterday. Fuck. I don't have anything in there that will cut through it." He nodded at the knife in Colin's hand. "The best bet is to saw through the wire with that. It will take longer, but that's an ace knife. It will do the job."

"What about me?" François' voice had a hysterical tone to it. "What are you going to do to get this off me?"

"We're waiting for the bomb squad." Vinnie pressed down on François' shoulder when the injured man started to move. "Just don't fucking move."

"I can't do this. I don't want to do this. Get this off me."

The thought of François acting on his neurotypical panic and mindlessly struggling to get away brought more darkness to my mind. I pushed hard at it and tried to concentrate. There had to be something I could do to help. It felt like I was fighting against an invisible force to get my mind to let go of the panic and focus on something proactive. "Why did Shahab torture you?"

François took a sharp breath and looked at me. "Because he found out I wanted to take his business away from him."

His frankness surprised me and also didn't surprise me. In Phillip's conference room, he'd appeared desperate to share whatever had caused him such fear. It was, however, unusual for someone from his background to disclose criminal activity so quickly.

"What business?" I asked.

"You know." He started shrugging, but stopped when Vinnie increased the pressure on his shoulder. He winced. He sighed heavily, then winced again, his arms moving closer to his torso, to his broken ribs. "Drugs. I was going to take *some* of his drug business to fund my art business."

"You had a plan." And I wanted to know what it was.

"Yes. Well, Élodie had a plan." His sigh was sad. "I liked her. It's awful that she died at Shahab's hand."

"Why did he torture her?"

"To find out where all the crates with Shahab's product were, of course."

"Let's get back to the plan." Manny took a step closer. "Tell me about that."

"Élodie had figured out most of Shahab's operation. She had it all mapped out. She knew how he got his product into France, she knew where he got his product from and she had figured out most of his distributors. It must have been one of those fuckers who told Shahab that we were offering them a better deal."

"What deal?" I asked when he glanced down at his

torso and his eyes widened. "Were you offering them more money?'

"No. A partnership. Élodie had it all figured out. She was working with the manager from this storage place. He was going to be the import point for us. The guy had been accepting all kinds of illegal shipments for years, including Shahab's stuff. He got all this at his courier business. Somehow, Élodie found out about that and made him an offer he couldn't refuse."

Something in his tone made me frown.

"You mean she blackmailed him." Vinnie must have also heard the tone.

"It was her original plan. But when she went to Gilles, he was so excited about the quantity and the kind of money she was talking about, he immediately agreed to accidentally lose one shipment. He would then bring it here. From here, Gilles and I would co-operate in future deals. Élodie only wanted to do this one deal. Nothing more."

"How're you doing there, Frey?" Manny narrowed his eyes to see past Colin's hands.

"Slowly, but surely." Colin didn't look up.

"An African elephant is pregnant for twenty-two months!" Caelan had slowed his rocking, but now it increased again.

"Oh, God." François groaned. "We're going to die here. I should never have gone against Shahab."

"Where did Shahab get his heroin from?" I needed François' attention away from the situation. And I needed something to focus on.

"Rudbar. It's a small town in Iran. Shahab has a registered vineyard there. And they don't produce wine."

"He used the vineyard as a cover."

"A great cover, as it turns out. He's been importing crates of wine bottles to France for nine years already. His shipments were always about the same size as the one Gilles had brought here. Twelve crates." He closed his eyes again, a tear rolling down his cheek. "We really thought we had planned it all out."

"What went wrong?"

"Shahab has many contacts. He would never have known that Gilles had changed the recipients. Élodie helped him and they covered their tracks really well. They made it look like the crates never left Iran. But Shahab had someone at the port in Iran who told him the crates made it to France. His contact at the French port confirmed it."

"That's why Shahab came to Strasbourg."

"Yes." François swallowed. "He went straight to Élodie's house. She'd only taken four crates. Shahab told me that she wasn't able to tell him a lot before she died."

"She had a pre-existing heart condition. The stress of the torture gave her a heart attack."

"Shit. I didn't know that." François took a shaky breath. "Shahab took the four crates from her house and went looking for the rest. When he didn't find it and those people he tortured knew nothing about this, he went back to her house to see if she'd lied and maybe had it hidden somewhere."

That explained why Shahab had spent an hour in Adèle's

house after he'd sent the officers away. Colin grunted and I looked over. He was still sawing away at the rope. It looked like he was almost halfway through. Caelan had calmed down a bit, but was still rocking.

"Did Adèl... Élodie tell him about this warehouse?" Manny asked.

"No." François groaned. "He told me she only had time to tell him she had stored the crates in a warehouse, but not which one. It took him a few days to figure that out. Then he found out about the treasure-hunting young people."

"Geocaching," Vinnie said. "Not treasure-hunting."

"Well, he went after them." He shivered. "First that young man. Then those other two. He made me take them out of his SUV and hide them in the forest. The first time I was lucky. The second time... those women saw me before I could get away. Shahab had already left and I was stuck there with the police. And somewhere in the process of killing these young people he found out about Gilles' role in this takeover."

"When did Shahab tell you this?" Manny asked

"When he still considered me a business partner."

"Business partner?"

"I was his distributor in Rotterdam and sometimes supervised distribution here."

"That's how you knew Gilles." I thought back to his reaction when Daniel had given the news about Gilles' death. "You suspected Gilles would tell Shahab about your plan."

"He was always a coward." François sighed. "When I heard Gilles had been tortured, I knew my time was limited. Gilles would've told Shahab after the first punch. He was terrified when we found out Élodie was dead. That's why he gave those other crates away. He didn't want anything in his possession if Shahab came around asking him questions. And look how that worked out for him. When I left your office, I tried to play it cool so I could get away, but that stupid lawyer Shahab hired for me took me straight to that monster."

"That was Shahab's lawyer?" Manny asked.

"Oh, they're best pals. Bastards."

I thought about everything he'd told us so far. "How did you find out who Shahab's distributors were?"

"I don't know how Élodie did her research, but she was able to track down all of them. I think she did a lot of stalking. She told me that she knew where they were, but wasn't sure about their names and exact details. So I used my contacts to find out more about the vineyard. Turned out that all of the workers are there because Shahab threatened to torture and kill their families. We made contact with one who was willing to give us everything she could find in Shahab's books. For a price."

"Élodie sent her the money through the hawala system."

"Yes. And we got what we needed."

"How did this worker get the information to you?" I asked even though I was sure I knew the answer.

"She was very clever. She worked in Shahab's office.

She was the one who printed the labels for the bottles. She told us she would put the names and towns of the distributors on the labels. It would be in the lines of the background." He huffed softly. "We never got it. Élodie took those four crates to check the labels and get the names. But then Shahab killed her."

"You used the past tense for the woman who gave you this information."

"Oh. No. She's not dead. She managed to escape with her family before Shahab found out about all of this." He glanced down at his chest. "Where is that bomb squad? You must get this off me."

"They will be here soon." The doubt on Manny's face couldn't be about their arrival. Did he doubt they could disarm the bomb? I glanced at Colin still sawing the rope. It looked like he'd cut through the centre and was now struggling with the last half.

Panic crept up on me and I forced myself to focus. "What was Élodie's plan?"

"She wanted out." François shuddered and tried to control his breathing. "That's why she sold me Shahab's business model for one million euros. I negotiated of course. For that money I wanted her to help me plan the first shipment, use her hawala contact to pay our informant in Iran as well as pay for the artefacts."

"You mean the artefacts you stole from the Iranian people?" Colin's voice was strained.

"I didn't steal it. Someone else got 3D-printed copies made and paid a worker at the museum to replace the originals. I only paid for it." He winced. "Élodie told me it was as good as stealing it myself. But she was no better than me. She dealt in drugs. Art is actually better. It's a victimless crime."

Colin stiffened, but didn't respond.

"All I wanted was for the drugs to give me enough money to build a healthy portfolio of art."

"To sell illegally." Colin's anger gave him more strength to cut through the rope, but the progress was slow.

"Doesn't matter now." François looked at his chest again. "Élodie will never get to study music. And if you don't get this off me, I'll…" His head jerked up when the sound of sirens came closer.

"Deep sea perch can live up to a hundred and forty-nine years!"

"We're getting there, bud." Colin increased his sawing. "Almost through."

I wasn't sure how many vehicles were outside, but it sounded like more than three came to a screeching halt close to the door we'd entered. Within seconds footsteps sounded in the warehouse. I didn't move.

"Over here," Vinnie called out. "The old man and I are armed and there's one bomb here."

"Clear!" a few male voices called out from around us.

"Can't stay away from the action, Genevieve?" Daniel walked to us, his assault weapon lowered.

I frowned. "I don't like action."

"I know." His smile was genuine. Then he sobered as he looked over the situation. "Well, you sure find a lot of it."

"Where's your bomb guy?" Manny asked.

"Where is he?" François searched the aisle. "You need to get this off me."

"I'm here." A muffled voice came from the end of the aisle. A suited man was slowly walking towards us. He was dressed in a blast-resistant suit, his large helmet obscuring his features. "Why are there so many people here?"

"The Sumatran-Andaman earthquake in 2004 lasted five hundred to six hundred seconds!" Caelan was slapping his thighs again. "Doctor Lenard! The three-toed sloth can move maximum five metres a day."

Everything slowed down in my mind. I looked at François, his badly injured face, his broken hands and the bomb strapped to his chest. He'd used the last nine minutes to confess his entire criminal career and plan. I wondered if he'd accepted that he would die. Or was it that he desperately needed to relieve himself of the guilt he suffered for playing a role in the deaths of so many people?

"You need to get these people out of here, Daniel." The bomb disposal technician stopped in front of François and leaned over to look at the device.

"It took more than two thousand years to build the Great Wall of China!"

"I'm almost done, bud." Colin glanced over his shoulder towards François and the technician, but quickly turned back to continue sawing.

Caelan was losing control, his movements becoming more erratic by the moment. Then a realisation crashed into my thinking brain, followed by a rush of adrenaline. Caelan's facts had first been about volcanoes to warn us about the bomb. All the other facts had been somehow related to time. I gasped.

"Jenny?" Colin looked at me.

I stared at the bomb disposal technician. "There's a timer."

"What?" The technician stilled. "Why didn't you tell me earlier?"

"Because we didn't bloody know." Manny took a step away from François. "If there's a timer, there's a countdown. What are we looking at?"

"Give me a moment." The technician's hands were steady as he took a device from his bag and aimed it at the bomb. The device immediately showed a red light. "A lot of explosives here."

He took another device from his bag. A mobile x-ray machine. He aimed that at the bomb. The display showed a lot of wires. The technician put the machine down. "There are no wires under the lid. I'm going to remove it to see what we're looking at."

"It takes twenty-seven point three two days for the moon to orbit around the Earth!"

"Shit." Colin's jaw was tight as he worked harder to cut through the last wires on the rope.

"Oh, God. I don't want to die." François was crying, yet trying hard to control his breathing.

The technician carefully removed both the ropes that held the lid in place. With steady hands, he removed the lid. And tensed. "Evacuate. Now."

Daniel didn't hesitate. "Evacuate! Evacuate! Evacuate!"

The sound of boots running towards the door filled the warehouse. I stood frozen.

"I'm not done yet." Sweat was forming on Colin's forehead. "How much time do we have?"

"Twenty-three seconds." The technician grabbed a wire cutter from his bag and tossed it to Colin. He lifted his bag and looked at François. "I'm sorry, sir." Then he looked at Colin. "Don't waste time." He grabbed his bag and ran to the exit, slowed down by his bulky suit.

"Ninety percent of Earth's population lives in the Northern Hemisphere!"

"Oh, God. Oh, God." François looked at me, tears streaming from his eyes. "Tell Phillip I'm sorry."

"Done!" Colin threw the wire cutter on the floor and got up. "Vin! Grab Caelan. I've got Jenny."

Blackness rushed towards me, but I kept fighting it. Caelan wasn't safe yet. Colin, Vinnie and Manny weren't safe yet.

Vinnie ran to Caelan and picked him up like a baby. Caelan was jerking and keening, but he didn't fight Vinnie as they ran to the exit, followed by Manny.

"Let's go!" Daniel was waiting for us. Colin looked at me once, then lifted me over his shoulder and ran as fast as he could, Daniel by our side. I was looking back towards François still tied to the chair. He was sobbing, his one hand reached out towards us, his broken fingers stretched out.

That was the last image in my mind as we left the aisle and a few seconds later ran into the frigid night air. Manny, Daniel, Colin and Vinnie continued running towards the GIPN vehicles, their red and blue lights still flashing.

The bomb exploded.

The warehouse lit up, followed by intense heat and a rush of air so strong that it pushed Colin off his feet. His legs buckled under him and we fell. I watched the snow-covered ground rushing up towards me and surrendered to the safe warmth of a shutdown.

Chapter TWENTY-ONE

"COMPLAIN ONE MORE time and I'm... I'm going to—"

"You're going to what, little punk?" Vinnie grinned at Nikki when she threw her napkin at him. "Cook again?"

"Not if you keep on criticising everything I made." Nikki turned to me. "Tell him, Doc G. A good friend supports you and doesn't rip apart your labour of love."

I valued Nikki's cheerful and buoyant personality. Now more than ever. It had been a very difficult few days. But I couldn't lie. "Vinnie is right. You forgot to add salt to the pasta. It doesn't taste good."

"Argh!" Nikki threw her hands in the air before she took the salt shaker and added more salt to her food.

It had been three days since the explosion and we hadn't found Shahab. Francine had scoured through every camera in the vicinity of the warehouse. She'd found nothing. She hadn't even been offended when I'd found it hard to believe and had looked through the footage myself. I also had found nothing.

We had come to the conclusion that Shahab must have worn a very good disguise to have avoided detection when he'd left the president's residence and then the warehouse. It had been a very intense three days.

It was improving, but the first day after the explosion I'd seen the unadulterated fear on François' face every time I closed my eyes. I hadn't expected such strong emotional repercussions from leaving behind a man who'd played a role in those brutal deaths. I had trouble sleeping.

Colin had insisted we visit the hospital after the explosion. I had been in a shutdown for three hours before we could go. The doctor had examined the numerous small lacerations on my hands where the debris from the explosions had cut my hands when I'd lifted them to protect my face.

Fortunately for all of us, our winter coats had protected us from any deeper cuts. Had I worn my gloves, my hands would most likely not have been injured at all.

The destruction to the warehouse had been extensive. One of the GIPN trucks that had been parked close to the door had also been damaged quite severely by the flying debris. All the officers that had taken cover behind the vehicles were unharmed. As were Daniel, Manny and Vinnie.

It had been an immense challenge to get Caelan into a hospital room. Not even Francine or Phillip had been able to calm him when they'd arrived at the hospital. His hoarse keening had become too much for me and I'd left my room to admonish him.

But his tear-streaked cheeks had caused a heavy weight to rest on my chest. So I'd sat with him and given him incorrect geographical facts until he'd calmed down enough to admonish *me*. Francine had laughed and cried at the same time.

She'd been affected by François' death as strongly as if she'd been there. The horror on her face had been severe when she'd recalled seeing the video footage blink out when the bomb had exploded. Vinnie had suggested she go to the therapist at GIPN. Daniel's whole team were going for sessions to deal with leaving someone behind, the bomb squad as well.

I took another bite of Nikki's unsalted pasta and allowed the bickering to wash over me. I needed this. I needed the normality of having dinner with the people who had become my family.

Knowing that the man who had killed Caelan's friends was free caused me great distress. Even without any resources, he would not have any financial problems if he managed to sell the heroin in the wine bottles he'd taken from Adèle.

"Okay, wait." Nikki wiped Eric's chin and turned to Francine. "What happened with François' lawyer?"

"He's gone. His legal firm hasn't seen him since the meeting at Rousseau & Rousseau. And he's cleaned out his personal accounts." Pink took the cloth from Nikki, frowned at her, then cleaned Eric's cheek and neck as well. I found it most repulsive to watch the little one eat. He'd recently insisted on feeding himself with his plastic spoon. A large percentage of his food didn't make it to his mouth, but had to be wiped off his tray and his body.

"Huh." Roxy pulled the serving dish with grilled

vegetables closer and added two heaped spoons to her plate. "Do you think he's with Shahab now?"

"We don't know." The dark shadows under Francine's eyes were mostly gone. But they'd been replaced by a new tension—the kind observed in victims of violence. I decided to encourage her to see that therapist. After I vetted him. She sighed. "I'm looking for him. And for Shahab."

Roxy put her knife and fork down. "He's a... a... monster."

"And that's putting it lightly," Francine said.

"What about Claire?" Roxy asked. "Will there be any legal fallout for her?"

"No." Pink helped Eric scoop food onto his plastic spoon. "Dan and Fabien worked with the prosecutors on this. Claire and her husband will tell the prosecutor everything they know and also give them access to all Adèle's accounts. Claire no longer needs or wants the drug money."

"Wow." Roxy shook her head. "What a crazy case. I'm just glad you're all safe. Car chases. Bombs. Scary stuff."

Both had been terrifying. The bomb squad had confirmed there had been explosives in the SUV that had exploded and had told us we'd been lucky.

Francine sighed loudly, then frowned. She shook her head as if to stop an internal process and straightened in her chair. Then put one fist on her hip and flicked her hair over her shoulder. "Okay, that's it. If no one's going to say it, I will." She looked around the table, then rolled her eyes and looked back at Roxy. "I don't like your hair like that."

Roxy's eyes widened. My groan came out louder than I'd intended. I'd become quite familiar with the fake shock. She put her one hand over her chest. With the other, she played with her long straight hair. "You don't like it all neat and tidy? I look just like you." She moved her chair back and waved both hands over her body. "Look. Designer jeans, a gorgeous blouse just like the one you bought last month. And my new boots are standing there by the door."

Francine's lips thinned. "That blouse looks nothing like mine."

"But look." Roxy's eyes widened even more. "It has the same cute little buttons like yours does."

"Bloody hell." Manny muttered a few more rude words under his breath and pushed his plate away.

"See?" Roxy looked at Manny as if he'd given her a beautiful gift. "Even Manny loves my new look."

"Well, it doesn't work." Francine crossed her arms.

Nikki's loud laughter startled Eric for a second. Then he looked at his mommy and also started laughing. That set Nikki off even more until everyone around the table was smiling.

"What's so funny, Nix?" Francine looked perplexed, yet was smiling. Some of the weight on my chest lifted. It was good to see Francine's smile.

"You... oh... I can't." Nikki laughed harder.

"Nikki helped Roxy do her hair." I'd heard the giggles coming from their side of the apartment for more than two hours before Francine and Manny had arrived for dinner. "I think I overheard Nikki say that she stole that blouse from your wardrobe."

"You little minx!" Francine glared at Nikki, but there was no malice in her micro-expressions. "You betrayed me. You stole from me. I thought we were in this together."

"Nah." Nikki wiped laughter-tears from her cheeks. "I'm in it with the one who gives me the most wicked fun."

Roxy raised her fist and bumped it against Nikki's. Then she turned a fake loving smile towards Francine. "At least now I know you love my curly, messy hair and my unique sense of fashion."

"Oh, man." Francine leaned back in her chair, looked at the two women, then nodded reluctantly. "Well played, ladies. Well played."

"What's happening at Interpol?" Colin's question put an immediate damper on the atmosphere around the table.

Manny stabbed at his food, then put his utensils down. "They've agreed to put the blame where it belongs. Three of the officers who ordered the op took responsibility. I think they're also making this out to be a teachable moment so everyone can see that even the higher-ups are willing to take responsibility for their screw-ups. Bloody hell. Anyway, the two team members who survived will receive full pension with benefits when they leave."

"They're leaving?" Colin frowned. "Do they want to or are they being asked to?"

"They want to. These poor buggers are badly hurt. It will take months of physio before they're able to get around. I doubt they'll ever pass another physical that would get them into the field." Manny's lips thinned. "They are also emotionally banged up. That might take years of therapy before they're okay. If ever."

"That's rough." Colin looked at Francine as he said this. He had been more concerned about me and Caelan than François' demise. He'd told me he hated how that situation had ended, but knew and accepted that none of us could have prevented the outcome. I agreed. I wished Francine looked at it the same way.

"Yes, those two are taking it hard." Manny sighed. "I can't remember the last time I was that bloody angry. I was going to get the big guy to go and beat up those idiots in charge."

"Aw." Vinnie tilted his head. "You know I would've done it for you, old man."

The doorbell rang. Vinnie's light-heartedness disappeared. He and Pink both got up, their hands going to the backs of their pants where their guns were hidden under their shirts. At the door, Vinnie looked through the peephole, then relaxed as he opened the door. "I hope you don't mind, but we got started without you."

"No problem." Phillip came in, took off his winter coat and hung it on the hanger next to my coat.

Daniel followed him and smiled when he looked at the table. He walked towards us, his eyes on Eric. "How's the little man doing?"

"He's loving his mommy's food." Nikki got up and kissed Phillip on his cheek. Then she wrapped her arms around Daniel and gave him a long hug before pushing him towards the table.

"Good evening, everyone. My apologies for being late." Phillip sat down in his usual place and looked at the dishes on the table. "I won't be eating. We had dinner with Caelan."

Daniel nodded. "I'm surprised that white food can be tasty and filling."

"How's he doing today?" I had visited Caelan the first two days after the explosion. Today, I'd needed to be away from his intensity.

"He's struggling." Phillip nodded when Vinnie held out a bottle of red wine. He took it and slowly poured it into his glass. Phillip was back to his usual composed self. He'd told me he had long ago accepted that François would never live up to his potential. Phillip put the bottle down. "His legs are still hurting from the bruises."

"The dude really did a number on himself." Vinnie shook his head. "I saw his legs at the hospital. Scrawny little sticks, but he managed to beat the shit out of himself."

"Vinster." Francine opened her eyes wide and tilted her head towards Eric. "We want his first words to be 'Mommy' and 'Francine is fabulous'."

"Dream on, girl." Roxy winked at Francine. "He'll say 'Roxy rocks'. Then he'll say 'Mommy'."

Francine stared at her for a second, then both women burst out laughing. I sighed.

"We missed you, Rox." Nikki handed Eric a slice of red pepper. "Don't leave us again for so long."

As Nikki said this, my eyes narrowed. I pointed at her face. "What was that?"

"What was what?" She looked up, then fell back in her chair. "Dammit. You saw that? Why did you see that?"

Manny jerked at the worried sound in Nikki's voice. "What did she see? You're not pregnant again, are you?"

"What?" Nikki's shock was evident in the high pitch of the word. "No."

"Oh, little punk." Vinnie crossed his arms and shook his head. "What the... something have you done?"

Nikki laughed. "Something? Really?"

"Hey, I didn't have enough time." He lowered his chin and stared at her. "Whassup, little punk?"

She swallowed, then looked at Pink. My eyes narrowed even more. I was watching her inner conflict playing across her face. She inhaled deeply, pushed her shoulders back and lifted her chin. Then her shoulders dropped, her voice low. "I don't know how to say this."

Pink reached out and put his hand over hers. "Do you want me to do this?"

"You motherfucker." Vinnie jumped up and shook his fist at Pink while staring at their hands. "What's that? Huh? What's that?"

"Oh, keep your panties on, big punk." Nikki rolled her eyes. Then she turned her hand and interlaced her fingers with Pink's. Her fingers tightened around his until her knuckles turned white.

I could no longer watch her discomfort. This was extremely difficult for me, but I knew how important it was for her. "Nikki." I waited until she looked at me. "Ignore the posturing. Tell us about your flat and about Pink."

"Huh? What?" She stared at me, everyone else forgotten. "How do you know?"

"Really?" I gave her a look that she had once said is my 'are-you-really-that-dumb' look. "Your nonverbal cues the last few months have been increasingly obvious." I looked at Pink. "As have yours."

Colin winked at Nikki. "So are you going to let us tell everything or would you two like to say something?"

"You were right." Pink squeezed Nikki's hand and blinked a few times. "This is much harder than I thought."

"They see and know frigging everything." Nikki inhaled slowly and cleared her throat. "I bought the flat downstairs. I signed the final sales agreement yesterday. Pink and I... well, we've kinda hit it off and he—"

"I care deeply for Nikki and Eric." He looked at me. "I know you can see it."

"I do." And it reassured me. Even though it didn't make this easier.

"Then you know that I'll be okay to move into my new flat, because Pink will be with me."

I stared at Nikki. "You will be okay because you are you. Being with Pink will enrich your life."

Tears gathered in Nikki's eyes.

"Now just wait a bloody minute." Manny slapped his

hand on the table. "Why are you moving?"

"Um, because I'm an adult? Because I want to build my own life." She sniffed and looked at me. "Like Doc G did."

"Well, I don't know about this." Manny rubbed his hand over his head. He jerked when Francine took his hand and held it against her heart.

"Well, I know about this." She winked at Nikki. "Nix is fabulous because she's a part of us. She's smart and she'll be just fine."

"And I'll most likely be here every night to eat," Nikki added.

"I second that." Pink glared at the pasta on his plate. "We might both need to take some cooking lessons before we're really ready to fly the coop."

"Oh, I'll miss you." Roxy wiped tears from her cheeks. "You'll be just downstairs, right?"

"Nikki will keep her keys for our apartment." I looked at her. "This is your home and you're always welcome here."

"Oh, Doc G." Nikki got up and walked to me. "I'm going to hug you."

"I wish you wouldn't." This time I didn't mind so much when she leaned over and rested her head on my shoulder and wrapped her arms around me.

"I thought you would be so mad."

I shook my shoulder until she giggled and straightened. "I'm not angry. I'm scared because you're bringing change into my life. Again. But I have watched you grow. Nikki, you're a strong, amazing young woman. You're responsible and kind. And you deserve the life you want to build."

"Oh, Doc G," she said again as she swallowed. "I'm gonna hug you again."

I sighed and nodded. Even though I didn't like the physical closeness, I knew she needed it. And in a sense I also needed it. When I'd confided in Colin my observations about Nikki and Pink's body language as well as my suspicions about the flat, he'd given me practical advice. Including what I should say to her.

She gave me one last squeeze and went back to her seat. "Now tell me how you knew about the flat."

"We also received the notice that the flat was for sale," Colin said. "I was going to buy it."

Her eyes widened. "They told me they'd had another offer, but then that person withdrew it."

Colin smiled. "When I found out you had also made an offer, I was thrilled. I think that place is perfect for you."

"Did you tell Doc G?" Nikki asked.

"He didn't. I saw how you looked at the flat every time we went past it." It would've been hard to not see the longing in her expression. "I also overheard a conversation you had with what I assume was your lawyer. If you want to hide your actions, you should close your door when you're having confidential conversations."

"Who's your lawyer?" Phillip's concern was sincere. He'd been quiet this whole time, his eyes narrowed.

"I used the lawyer you suggested." Her smile was embarrassed when she looked at me. "I told Phillip that my new boss wanted to buy a house and he needed the best lawyer available."

"So you asked me to recommend the lawyer I would recommend if you were going to buy a house." Phillip's smile was proud. "I fell for your ruse."

"Why all the lying?" Manny slumped back in his chair. "Why not just ask for help?"

"Manny, I love you, but seriously?" Nikki rolled her eyes. "How can you not see that I wanted to do this on my own?"

"Well, you still should've asked."

"I'm proud of you, Nikki." And I knew Manny was too. He was just struggling with the change. At least I'd had a few weeks to process this. "You were wise to get a lawyer to help you and you did a very good job. On your own."

Her smile was sweet as her cheeks reddened slightly.

"I'm so not done with this." Vinnie sat down heavily, glaring at Pink. "You and I are gonna talk."

Pink laughed. "Sure, dude."

Vinnie's phone pinged. He grunted when he looked at the screen. "Jen-girl, I'm being harassed and it's all your fault." He shook his phone at me. "You need to go get that rug."

"Hassan SMSed you again?" Colin smiled. "I'll phone him tomorrow morning."

"What's this about?" Roxy looked from Colin to Vinnie to me.

"The hawala broker sells Persian carpets." The more I

thought about this, the more I loved the layout of his shop.

"Jenny saw a beautiful rug that Hassan now wants to give to her." Colin took my hand. "If she decides she wants it, we'll buy it."

"Oh, boy." Vinnie crossed his arms. "You haven't decided yet? Hassan's gonna drive me crazy."

I needed at least one more day to consider the change that rug would bring in my living space. Already there were too many changes coming.

I sat back in my chair and listened to Roxy begging Vinnie to buy an Aladdin carpet to fly on. Vinnie kissed her head, then turned to glare at Pink and Nikki. Threats ensued, then jokes, excitement and finally promises to never let Roxy help with the décor in Nikki's new flat.

I felt conflicted. Seeing Nikki so excited made me happy. But knowing that she was going to leave didn't. Most of all I was going to miss Eric's warm body pressed against mine. I was even going to miss Pink's quiet presence in the apartment. I watched him as he lifted Eric from his high chair and settled the baby on his lap. There was an ease that was unique to that man. An ease that I saw brought a balance and happiness to Nikki.

Colin took my hand and squeezed it until I looked at him. "They'll be okay."

"I know."

"You will also be okay."

I nodded. As always, I would work hard to make sure that was true. I would also work very hard to locate

Shahab so he could bear the consequences for what he'd done to Jace, Adèle and the others. But for now, I was going to enjoy the company of the people around this table. The people I loved.

Tomorrow, I would start looking for Shahab.

~ ~ ~ ~ ~

Look at the painting that was found under Jace's bed, learn more about Franz Roubaud, geocaching, liquid heroin cases and panoramic paintings at:
http://estelleryan.com/the-roubaud-connection.html

~ ~ ~ ~ ~

Be first to find out when Genevieve's next adventure will be published. Sign up for the newsletter at
http://estelleryan.com/contact.html

~ ~ ~ ~ ~

Other books in the Genevieve Lenard Series:

Book 1: The Gauguin Connection

Book 2: The Dante Connection

Book 3: The Braque Connection

Book 4: The Flinck Connection

Book 5: The Courbet Connection

Book 6: The Pucelle Connection

Book 7: The Léger Connection

Book 8: The Morisot Connection

Book 9: The Vecellio Connection

and more…

For more books in this series, go to
http://estelleryan.com/books.html

Please visit me on my **Facebook Page** *to become part of the process as I'm writing Genevieve's next adventure.*

and

Explore my **website** *to find out more about me and Genevieve.*